ARAPAHO

Larry Jeram-Croft

Arapaho

Copyright © 2013 Larry Jeram-Croft
All rights reserved.

Cover image: PO(Phot) PJ Packenas;@ Crown Copyright 1984

Also by Larry Jeram-Croft:

Fiction:

The 'Jon Hunt' series about the modern Royal Navy:

Sea Skimmer
The Caspian Monster
Cocaine
Arapaho
Bog Hammer
Glasnost
Retribution
Formidable
Conspiracy
Swan Song

The 'John Hunt' books about the Royal Navy's Fleet Air Arm in the Second World War:

Better Lucky and Good
and the Pilot can't swim

The Winchester Chronicles:

Book one: The St Cross Mirror

The Caribbean: historical fiction and the 'Jacaranda' Trilogy.

Diamant

1

Arapaho

Jacaranda
The Guadeloupe Guillotine
Nautilus

Science Fiction:

Siren

Non Fiction:

The Royal Navy Lynx an Operational History
The Royal Navy Wasp an Operational and Retirement History
The Accidental Aviator

Chapter 1

Night; black, vibrating, roaring, night. Little could be seen with the naked eye except for the dim glow of the instrument lights turned to their minimum brightness and hiding behind sheets of blue glass. The two men, sitting in the cockpit, looked like Martians, with broad helmeted heads and strange black eye stalks sticking out of the front. These were the latest night vision goggles and they were allowing the Sea King helicopter to be flown almost suicidaly low across the North Sea in the pitch darkness of a winter's night.

Lieutenant Commander Jonathon Hunt, Commanding Officer of the Royal Navy's newest helicopter squadron wasn't flying the lead aircraft as he should have been. Nor was the squadron's Senior Observer and his friend Brian Pearce, sitting in the back looking at the radar. They were both dead and bloody annoyed about it.

The squadron had been formed earlier in the year, as the third Fleet Air Arm, Commando Helicopter Support squadron but with the additional task of Maritime Counter Terrorism. They had been working up tactics and procedures for months and tonight was the big final exercise to prove that all the concepts would work. Royal Marines from the elite specialist Comacchio Group were being taken out to a 'hijacked' oil rig to deal with the bad guys. On the rig were representatives of the Squadrons Operational Command, Flag Officer Third Flotilla or FOF3 for short as well as some goon from the Ministry of Defence. Jon had been given command of the squadron at its formation and it was made clear from the start that this was all a bit of an experiment and would need justification for continued funding. That justification was happening tonight and Jon was stuck in the mess at RAF Lossiemouth instead of leading his people as he bloody well should be.

The bar area was silent. Everyone else had gone to bed long ago. Jon and Brian had thought about staying in the station control tower in case any radio traffic was heard but as the exercise was totally covert that wasn't likely. Neither of them had wanted to go to bed either, so the bar had been a compromise.

Brian had nodded off and was snoring gently, his head lolling against the back of the arm chair he was sitting in. Jon couldn't sleep. He was continually wondering how things were going. He understood why the FOF3 Commander had decided to take the squadron hierarchy out of the equation at the last minute by telling them their aircraft had conveniently 'crashed' on the way up here from Yeovilton. In some ways, it was a good test of how well trained everyone was. It also proved that there was a degree of redundancy and spare capacity in the process. It didn't make Jon feel any the happier though. His place was out leading, not sitting in some bloody bar waiting to hear how the others had got on.

Suddenly, the phone rang. The tower knew where they were, so Jon wasn't surprised when the voice at the other end asked for him. He listened for a few moments, grunted a reply and walked back over to Brian, giving him a gentle kick in the process.

'Wake up sunshine, the boys are on the way back, let's go out and meet them. At least we can be part of the debrief.'

'How did it go? Did they say?'

'Very well apparently. Seems we are superfluous after all.'

Two days later was a Friday. With all the aircraft returned to their respective hangars, 844 Squadron stood down for the weekend. 'Standing down' traditionally started in the bar for happy hour and today was no exception.

Jon and Brian were propping up the bar in time honoured fashion and watching the rest of the squadron officers in an avuncular way as the level of noise slowly rose.

'I must be getting old Brian, some of my guys look like they should still be at school,' Jon observed as he looked around the throng.

'Tempus fugit old chap,' came the slightly slurred reply. 'Or something like that. Who would have thought you and me would be allowed to be in charge of a squadron? Poachers and gamekeepers spring to mind.'

Jon grunted acknowledgement. 'Oh by the way, I had a phone call just before I came over. Apparently, the powers that be liked our little demonstration the other night and so we get to keep said squadron and her role of taking out the bad guys.'

'I should bloody well hope so. I wonder if we'll ever have to do it for real?'

Jon looked thoughtful for a second. 'For God's sake don't repeat this Brian but I do wonder if it would work against someone who was properly prepared. There are so many things that could be done to make it just about impossible for us to get close enough.'

'Yeah but we're not meant to be going up against clever sods are we?'

Brian was about to continue talking when he realised that his friend wasn't listening. His gaze was fastened on something over his shoulder. He turned and looked at what was engaging Jon's attention and wasn't surprised when he saw three WRNS Officers walking into the bar. Two, he immediately recognised. One was from Air Traffic Control and the other was the Staff Officer of one of the other squadrons but he didn't recognise the third. Nor apparently did anyone else in the bar as all heads turned as if they were on strings. It was quite clear the newcomer was aware of the effect her entrance was making and she didn't seem to mind one little bit.

'Jesus Jon, she hasn't got her legs on upside down like most WRNS,' observed Brian admiringly.

Tall and very slim, even under the rather long regulation black skirt, her legs disappeared upwards to God knew where. She was blonde with short curls around her ears and the rest of her hair tied up. Even from this far away her deep dark blue eyes could be seen appraising the room. Brian turned back to Jon who immediately turned away and looked back over at the back of the bar.

'Come on mate, I saw you drooling, just like the rest of us.'

'Not me, I've given up women for Lent.'

'Jon, come on, it's almost a year now since we got back from the Caribbean. You've got to put it behind you.' Brian could see his friend's lips tightening at the remark but he ploughed on. 'Life goes on you know.'

Jon's face was set. 'Thank you for the homely advice but drop it please Brian. When I decide I need female company I will make the bloody decision myself. Oh and it certainly won't be over some self-centred tart who is clearly in love with herself.'

Neither man noticed it but the three girls had just reached the bar next to them and Jon's words had obviously been overheard. The new girl flushed bright red and an angry frown appeared on her face. It was clear she was about to say something when one of the other girls whispered in her ear and pulled her away. Brian turned and caught the end of the exchange and immediately worked out what had happened but it was too late. To groans from some of the men present, the three WRNS left the bar without another word.

Chapter 2

1967 - The Sinai

The two boys were playing outside their house when their father came striding up the dirt track from the little village. They both looked up as he approached and he tousled their hair in an offhand, affectionate manner.

'Boys, one of the goats has gone for a walk again, will one of you please go and find him.' Before they could reply, he went into the little house, clearly expecting to be obeyed.

Karim looked at his twin brother Khalid. 'You go, I had to find one yesterday.'

Khalid wasn't going to agree. 'Yes but I had to carry mother's washing today and you did nothing.'

Karim's look of determination was mirrored almost exactly on his brother's face. They were in all respects identical, complete mirror images of each other. But like all twelve year old boys, even that wasn't going to stop them bickering.

Unfortunately, before they could build up a good head of steam, their mother heard them and her voice carried out of the window above their heads. 'Karim, your brother is right, do as your father says.'

Khalid grinned at his brother in victory. They both knew that mother's word was law. Karim got up grumpily and Khalid easily avoided the half-hearted kick that was aimed at him. 'Off you go brother. I'll stay here and guard the house.'

Without another word, Karim headed off up the dry gulch behind the house. The goats always headed there. They may have only been dumb animals but they knew where there was water and some vegetation even in the barren, Sinai, semi-desert. As he trudged up the hill and the house was lost from sight, he cheered up. He loved being here in the silence of the land. The oven heat of the day was waning now and he knew the evening would be cool as he listened to the sounds of the rocks slowly dissipating the day's heat. Suddenly, he heard the bleat of his quarry and realised that the goat must have run much further than normal. Cursing the animal, he continued his climb as the gully became narrower and steeper. It saved his life.

Arapaho

The pilot of the Israeli Mirage 3CJ was annoyed. The lightning strike by his Air Force had all but annihilated the Egyptian Air Force in a matter of days. At first, it had been exhilarating but now it was just a mopping up operation. There was no longer anyone in the sky to offer any resistance. He knew that the ground offensive would be starting tomorrow so they would all be busy again. His wingman had suffered an engine problem shortly after take off and had had to return to base. Command had wanted him to go back as well but as he had a full load of ordnance on board he had convinced them to let him continue and look for targets of convenience, as long as he stayed away from the main area of the forthcoming ground attack. They didn't want any warning being given.

Flying at ten thousand feet was no good. Although he could see a great distance, it was too high to pick out any detail. He throttled back and put the aircraft into a dive. Just as he passed through three thousand feet he felt a jolt through the airframe. He quickly scanned his instruments and control panel but could see nothing amiss. Craning his neck, he looked back at as much of the aircraft as he could see but being so far forward it wasn't that much. Suddenly an amber warning started to flash. His engine was starting to lose oil pressure. It wasn't critical yet but all thoughts of continuing with the sortie left his mind. This was not the place to be, over hostile territory with a sick engine. He turned for home and raised the nose. Any spare height he could get would be a bonus if things got worse. The aircraft was sluggish in the climb and the bomb load he was carrying didn't help. Without thinking or looking exactly where he was, he hit the bomb release switch. The aircraft seemed to jump skywards as the extra weight and drag was shed. It was only after he eventually landed safely that he realised he had released the bombs in an armed state, rather than jettisoning them safely. With a mental shrug, he dismissed the minor error from his mind. After all, he was over a desert and an enemy one at that.

'There you are you stupid animal,' muttered Karim through his laboured breathing as he finally saw the missing goat. It had obviously seen a tasty bush far up the narrowing gully and with the single mindedness only a goat can achieve, had gone after his supper. Unfortunately, it was now stuck and bleating its distress. Karim stopped and looked carefully at how he was going to conduct the rescue. The animal was in severe danger of slipping. The slope was so steep that he could see that the approach was going to tricky. The ground was rough scree and he could easily lose his footing. Suddenly, he was distracted by the sound of an aircraft. They had been going over their house for days now and father had been close mouthed about what it all meant. Even mother was strangely reticent but both boys knew that their parents were worried about something. Today had been the first day for some time when the skies had been quiet, so he stopped for a second to look up. However, the close shoulders of the gully cut out most of his view and as the noise of the jet engine started to recede he shrugged and started back to consider his primary job.

The blast, when it came, simply lifted him off his feet. One moment he was standing looking up at the goat, the next he was flying. He hit the side of the gully with a thump which knocked all the wind from his lungs and then he started to slide. Afterwards, he found he couldn't remember any noise. He was sure there must have been some but it all seemed to happen in a numb silence. He slid and tumbled for what seemed like forever but was probably only seconds and came to a slamming halt on a boulder as smaller stones and sand cascaded past him. He whimpered with pain. His bare arms and legs were covered in cuts and his ribs hurt where they had hit the boulder. He lay for an uncountable time recovering his breath, waiting for the stones to stop falling and then got shakily to his feet. Amazingly, as he stood up, the goat that had caused all the problems calmly walked past him. Without thinking, he grabbed the animal. Whatever had happened, father would be pleased that the animal had been recovered safely.

Tying a piece of rope around the animal's neck, he made his way around the shoulder of the hill. When he should have been in sight of his house he stopped. Even at twelve years old he was able to work out something of what must have happened. Half his home was missing, just not there. Where the garden had been was a massive smoking crater and further down the valley another crater smouldered. Completely forgetting the goat and all his cuts and bruises, he started to run. It only took minutes and he was standing looking at the wreckage of his home.

'Mother, Father, Khalid,' he called desperately but no one answered. He realised he could barely hear his own voice anyway. He climbed the remains of a wall and looked over. He saw his mother or rather he saw half of her. In a sight that would be seared onto his memory for the rest of his life, he saw his mother. The loving woman who had looked after him and loved him all his life. He knew it was her because her face was relatively intact but the rest of her looked like the meat he saw on the butchers slab down in the village when they went shopping. One relatively intact arm was thrown out as if pointing to something, her face looked surprisingly serene. There was blood everywhere, blood mingled with what he now realised were parts of the bodies of his parents. He threw up.

Suddenly, movement caught his eye. Looking to his left, he saw a foot sticking out of the rubble. He immediately recognised it as it was clad in the same sandals that were on his own feet.

'Khalid,' he cried as he saw the foot twitch and he carefully made his way down the treacherous rubble pile to his brother. He also realised he could hear his voice a little better and frantically started calling out his brother's name.

After what seemed like ages, he clawed the rubble off his brother's body. He was alive but deeply unconscious. All his limbs seemed intact but there was a terrible cut on his head from his right ear right over the crown. Not knowing what to do, he pulled off his own shirt and pushed it over the wound which quickly became saturated with his brother's blood.

That was how the men of the village found them half an hour later, the two little boys, one cradling the other in his arms, staring at the butchered remains of their loving mother. They never found a recognisable part of the father.

Chapter 3

The large hangar bustled with energy. Five Sea King helicopters were the centre of attention as the day watch of maintainers busied themselves with maintenance and rectification work. One machine was having an engine removed. Others were in a more intact state and would be out on the flight line later in the day.

Brian Pearce turned to the WNRS Officer at his side. 'So Helen, this is our hangar and as you can see it's fairly busy today. We had a pretty hectic time last week and the aircraft are getting some TLC.'

The girl looked suitably impressed as she took in the sight of all the activity.

Brian had been surprised that morning when she turned up announcing that she was the new squadron Staff Officer. She was expected but no one had realised it would the pretty blonde girl who had briefly visited the bar last Friday. He wondered if her entrance had been to make her introductions when Jon's unfortunate remark had scared her away. Luckily, Jon was away for the day in Portsmouth, debriefing the previous week's exercise. It gave Brian a chance to build a few bridges.

'So, you are now the latest member of 844 Squadron. We were formed at the start of the year, primarily as the third Commando helicopter support squadron but we also have the MCT role and it was deemed a good idea for us to have a couple of Mark Two Sea Kings as well for that little job.' He explained.

'I'm sorry Sir but you are going to have to go a little slower. I'm new to all this, I only finished training two months ago,' she smiled at Brian, looking a little confused.

'Oh, yes sorry, like much of the navy we have our own language but I don't suppose it will take you long to catch up. Right, the green helicopters are Mark Fours, which are designed as troop carriers and we've got six of them. The dark blue ones are Mark Twos and they are designed for Anti-Submarine Warfare or ASW in our language. The reason we have them is because of their radar, although they can also carry a limited number of Bootnecks.'

That got him another puzzled look.

'Right, sorry again, Bootneck is one of our terms of endearment for our Royal Marine chums although there are ruder names. Oh and

MCT stands for Maritime Counter Terrorism, our other role. Basically, anyone who wants to have a go at our oil rigs or merchant ships will have us to deal with, along with a large number of Royal Marines.'

'Oh, didn't something like that happen a couple of years back when a cruise liner was hijacked?'

'You probably mean the Achille Lauro, she was hijacked off Egypt. Yes, we were on standby for that but it got resolved quite quickly. The boys will tell you its because they heard we were coming. This squadron wasn't actually around then of course but quite a few of our guys were on 846 at the time. We have the role full time now, it's a bit of an experiment but we did a major test of it in the North Sea last week and it seemed to go very well. Come on let me show you the rest of the real estate.'

They spent an hour visiting all the various offices of the squadron building with Brian introducing Helen to as many personnel as he could. It was quite clear that the stunning new blonde girl was making an impression and he got quite a few cheeky grins when her back was turned. Eventually, they ended up back in his office. He offered her a seat and sat himself down behind his desk.

'SOBS?' Helen asked as she saw the name tally on his desk.

'That's me,' he replied with a grin. 'It stands for Senior Observer, we also have a SPLOT or Senior Pilot but just about everyone else just has a name or a simple title. Oh then there's the CO or Commanding Officer of course but he likes to be called Boss most of the time.'

'You mean Lieutenant Commander Hunt?'

'That's him. He has the office next door but he's away today. You'll probably meet him tomorrow.'

'I've heard quite a lot about him,' Helen offered.

'Hmm and yes let's be honest it was him you overheard in the bar on Friday. I'm sorry if he seemed rude but you have to understand that we had a pretty tough time last year and he's still not over it.'

'Wasn't that something to do with drug smuggling? There seem to be a lot of rumours around and didn't he do something special in the Falklands?'

'Listen Helen, Jon and I went to school together and also joined up together and we've been pretty lucky because for our last four appointments, we've managed to serve on the same outfits. Very simply, he's my best friend and yes he has an amazing track record. I'm afraid some of it is classified but that doesn't seem to stop the rumours and believe me most of them are rubbish. But last year we were together on HMS Chester doing anti-drug operations in the Caribbean. We managed to snare some bad guys and it all got a little hairy. Believe it or not, they managed to resurrect a war time German submarine and we had the task of sinking it. It wasn't pleasant. Jon took it quite hard, so just give him some slack OK? He's actually a fantastic bloke. It's just that he's a little raw even now.'

'OK Sir, I get the message, Friday never happened.'

'Good and you can stop calling me Sir. We're reasonably informal here. SOBS is good or Brian in the bar. The Boss is normally just that but again we don't worry when we are socialising OK?'

She smiled at Brian and once again he noticed how deep blue her eyes were. Having such a pretty girl on the squadron was going to be a potential problem and he decided he ought to say something early just in case.

'Now look Helen, let's get a few things out in the open. Firstly what's your background?'

'Well, I did a law degree at Oxford and then decided sitting in a solicitor's office wasn't for me. I wanted something a little more exciting. My father was in the navy during the war and so I decided to try the WRNS.'

'And what did you get told about your duties in the squadron?'

'As I understand it, I run the admin side, correspondence and records that sort of thing.'

'That's right, I'll introduce you to the guy who has been doing the job while we waited for you to arrive. He'll be delighted to hand it all over I assure you. But look, I'm going to be honest, you are a very attractive young lady and I just want to prepare you for some of the more basic realities of squadron life.'

He saw the blush appear on her face but soldiered on. 'Look, I guess what I'm saying is that some of our chaps can be a little coarse on occasions. I've seen it before where it can get out of hand. Don't worry, I'll be keeping an eye out for you but don't let some of the buggers take liberties alright?'

Helen laughed and held up her hand. 'It's alright Sir. I grew up with three brothers. I'm pretty sure I can manage the advances of all those rampant males.'

'Alright but let me know if you need top cover. So, let's go to the crewroom and meet all those rampant males, those that aren't flying at the moment.'

The next day, Jon was back in his office staring morosely out of his office window over the large expanse of concrete of the flight line. A Harrier had just taxied in and further away one of his Sea Kings had just engaged its rotors and was about to taxi out.

Brian stuck his head around the door. 'Bloody hell Boss, you look like someone just nicked your pint, anything up?'

Jon sighed. 'Not really, the debrief went well. But look, one day out of the bloody office and all this paperwork just appears by magic. I joined the Fleet Air Arm to fly, not shuffle bloody paper.'

'Ah, well, that might be also because the new Staffy joined yesterday and she's already got stuck into the backlog. Jonno was doing a reasonable job but this girl is like a bloody dervish, apparently, she was here until midnight and you're seeing the results in your in-tray.'

'Oh God, I'd forgotten all about her. What's she like? Have you given her the guided tour yet?'

'Ahah, yes well, she's fine, more than fine actually. I showed her the ropes yesterday and as your in-tray testifies to, she's already making an impact.'

'Let me guess, fifteen stone, built like a Sumo wrestler, with spots.'

Brian tried to hide his grin. 'No, not exactly, in fact you've already met her.'

'Eh? When was that?'

'Remember Happy Hour last week? The blonde you managed to piss off?'

'Oh, you've got to be joking, she's our new Staffy?'

'Yup and don't worry, I've already apologised on your behalf.'

Jon looked stricken for a second and then grinned at his friend. 'Thank you Brian but I guess I'd better do the same.' So saying, he jumped up from around his desk and made his way down the corridor to the staff office. Brian contemplated following but decided it would be better if Jon dug himself out of his own hole for a change.

Chapter 4

The rows and rows of dirty, dilapidated tents were full of the chatter and smell of overcrowded humanity too long in one place and without adequate sanitation. The heat and flies added to the brew of the miasma that hung over the refugee camp like a virulent fog. Most of the inhabitants didn't even notice it. They were far too concerned with the simple act of living day to day. The United Nations, the Red Cross, even the Israelis themselves poured support into the camp but it was never enough. More people fleeing the chaos of the region turned up day after day and swamped the meagre capacity the authorities provided.

Families lived crammed together in one tent but they were the lucky ones. Old people with no one to help them were often just found dead where they had been sitting. They had just enough to survive on but many simply didn't want to keep on living in such a human wasteland when all they loved and owned had been stripped away from them by the inhumanity of war. Then there were the children, the orphans and there were so many of those. Attempts to manage them met with scant success. Makeshift schools had been set up but attendance was tiny and the volunteers who had come from all over the world to help, slowly sank into the apathy of acceptance.

Karim and Khalid loved it. Ever since their parents had been killed they had lived here growing up amongst the chaos. They knew every tent, every alleyway and every trick to ensure they got more than their share of food. Of course, they didn't achieve this all on their own but the gang they belonged to formed a cohesive unit and exercised considerable power through the threat and sometimes the act of violence. But that was life in the camp. No one was surprised.

Today was different. The two young men were seated in the dust outside a yet another nondescript tent. Much of what they had been doing and planning for the last five years depended on the outcome of the meeting they had been told to attend. They had been kept waiting for some hours and neither knew when they would be called but one thing they had learned was patience. Lean and well-muscled, unlike many around them, they had the glow and energy of youth. However, unlike when they were little, it was now possible to tell them apart. Physically they still resembled each other with long

Egyptian features and thick dark hair, the first wispy stubble of adolescent hair on their chins. An onlooker would see the similarities but now also the differences. Karim looked handsome and fit, his face was often smiling and his eyes open and guileless. It would have been a mistake to assume that reflected his nature because he could be as ruthless and vicious as life in the camp required. Khalid on the other hand, always looked cruel and angry. It was in the pinched look around his eyes and the way he held himself. There was an almost feral gleam to his expression. No one would make the mistake of thinking this was just a boy. And then there was the scar. He wore it as a badge of pride. Only some of it could be seen. Even now it looked slightly raw extending from in front of his right ear and up into his hairline. His hand strayed up and started rubbing it in an unconscious habit as he looked at his brother.

'If he keeps us waiting much longer I will go in and force it out of him.'

His brother snorted in derision. 'He will have at least four other men with him you know that. You won't stand a chance.'

Khalid grimaced in anger. He knew his brother was right but he could feel the rage building inside him again. The rage that had never gone away since he had recovered consciousness in his brother's arms five years ago. The rage that might finally have an outlet if the man could give them what they sought.

Karim looked at his brother and sympathised. 'He may not have all we need anyway. I don't trust him, I never have.'

Khalid nodded in agreement. 'Then I will kill him.'

For a second, Karim almost laughed at the ludicrous idea, then realised his brother meant it and was probably focused enough to try. There could only be one result of such foolishness.

'Then you will die too and how will that help us in our vengeance?'

Khalid heard the truth in his brother's words and bit down hard on his anger. Karim was right, they needed patience. This was the only way to get what they wanted. It was just that it was so hard.

The flap of the tent was thrown open by a burly arm and a hand gestured to them to come in. Standing and wiping the dust from their backsides the two boys moved into the relative gloom, their eyes seeking the man they had come to see. He was seated behind a makeshift desk and two armed guards stood either side of him. No one seemed to have told them that weapons weren't allowed in the camp. It wouldn't have made any difference if they had. It was a show of power and authority in a place where that mattered a great deal.

The man looked up at the two youths. His expression gave nothing away. The long beard fell from his chin and his dark eyes looked hooded and dangerous.

'Did you do as you were told?' he asked them.

The brothers looked at each other and as usual, it was Karim who answered. 'Yes, they are all dead. Now, do you have the information you promised us?'

'They are not all dead. Did you think I wouldn't check? When you strike a bargain you have to keep to it.' His words echoed into the silence. 'That was a test to see if you could follow orders, clearly you cannot. As far as I'm concerned you have failed and I no longer wish to use your services.'

Khalid took a step forward and the two guards did the same. 'We did as you asked not ordered,' he said in a tight voice. 'The two old men are dead, but we did not kill the woman. She is no threat to you.'

'Wrong,' the man shouted as he stood angrily and slapped the desk in front of him confronting Khalid. 'Your orders were to kill everyone in that tent and that included the old woman. She is just as much a danger as the men, she knows too much.' And then he sat down and smiled. 'Or maybe I should say she knew too much, as my men have finished the business. I thought you would do this, you clearly don't have the courage and resolution that I need. You are just boys. Get out and never come back.'

Karim was glowing with rage now as well. It didn't happen often but when it did he could lose himself in it. 'You promised to find out who he was and where he lived. Did you even bother to do that?' He asked through tight lips.

'That is no longer your business child, leave me now. I no longer have any use for you. Leave.' The last word was accompanied by a gesture to the two guards who stepped forward and levelled their rifles.

It was too much for Khalid and he lost control. Screaming incoherently, he rushed towards the man, only to be contemptuously knocked to the ground by a rifle butt. Karim instinctively leapt to the defence of his brother and was treated the same way. As they fell to the ground the two guards kicked them both several times and then dragged them to the tent flap and simply flung the two inert bodies out into the dirt. It was testament to the atmosphere in the camp that no one took any notice and certainly no one offered any help.

That evening, the two boys had dragged themselves back to the little tent they had acquired to lick their wounds, almost literally. There was little in the way of first aid available. Khalid was still beside himself with rage. Karim did all he could to calm him down but it was difficult. He felt very much the same.

'He knows. He did find out,' Khalid muttered through clenched teeth as Karim bathed the lump on his head with some clean water. There was a small cut and a large lump but nothing more. They both had sore ribs as well but nothing that time wouldn't heal.

'I agree but now that he has thrown us out there is no way to get back. You know what he is like.'

'Then we will have to ambush him and force it out of him.'

'And how? You know he is always guarded. There are only two of us.'

'Then we will have to use our brains brother.'

Karim was surprised by the reply. Khalid was always the one to act first and think afterwards. But he was right. There was no way that brute force would get them what they needed.

It took them two weeks to work it out and hours of stealthy surveillance. They had to be very careful not to be seen but they soon worked out the man's routines. He seemed to have the trust of the authorities and would often be out of the camp but when he returned, he returned to his habits and so they found what they needed. At the same time, they worked on the other plan, the one that would get them the vengeance they had looked for, for so long.

The smell was dreadful but everyone was used to it. With thousands of people in a small area, sanitation was always going to be a problem. The pit was re-dug almost weekly and this one was almost ready to be filled in and replaced. It was also the last place anyone would expect a threat to come from. The two boys had rags tied around their mouths and had stuffed their nostrils with more. Even so, the stench was making them gag. Just behind the trench, they had hidden some large water containers. Hopefully, they would be used to wash themselves off when they had been successful. They had crept into the pit half an hour before the man was due to make his daily visit and had waded carefully through the muck to get into position. Luckily for them, he was a prude and insisted on a tented off area for his daily crap. His guards would be outside. It wouldn't help him.

Suddenly they heard voices. Karim looked up at the wooden shelf above him. Sure enough, a large hairy backside appeared over the edge. He looked at his brother and nodded. Luckily it was before the man had started and they stood up silently like two shit covered ghosts and grabbed him by the shoulders dragging him backwards off the bench and into the filth. He didn't cry out, so unexpected was the assault but he did start to struggle as the two boys held his head under the crust of faeces. They held on for dear life, he was strong but so were they and they were motivated by weeks of pent up hatred. Slowly the man's struggles started to subside and they pulled his head back up. He took great gasps of breath and then vomited. Before he could do anything more Khalid had a knife to his throat.

'You have one chance at life and you know what it is. A name and an address is all we want.'

The man felt the knife and saw the look in Khalid's eyes. He knew with certainty that the boy wouldn't hesitate to use the blade. He then felt something around his genitals and realised the other brother held another knife there. He slumped in defeat and told them. He struggled even harder when they held him under again but this time they didn't let him up until his struggles stopped.

Minutes later his guards finally realised something was wrong. The two boys were never seen in the camp again.

The suburb of Jerusalem was busy as it always was this time of day. The husbands had all gone to work. Many of them were part of the military but that could be said of most men in this county. The wives were bustling their children and getting ready for school. The house of Major Binyamen Melamed looked like all the others in the row and his wife Gabriela was doing just the same as all the other wives. With muttered threats and imprecations, she finally managed to get her little boy and girl into the car along with all the assorted equipment needed for another day at school. With them finally seated in the back, she went round and got into the driver's seat. It was only a couple of miles to school and once she had deposited the children, she was looking forward to spending the day with her mother. Shouting into the rear of the car at them once again to stop fighting, she turned on the ignition.

Karim and Khalid had learned a great deal in their time in the camp and now it was being put to good use. They hadn't been able to get any sophisticated explosives but had managed to make a basic device using fertilizer and petrol. The bomb wasn't very powerful but it was designed to fling burning fuel a good way.

Hiding behind a hedge some distance away, they were initially disappointed when it went off. Karim had simply clipped the detonator to the wire that went to the starter motor, something he had done from under the car late last night. The sound was only a muffled crump and the car hardly moved but then it turned into an inferno and the screaming started. Neither of the children made it out but Gabriela did. She was on fire from head to foot and although she managed a couple of paces she was mercifully dead before she crumpled to the ground. The two boys smiled to each other and carefully made their exit just as everyone else started running in the opposite direction.

Sometime later Major Melamed received a phone call. He went white and crumpled into his chair as the voice on the end told him what had happened. Although the accent was odd, he thought he was talking to a policeman but then his blood ran cold as the man continued to speak. 'So, now you know what it is like for your whole family to be murdered. I hope you live for a long time to think about it you bastard. Maybe you won't drop bombs on helpless people ever again.'

Chapter 5

Helen Barratt was excited and not a little nervous. Her reception on the squadron had been everything she had hoped for. She knew she was very lucky to get such a plum job straight out of training but that didn't stop her wondering what it would really be like. She had quickly found that she needn't have worried. The work was straightforward and everyone had made her welcome. Being one of the few girls on the squadron had helped and anyway she knew her looks would make her popular, it was something she had grown up with. But even so, she soon realised there was a real buzz about the place. It was clear that morale was high and everyone was motivated and keen to get on with the job.

And today the Training Officer was taking her flying in a Sea King. When the offer was first made she was cautious and her suspicions only got worse when she had been taken to the Air Station's Survival Equipment Section to have her safety equipment issued and get briefed on its use. Her father's dire warnings sprang to mind about some of the dreadful wind ups the navy inflicted on its new joiners. She slowly came to realise that this wasn't going to be the case today, although she vowed to herself to keep on guard. Little did she know that there had been some debate about doing just this in the crewroom but in the end, none of the men wanted to be the one to get the blame. Her presence was already making itself felt.

Now here she was, dressed in a green flying suit with her Mae West lifejacket around her shoulders and her helmet in her hand as she and Geoff Gregory or GG as he was known, walked towards the massive machine.

GG looked at her and gave her a grin. 'Right Helen, I'm going to do the walk around and you get yourself strapped in as I showed you in the hangar. I'll be along in a minute. If you have any problems one of the ground crew will help out.'

They had reached the forward door with the steps hanging down on their flimsy looking wires and Helen carefully climbed in and seated herself in the left hand seat. The aircraft had a peculiar smell, a mix of hydraulic oil, plastic and aviation fuel. It wasn't unpleasant but very distinctive. She wondered if all helicopters smelled like this as she carefully did up all the straps as she had been briefed to do.

She then adjusted her seat using the various handles until she was comfortable, finally fitting her helmet, realising she should have done that first. With nothing else to do until GG joined her, she tried to make sense of the enormous number of gauges, switches and controls that confronted her. She was completely amazed that anyone could know what they were all for, let alone manipulate them to actually get this incomprehensible machine off the ground. Suddenly, there was a clunk from behind her as GG shut the personnel door and jumped into the seat next to her. She couldn't believe how quickly he managed to do up his straps and get settled.

With another smile, he turned to her. 'Right, I'm going to start her up. Please feel free to ask what I'm doing but I'll try to keep up a running commentary. As you can imagine it's quite complicated but I'll try to explain it all as we go along.'

So saying, his hands flashed with blinding speed around the cockpit and after a few moments and some hand signals to the ground crew outside, she heard the distinctive sound of a gas turbine engine starting up.

'That's the number one engine going,' said GG. 'It isn't connected to the rotors yet but is giving us hydraulic power. So now we can unfold the wings.' His hands danced over the switches on an overhead panel and suddenly Helen saw that the rotor blades that had been folded neatly along the tail of the helicopter were slowly opening and spreading into position. 'The boss insists we always fold the blades,' GG explained. 'We could just leave them spread but the folding system is hydraulic and if it's not used, it tends to not work when you need it. On my last squadron, we came back from Germany last year after three weeks away. The whole squadron taxied in and shut down together. Unfortunately right in front of all the families, several of the aircraft spewed hydraulic fluid everywhere as they tried to fold the blades. So now we always use the system. It's like a lot of things in a helicopter, the more you use it the better it works and if we need to go to sea, the blade fold system is imperative. Right starting number two.'

Once the second engine was running, GG made a spinning signal to the ground crew who gave a thumbs up in response. He then reached up and released a large handle near the ceiling and the rotor blades slowly started to rotate. 'Gotta be careful here,' he explained. 'If it's windy, especially on the deck of a ship, when the blades are going slowly they can dip down and get bloody close to the deck. They could easily take of a bloke's head so we have to watch it.' But soon the rotors were up to speed and the aircraft was thrumming with their vibration. Some more signs to the ground crew and the chocks were pulled away from the wheels. Releasing the brakes, GG pulled up on the collective lever a little and the aircraft started to taxi slowly away from the hardstanding.

Helen was surprised. 'I didn't realise a helicopter could do this.'

'Well, that's why we have wheels. The thing is, the downdraft from these aircraft is pretty fierce when they're in the hover and we don't want to blow over any of the ground equipment or people for that matter. So we'll get to a clear area down this taxiway and then we can play at aviation.'

They taxied until they were near the end of the main runway and GG called for take off on the radio. The tower responded saying that the circuit was clear as GG finished the final pre-take off checks. 'OK Helen, just put your hands lightly on the controls and feel what I'm doing as we lift into the hover.'

With some trepidation, she did as she was told and GG pulled smoothly up on the big lever in his left hand. Helen felt it move and the aircraft's movement changed until with a little jerk it lifted off the ground. She was enchanted. One moment they were a lumbering vibrating ground beast and suddenly they were floating only ten feet up. She felt the rudder pedals move and the nose of the aircraft rotated until they were facing the way they had come.

'Just checking there's no one behind before we take off and all looks good. Tower, this is Whiskey Charlie at point west, request clearance to Merryfield over.'

The control tower responded giving them clearance and Helen felt the pedals move again until they were facing into the wind and then GG pulled even more on the lever and pushed the nose forward. Nine tons of helicopter smoothly accelerated forwards and upwards.

The next hour passed in a blur. There was so much for Helen to take in. GG flew the aircraft to the satellite airfield at Merryfield ten miles away where there was more room to play around as he put it. The first thing he did was get Helen to try to hover the aircraft. When he demonstrated how he did it she was amazed at how little he moved the controls. As soon as he let her have a try she immediately started over-controlling and the aircraft slowly diverged out of the

Arapaho

hover until, with a laugh, GG took control and with an amazing minimum of effort put the Sea King back where it had been.

'How long does it take to learn how to do this?' she asked in frustration.

'Surprisingly, not long. It is literally like riding a bike, the knack suddenly comes. Look, have another go.'

Placing her hands on the controls, Helen once again tried to keep the machine steady. It started to move sideways so she forced herself to make only a small correction, then it started to descend, so she pulled on the collective lever a fraction and the same time pushed on one rudder pedal to keep them straight. Every time the damn thing tried to escape her she forced herself to be gentle with her response.

In the other seat, GG was surprised and quietly impressed. He had been instructing for years and never had a pupil managed to learn to hold a hover so quickly. After a few minutes, he called over to Helen. 'Well done, you realise you are doing all the work now. I haven't nudged the controls once in the last few minutes. Take a rest. I'll take her now.'

With relief but tinged with a little reluctance, she relinquished the controls and only then did she realise how hard she had been concentrating.

GG then flew around the airfield and demonstrated a few more helicopter tricks. He showed her how if he lowered the collective lever completely, when they were in flight, the aircraft descended but the airflow up through rotors allowed for a controlled descent, even a controlled landing. 'But we don't actually do that in twin engine machines like this. However, in the training aircraft the Gazelle and the little Wasp, it's practised regularly. Quite fun but a bit of a bugger if you get it wrong because you only get one chance at it.'

Helen was even more impressed but simply nodded.

'Right, how about a bit of sight seeing?' GG suggested and before she could reply he pushed the nose forward but this time didn't allow the aircraft to climb. They shot along the ground at a height that seemed almost suicidaly low. She swallowed a lump in her throat as GG artfully dodged several trees before allowing the machine to climb just a little.

'This is where we operate Helen, this low it's hard for the bad guys to do anything about us and more to the point its fantastic fun.'

He added with a cheeky grin. 'The stovies don't go below two hundred and fifty feet even if they are doing five hundred knots. Quite often we do a complete sortie not above fifty feet.'

'Stovies?' she managed to croak out as they crested a small hill and shot down the other side with a flock of sheep scattering before them.

'Oh, that's what we call the little boys with the noisy toys, the fixed wing lot. Always posing on about how fast and high they go. Well, I'd rather be down here in the grass.' The aircraft suddenly banked hard to the left and they just missed a little ruined chapel on the top of a small hill.

GG looked over at her and from the look on her face decided that enough was enough and pulled the Sea King up to five hundred feet and settled down to a more leisurely cruise.

'Sorry Helen, are you alright?'

She looked slightly green but it was clear she wasn't going to be intimidated. 'No, I'm fine. So what are we going to do now?'

'Well we've got a little time left so let's go and look at the local area and you can try flying her normally.'

GG climbed the helicopter to a relaxing thousand feet and explained how to fly when in the cruise and then slowly let Helen take control. Once again he was surprised at how quickly she picked it all up.

'You know Helen, it's a shame we don't allow girls to fly or even join up as full officers because frankly, you've picked this up faster than most males I've flown with.'

She looked over at him to see if he was joking but his face looked completely serious. 'I'm flattered GG but I can't see the navy ever letting girls fly or go to sea for that matter, can you?'

'Well, actually, you're wrong about that, not on warships but we often take WRNS to sea in the Royal Fleet Auxiliaries. RFA's are merchant navy vessels, so you never know, you might get the chance as we operate off them quite often. Anyway, how have you found your first few days with us? It must be a bit of a culture shock?'

'Actually, it's not been too bad. Everyone's been very helpful and I've got a fair feeling for the job now.'

'Yes, you've been lucky. We've been very busy for the last few months working up the full MCT capability but that's all done and dusted now. Things should be fairly static until summer leave. This is the ideal time to get your feet under the table.'

'Yes, SOBS said the same thing but can I ask a question?'

'Of course.'

'Well, it's about the CO. I hope you don't mind but I've heard a few stories about him but he seems a bit stern and reserved.'

GG stifled a laugh. 'You should see him with a few beers inside him. He's neither stern nor reserved then.'

'Is there anything I should know? I'm going to be working closely with him after all.'

GG thought for a moment. 'Look Helen, I don't know the whole story but you probably heard about his exploits in the Falklands. That's where he got the big shiny medal but some of that is classified as was the work he did up in the Arctic soon after and no one really knows what went on. But it was his last job that seems to have affected him the most. He was in a frigate, HMS Chester and they got involved in some rather nasty anti-drug operations. Believe it or not, some Columbians got hold of an old war time submarine and Jon was responsible for sinking it. Most people think he did a bloody good job but it seems to prey on his mind a bit. Just give him some space. He's a bloody good boss and the boys all think the world of him, including me I might add.'

'Thanks GG. I'll keep all that in mind.'

'Good, now we have another problem.'

'Oh, what?'

'With all that yacking, we've not really been looking where we've been going. Have you seen a bloody great air station around here anywhere?'

Chapter 6

The Minister sighed to himself in frustration. They had been sitting around the table for several hours and despite an enormous amount of talking nothing was being achieved. He looked out of the conference room window in the Ministry of Defence Main Building at the grey, sluggish Thames, drifting slowly down to the sea and wished he could be on one of the boats he could see, anything other than this permanent in-fighting. He couldn't say he hadn't been warned. His permanent under-secretary had briefed him, the navy and army had been at loggerheads with their light blue RAF cousins ever since the service was formed after the First World War. But you would think that maybe almost sixty years later they could at least make an effort to cooperate.

The Air Vice Marshall had just stopped pontificating about how all air power should be concentrated in the RAF and the Minister was about to have his say when the Admiral got in first. 'Minister, do you know how many enemy aircraft have been shot down since the end of the Second World War?'

The Minister shook his head knowing that he would get the answer anyway.

'Almost thirty and Minister, do you know how many of those have been shot down by the RAF?'

'I am assuming you are going to tell me Admiral.'

'None, the Fleet Air Arm have done it all.'

'That's a cheap shot,' muttered the Air Vice Marshall.

But the Admiral was just getting into his stride. 'Oh no, it's not. It proves that flexible, deployable, airpower is the most effective way of engaging the enemy, especially in the sort of conflicts we find ourselves facing these days. Yes, if the Soviets come over the horizon then things will be different but we have to be realistic. Look at the Falklands, if we had actually had the nuclear carrier we were building in the sixties, with two Phantom squadrons and one of Buccaneers on board do you think the Argies would have been stupid enough to invade? And why didn't she get built? I'll tell you why. It was because the RAF convinced Dennis Healey that all British interests could be defended by RAF aircraft operating from ashore. The only RAF aircraft that were involved in the Falklands either flew out of Ascension and were virtually useless or had to fly from the decks of our carriers, so that argument was clearly a little disingenuous.'

The Minister could see that tempers were getting frayed. The Air Vice Marshall was getting particularly red in the face. 'Gentlemen, this meeting is meant to be considering broad strategy for the next decade. It's quite clear to me that aviation is a discipline that is relevant to all three services. General what are your views?'

The General sat quietly for a moment. A man of few words, people knew that when he spoke, he did it from the heart. 'As far as I'm concerned Minister, I agree with your assessment. There are elements of aviation that are so embedded in the tactical and even cultural ethos of each service that it would be madness to try and split them out and if we did, we would be the only country in the world to try to do so. The Canadians tried a common defence service some years ago and that was a complete disaster.'

The Air Vice Marshall was clearly about to launch into another diatribe but the Minister cut him off. 'Right gentlemen, let's move onto the next item on the agenda, I think we've done that one to death.'

'Sorry but before we do that Minister,' the Admiral intervened. 'There is one issue I would like to advise you about and it's relevant to our discussion.'

'Alright, if it's not going to take too long Admiral.'

'Simply put Minister, we are still short of decks for aircraft and as recent history has shown, you can never have enough aircraft. In particular with our Fortress Falklands concept, we need to keep an anti-submarine presence in the South Atlantic. We are doing this with five Sea Kings operating from RFAs at the moment but a more permanent solution is needed. Clearly, a new carrier is not on the cards and the Invincible class of ships are relatively small and heavily committed. Of course, now that Hermes has gone to the Indians, they are all we have. There is, however, another option we have been working on for some time. We would like to try it out.'

Looking intrigued, the Minister nodded assent.

'It's something the Americans have already tried and we see enormous potential especially if we have to react quickly again, it's called Arapaho.'

Chief Petty Officer, Air Engineering Artificer, brackets 'Mechanical', Jim Merryweather sat in the car in the passenger's seat looking over a particularly scruffy part of Devonport dockyard and a particularly scruffy looking RFA. 'Jesus whose idea was this Sir? This will never work.'

Lieutenant Commander Robin Michaels could only agree. The two of them were normally based down the road in Cornwall, at the Naval Air Station at Culdrose. Both of them had been at a loose end, something that was an anathema to the navy. Robin had just left his Sea King squadron as the Air Engineering Officer and Jim was also between drafts. Two days previously, they had both been summoned to the office of the Air Station AEO and given the proposition. At first, it had seemed an exciting challenge, something different and possibly even revolutionary. After leaving together, they had been given some time to read into the project and set up some office space before they travelled to the dockyard to see the key element of the whole concept.

'Apparently, she was a conventional container ship that they commandeered for the Falklands War and we decided to keep her. She was damaged slightly during the war and has only just been put back into service,' Robin observed, looking at the rust streaked ship in front of them. 'But you can see from her layout how suited she is to the idea.'

'Maybe Sir but being able to float is surely a prerequisite?'

'Don't be such a cynic Chief. I'm sure the dockyard know what they're doing.'

That remark only got another snort of derision from the passenger seat. Privately Robin agreed. The workforce at the dockyard hardly had a reputation for unbounded professionalism. He could only hope that those on high knew what they were doing when they picked this ship and authorised the project.

'Well, let's stop worrying and go and meet her people. We've a great deal of work ahead of us that's clear.'

They left the snug comfort of the car for the bitter wind blowing across the Hamoaze straight into their faces. Robin pulled his coat collar up around his neck as they mounted the dirty gangway that led up to the rear of the ship. As they got higher, he could see the large space of the empty container deck and the idea didn't seem quite so daft.

There was no one to meet them, so using his instincts Robin led them into the ship. More by luck than judgement they found the ship's lounge and entered, grateful for the sudden warmth. The room was palatial by military standards and belied the exterior state of the ship. Comfortable lounge chairs were spread about and a long bar covered almost the whole of one wall.

'Bloody hell Sir, maybe we'll be more comfortable then we though after all,' Jim muttered.

At first there didn't seem to be anyone about but then Robin noticed the back of a bald head peeking above one of the large leather armchairs. He went over and addressed the head.

'Excuse me, I'm Lieutenant Commander Michaels from Culdrose, is anyone expecting us?'

The head turned and put down the newspaper that it had been reading. 'Ah yes, I've been waiting for you.' The man got up and thrust out a hand. Robin took it and looked into the eyes of a tall, middle aged man. The man continued, 'so you're the first of the naval contingent then, welcome on board, I'm John Pipe, the First Officer. I don't suppose you know when all the stuff is due to arrive? We've been kept pretty much in the dark so far.'

'Welcome the club. Oh and this is my Chief, Jim Merryweather and to answer your question, we expect it at the end of next week. It's due in on an American ship. Some will be taken to Culdrose for modification and the rest will be set up on board.'

The First Officer smiled, 'so, in quite a short time we will be the Royal Navy's newest aircraft carrier. I can't wait.'

Chapter 7

Beirut was hot. It was always hot but at least it had the sea breeze to help keep things bearable. Karim sat at a beach side café enjoying a beer, something he shouldn't be doing of course as a devout Muslim. He laughed inwardly at himself at the thought. He was only a Muslim when it suited him. He wondered idly where Khalid was but not for long. His brother led his own life these days. They still worked together and had been moderately successful but Khalid was always a little strange. Ever since their revenge in Jerusalem, he seemed more withdrawn although it didn't stop him dishing out the physical side of the business when it suited him. In fact, he seemed to enjoy that sort of thing more and more these days.

And business was what it was all about today. A short fat man in a greasy white suit approached and Karim nodded to him as he sat at the table, while at the same time signalling to the waiter for another beer.

'So, Ahmed, what news?'

The fat man grimaced. 'Not good, now that the PLO are arriving in strength, it looks like the balance of power is shifting even more.'

'And why should that bother me?' Karim was well aware of the heightening tension in the city and the country but didn't really expect it to amount to much.

'It should, because they are very much against the Christian Government and in turn, the Government won't accept their interference. Many think that there will be fighting before the year is out.'

'Civil war?'

'In my opinion yes and with all the vested interest from Israel and other western nations who knows where it will end?'

Karim was amused at his colleague's nervousness. 'I have seen war my friend and its ugly but it is also an opportunity as well. So far we have made some money by trading information and other commodities. Maybe we will be able to increase the size of our operations. So who do you think will win?'

'That depends on who gets the most outside help. With the West supporting the government and Syria and others on the side of the Muslims who knows what will happen?'

Just then they were interrupted as someone else seated himself at their table. It was Khalid and he looked angry. The waiter had just appeared with the beer that Karim had ordered and Khalid took it without a word and drank half the bottle in one gulp.

'That bloody man has gone too far this time,' he snapped angrily as he stopped drinking. 'I think it's about time we did something about him.'

Karim looked at his brother, not surprised by his sudden appearance but worried about the import of his words. 'I assume you mean the Monk?'

'Who else?' Khalid spat back. 'He has just doubled the price. I have buyers lined up and made commitments on price and the bloody man just decided to charge me more and there is nothing I can do. No one else in Beirut has the quantities of Heroin that I have committed to supply and he knows it.'

'So, will you lose out on the deal?' Ahmed asked. 'Or do you still have some margin.'

Khalid turned to the little man with a look of contempt. 'It's nothing to do with the numbers little man, I don't like being shafted.' And turning to his brother, 'we are going to have to do something.'

Karim had seen the look in his brother's eyes before and knew he wouldn't rest until he had caused mayhem. However, they needed to live somewhere and he still liked Beirut. An out of control brother could ruin all their business in this town.

'Alright. Ahmed, you know where he lives don't you?'

The small man nodded but looked uncomfortable. 'Don't mess with that guy. He has some powerful friends and is always well guarded.'

A glimmer of an idea was forming in Karim's mind. 'No I don't think we should go after him.' Then seeing the look on his brother's face he quickly continued. 'Khalid, he will be too difficult to take but there is another way,' and he outlined his idea.

Two weeks later, they were ready. They had staked out the man's house and had a pretty good idea of his movements. To Karim, it was just like three years ago in the refugee camp only this time the final aim was going to be different. Khalid was driving and Karim was in the passenger's seat. The road was in good repair as would be expected of a rich suburb and the legacy of the French occupation.

Their target appeared around the corner. It was just after four in the afternoon and the road was crowded with cars as the families of the school children waited for their charges to appear. Khalid parked the car alongside the road and they waited like all the others. Their target would recognise the car. They had made great efforts to get one identical to the normal one, in this case, a silver Mercedes. It had been a simple exercise to replicate the correct licence plate and in all respects, it looked like the original.

'Are we sure that the mother has been taken care of?' Khalid asked in a tense voice.

'For goodness sake brother, you know she has. We saw the accident as we drove up.'

It had been easy enough to pay a local to accidentally rear end the real car at the lights only half a mile away and it hadn't even cost them that much. It would take at least an hour to sort it all out and that was more than they needed.

'Here we go,' Karim called and quickly got into the rear of the car as the school gates opened.

At the same time, Khalid pulled the Burka over his head and was immediately unrecognisable. The children streamed out of the gate. The young girl they were targeting saw the car and ran gaily over towards it. Khalid raised his hand in acknowledgement and the girl opened the rear door, threw in her satchel and jumped in. Before she could react to the presence of the man in the rear, Karim had clamped a hand over her mouth and pulled her down out of sight. Khalid immediately drove out and headed down the road while his brother finished subduing the struggling girl.

Two hours later, they were secure in the little house out in the countryside that Ahmed had arranged for them. The girl was locked securely in one of the rooms and it was time to make the telephone call. Karim insisted he do it, he didn't trust Khalid to keep his temper and this needed to be done the right way.

The ringing tone stopped and a man's voice answered. Karim kept it simple. 'If you want to see your daughter again it will cost you a million dollars.'

There was silence for a second and then the man started to bluster that he didn't have that much. Karim knew it was probably true but wanted the man to sweat.

'A million dollars, you have one day and when I ring again. If you don't have it, I will send you your daughter's right ear to encourage you.' He put the phone down before the man could respond.

Two days later, the girl was released to her frantic father, minus her right ear, which he already had. Karim and Khalid pocketed almost a quarter of a million dollars. They had found their vocation in life. They had a working business plan.

Chapter 8

The bar of the King's Head was smoky and crowded. The open fire was throwing out heat and not a few sparks but no one was taking any notice. Morris the landlord was at last about to open the wooden cask of bitter that had been maturing behind the bar for several weeks. Despite ever increasing pleas from his customers, he had refused to broach the beer until he knew it was perfect. The anticipation didn't do any harm to his business either.

'Time ladies and Gentlemen,' he announced looking at the bar clock which was approaching eleven o'clock. The groan from the clientele was met with a grin. 'But as you are all now my guests we can lock the doors and sample some of this beer. As you all know, money cannot change hands as the bar is now closed but don't worry I will be keeping a note of who drinks what.'

A cheer went up as Morris's wife locked the doors trapping everyone inside and the bung was simultaneously knocked out of the keg. Morris knew he was technically breaking the law but as Derek, the village bobby, was sitting on one of the chairs around the fire he didn't feel he needed to worry too much.

Jon was sitting on a bar stool to one side of the bar and was one of the first recipients of a pint mug. He held it up to the light and appraised its murky depths. He then studied the head which closely resembled the froth of a good washing up liquid and tested the temperature which was perfectly warm. Finally, he sniffed the top and inhaled the pungent aroma of malted hops before taking a deep swig. The landlord looked over at him questioningly as he paused. 'Well done Morris, worth waiting for once again,' Jon commented before taking another swig. 'You know all that European frozen piss can't hold a handle to this.'

His remark was met with murmurs of agreement from around the bar.

'So Jon, not playing with your helicopters then?' The comment was in a broad Somerset accent and emanated from the red faced man standing next to him.

Jon looked deeply into his pint and considered the question. 'Not this evening Doug but there again you're not playing with your cows either.'

'Hah, but I will be at five tomorrow morning.'

'Ah well, just for once, I've got the weekend off and I'm going to drink as much of this fantastic brew as I can before staggering home and having a quiet Sunday at home.' Jon looked sad and wistful as he said the words.

His drinking buddy still had enough sense left to realise that Jon wasn't in the mood for banter and didn't pursue the conversation. Jon was well known in the little village and would have been surprised at how much they all actually knew about him and probably not a little embarrassed at how much he was admired.

Two hours later, he wandered down the main street towards the little cottage he lived in occasionally when the navy let him. It was one of those warm, calm summer nights that was full of the smell of growing things and the beauty wasn't lost on him despite his inability to walk in a straight line. He hummed a tune to himself as a full moon peered through the laden trees and an owl hooted somewhere in the distance. When he reached his front door it only took minutes to locate the key and not all that many more to find the lock. With a final effort he got the door open but before he entered the cottage, the owl hooted again. The melancholy of the sound struck a chord inside him and he sat down on the doorstep and contemplated the full white moon. Something tugged at his emotions and for no reason he could think of, he felt tears streaming down his face.

Then, just for a second, his actions of the previous year came back in awful crystal clarity. All the emotions and the sense of loss hit him between the eyes. 'Fuck it,' he said to himself. 'If I can't cry for her in private, when can I?' He sat there for an uncountable time mourning his loss, surrounded by the beauty and earthy aroma of the country he loved, all illuminated by the silver moon. Afterwards, he would swear even to himself that it had never happened and it was almost certainly a product of the late night and the beer but just for a moment he felt the touch of a hand on his neck and a familiar breath in his ear. No words were spoken but it was as if she was saying she was alright, that he was forgiven and shouldn't grieve any more. A shiver shot up his spine but of release not fear. He sat there for a while longer but the night was now still. Eventually, he decided that further self-pity was non-productive and if he didn't get to bed he would either get hypothermia or cramp or more likely both.

The next morning he woke late and as he focused on the motes of dust illuminated by the streams of sun coming through the badly drawn blinds, he realised that despite his obvious hangover he hadn't felt this good in ages.

'*Bugger me that beer must have been a really good brew,*' he thought as he turned over for another snooze knowing the rest of the day was his.

Monday morning and it was back to reality. Sunday had been nice but he had a squadron to run and he had let the Training Officer know that if his name wasn't on the day's flying programme there would be hell to pay. However, as soon as morning shareholders was over and he had seated himself behind his desk there was a knock on the door and the Staff Officer came in with a sheaf of files under her arm. For the first time, Jon really looked at her and realised what a beauty she was. He wondered who in the squadron had already made a move and how successful they had been. Putting the thought aside, he gestured to her to fill up his in-tray.

Helen smiled apologetically as she put the paperwork down. Jon appraised the top of her blonde hair as she leant forward. 'So, GG tells me you enjoyed your trip the other day Helen?'

'Oh yes Boss, it was absolutely fantastic.'

'He also tells me you're a bit of a natural and it's a pity we can't recommend you for flying training.'

Helen blushed at the compliment. 'Maybe one day Boss.'

'Indeed, well you'd better let me get on with all this as just for once I'm going flying today.'

'Oh and Sir, there was a phone call from a Commander on the Admiral's staff. There is going to be a briefing for all CO's over in the FONAC HQ this afternoon after lunch at two o'clock.'

'Did they say what about?'

'No Boss, it sounded quite mysterious.'

'OK,' and then a thought struck him. 'Hang on a second.' And he grabbed the copy of the FLYPRO and swore and then apologised when he realised Helen was still there. 'So much for getting airborne today then.'

That afternoon Jon and the COs of the other squadrons plus a host of staff officers gathered in the main briefing room of the offices of Flag Officer Naval Air Command or FONAC as it was generally known. Jon exchanged pleasantries with his acquaintances but was unable to find out what the briefing was about. It seemed that everyone was as much in the dark as he was.

The door opened and the Admiral walked in and everyone stood. He signalled for them all to sit and went to the front of the room.

'Gentlemen, thank you for coming. I'm sorry it's such short notice but what you are about to hear has only just become a practical reality and I'm sure you will all want to know about it. I won't say anymore as Commander Jones here from Fleet will tell you all.' The Admiral took his seat at the front of the room and was replaced by a tall thin Commander who went straight to the lectern and turned on the slide projector. On the screen next to him a black and white picture of a merchant ship appeared.

'Gentlemen, as you are all aware with the demise of HMS Hermes and Bulwark, we are now reliant on the Invincible class of carriers and any decks available from smaller ships and the RFA fleet. Frankly, our analysis of the amount of deck space we have, especially with the on-going need to patrol the Falklands, is that we have far too little. The Falklands showed us you can never have enough helicopters but the problem we have is that we don't actually have enough decks. So, we've pinched an idea from the Yanks. This RFA is an ex-container ship with a large well deck as you can see. We are going to line the front of the well deck with specially fitted out ISO containers and roof it over to make a hangar then lay a flight deck behind it. The containers will have all the stores workshops and other special equipment to support long term deployments. The deck will be big enough to operate three Sea Kings. In short, it's a modular mini aircraft carrier and if it's successful it will give us an option for creating decks space at very short notice. Not only that but we should be able to operate for quite some time away from shore support. I'll take questions now. Oh and the whole thing is called Project Arapaho.'

Chapter 9

James Merryweather looked out of the second floor window at the garden or what was left of it. Water had been in short supply for many years and lawns and shrubs were the first to suffer. With regret, he remembered the cool grassed-in space where he had hosted many official parties. It was now a dustbowl not even suitable as a place for his children to play. With a sigh, he dragged himself back to the present and turned to his two colleagues, Desmond Hughes, his deputy and Rupert Thomas, his head of station intelligence.

'So gentlemen, sum things up please.' He nodded to Rupert to be first.

The intelligence officer peered down at his notes. 'I won't go into the history too much as we all know it. The country has been in civil war since 75 and over half the original population has fled. Even though it started out ostensibly as a war between the Christians and Muslims there are so many factions involved now it's hard to tell what is really going on. Eighteen months ago, sixty French and two hundred and forty American soldiers were killed by two suicide bombers in their barracks and we're still not actually sure who was responsible. This was followed up by the bomb last year that killed several at the US Embassy. The Israelis have invaded but mainly to attack the PLO who seem to think they can use the place as their training ground. At the last count, there were twenty two identifiable organisations involved in the fighting ranging from Christian militias to Sunni and Shiite Muslims. We are pretty sure that at any one time they have allied with each other in some combination or another and then broken their agreements. On top of all that there is the criminal element. Just about every low life in the area has congregated here to take advantage. Theft and kidnapping seem to be the current favourites. Syria has also been meddling. Currently, a Syrian-backed coalition headed by the Amal militia is seeking to rout the PLO from their strongholds in the Sabra, Shatila, and Bourj el-Barajneh refugee camps. We expect a bloodbath if that happens.'

'So, why should we be worried now? It sounds like business as usual,' observed Desmond Hughes with a cynical smile. A career diplomat, unlike the Ambassador who was a Government appointee, he never seemed to empathise with the people of the country he lived in, unlike his boss who seemed to take every atrocity personally.

Rupert thought for a moment. 'All of our people who wanted to leave were evacuated from the city some time ago. But if this escalation into previously safe countryside continues we will need to consider a second evacuation. There are a lot of British subjects out there helping in the camps as well as in oil company compounds. And there is something else, we think we have an idea who sponsored those suicide bombs and there is good intelligence that they are going to have a second go at western organisations here in the city.'

'What are you suggesting Rupert?' the Ambassador asked with a worried frown.

'Put out a call to all British residents to leave the Lebanon, evacuate them and shut this Embassy down and go as well.'

Desmond gave a bark of laughter. 'Come on old chap, the place is a mess we all know that but pull out, why has it suddenly come to that?'

The Ambassador answered for him. 'Because this country has effectively no longer a government we can work with, because if we don't many of our subjects will die, that's why Desmond.'

As he finished there was an enormous, deafening, noise and all the windows blew in. The heavily weighted lace curtains did their job and contained the flying glass but nothing could stop the blast wave that threw all three men to the floor. Ceiling tiles, paperwork and sand flew around and settled on the three supine bodies. Then, for a moment, there was complete silence before alarms started shrilling. Rupert was the first to come to his senses and he carefully crawled to the window and looked out. The rear wall to the Embassy compound was no longer there but security staff were already running towards the breach. There was no sign of anyone trying to get in which was a blessing. He turned to the other two men. The Ambassador was getting groggily to his feet so Rupert turned his attention to Desmond. His body was still and Rupert carefully turned him over to check for a pulse. He stopped when he saw his face and throat. Some trick of the blast had hurled the coffee tray that had been resting on the conference table into his neck almost severing the head. There was blood everywhere coagulating in the dust.

Rupert knew that the man was well beyond any first aid he might offer. The Ambassador knelt down coughing next to Rupert.

'Time to go. You were right Rupert,' he said sadly, looking at the surprised face of his colleague.

'Right gentlemen, I will go to the PM now and we will table this for Cabinet straight away.' The Foreign Secretary looked worried and tired. The bombing of their Beirut Embassy had caught everyone by surprise as had the recommendation from the Ambassador to pull everyone out, if that were even possible given the state of the country. He turned to the Chief of the Defence Staff. 'Just take me briefly through the options please Admiral.'

CDS looked down at his notes. 'Well Sir, we've cleared this all with the Defence Minister as you know. As long as our other NATO and other national commitments aren't compromised, we think that it should be feasible. The main base closest to the Lebanon is Cyprus and we will activate contingency plans for evacuation by air but we must be realistic. Just getting our nationals to somewhere a commercial or RAF aircraft can get to or even will be allowed to land is going to be bloody difficult. And it's too far away to use shore based helicopters. We have ships stationed in the Mediterranean as well and they will be despatched but of our three carriers, one is in mothballs and one is not yet worked up. Our only operational carrier is committed to NATO exercises and is currently in Jacksonville in Florida and I can't see us getting her released soon.'

'Why is that a problem, why do we need an aircraft carrier?'

'Sir, we need helicopters and as many as we can deploy. If our assessments are correct, then the best way to get our nationals out will be to go to them wherever they are and pull them out to ships off the coast. The problem as always is that we don't have enough ships with operating decks.' He gave the Foreign Secretary a sour look, both men were well aware of the tension between politicians, always keen to save money and the military always keen to be given the tools they considered necessary to do what was asked of them.

'So, how many helicopters can we deploy offshore within a reasonable time?'

CDS looked at his notes. 'We can get HMS Fearless there within a few days with three Sea Kings and two of the RFAs with her can embark another two. There is one other thing we might consider as well. We have just finished converting an RFA, an ex-container ship to carry Sea Kings. Actually, it's a bit of an experiment and she is meant to be going south to the Falklands but she's just about ready. We could deploy her and we could get her there within ten days. That would give us four more aircraft. So that's a total of nine Sea Kings.'

'Is that enough?'

'How long is a piece of string Foreign Secretary? I think it should be and anyway it's all we've got.'

'Right, get it all underway and I'll sell it to the Cabinet.'

Chapter 10

The audience listened in rapt silence. The Yeovilton Air Station theatre was packed with officers and men from every unit on the base. They were all there to listen to the diminutive American Naval Officer who was talking quietly to them from the lectern at the front. His story and the simple way he recounted it was enthralling and horrifying his audience at the same time.

Lieutenant Commander James Willis had been an F4 Phantom pilot during the Vietnam War. He had also been a prisoner of the North Vietnamese for over four years and now spent his time lecturing on his experiences. He had started off recounting how he had been shot down over the North and the treatment he had received from the villagers that had found him, tying him so tightly with ropes that they dislocated both his shoulders and that was just the start. The troops they took him to were even worse and by the time he was taken before an interrogator, he was barely alive. However, for a while, the naivety of his captors worked in his favour. They didn't really know what questions to ask. That all changed when he was taken north to the capital and incarcerated in the infamous 'Hanoi Hilton' prisoner of war camp. The camp was a nightmare. Regular beatings were mixed up with psychological torture. There was no merit in interrogating the inmates as anything they knew was well out of date by then. They were kept as political hostages and treated as badly as their captors could devise without actually killing them.

'It's funny after a while, you start to live in the past,' he looked almost wistful. 'With no hope of an ending, you start to trawl your memories looking for happier times. At least that's what I did to keep sane. Others didn't cope as well of course. We had no idea how long we would be there. There was a ray of hope when we heard that some Hollywood actors had been given permission to visit us but were then amazed and disgusted when they condemned us in front of the world's press. Hey, we were just doing our job but of course we had no knowledge of how opinion at home was turning against the whole war. Even so, I've never forgiven those sons of bitches and never will. And then suddenly it was all over. One day out of the blue, a bus drew up and we were herded towards it. Several guys thought we were going to be taken out and shot for real this time but when we saw the American Embassy staff in their suits we realised it was really over. You know the hardest part was getting back to reality, some of us never really made it but I had a supporting wife and two kids and I guess they kept me sane but I'll be honest I saw a shrink for quite some time after I got home.'

There was silence in the room. No one knew what to say, everyone had been touched by the simple honesty of the man in front of them and his story which almost defied belief.

'So guys, I now spend my time telling people like you what to expect, what it can be really like. The first lesson is probably the most important and that is don't get caught in the first place. The best time to escape is when you hit the deck before they've got their hands on you. After that, your chances diminish very fast. When I landed, I was hurt from the ejection but it was nothing to what happened to me afterwards. And then you have to dig in, to find the strength inside you because believe me no one is going to help.' He looked up as a hand was held up in the audience. 'Yes Sir, you have a question?'

One of the pilots responded. 'Sir, it seems to me that we go through all this training for survival and resistance to interrogation and the rest but from what you say, I wonder if it's really worthwhile. How can anything prepare you for the sort of thing you went through?'

'You would be surprised how often I'm asked that and will probably be surprised by the answer. Get as much training as you can. Yes, in some ways you are right, nothing can prepare you fully for the reality but every ounce of prior knowledge is gold dust. Let me illustrate that for you in a rather roundabout way. In the Korean War, many prisoners were treated badly and they were from many nations. You Brits fared quite well but the one nation that drove the Koreans mad were the Turks. You see the conditions in the camps weren't far off what many of them were used to at home. Not one Turkish soldier cracked, not one. So as you can see the more you know, the more you are in a position to do something about it.'

There was some muted chuckling from the audience and the questions started to flow. It was over half an hour before Commander Air stood up and called the presentation over, thanking their guest and inviting him to the hospitality of the wardroom for lunch.

Jon and Brian headed back to the squadron, there wouldn't be time to spend propping up the bar unfortunately as Jon would dearly have liked to talk with their lecturer some more. However, he was once again on the flying programme and wasn't going to miss out.

'Jesus that guy went through hell,' he observed to Brian. 'And his answer to that first question was really interesting. I have to say I've often wondered about all that shit they put us through during survival training. I guess I'll have to think again.'

'Me too,' responded Brian. 'Let's just hope we never end up in a situation like that. Hopefully, there's nothing going on at the moment anyway.'

'Hah, we thought that in eighty two remember?'

'Good point, oh what does Helen want?' Brian asked as he spotted Staffy walking swiftly towards them both.

Helen quickly reached them. 'Sorry to be the bearer of bad news again Boss but we've just received a priority signal from FOF3. Full squadron recall and prepare for an emergency deployment. You're to contact them as soon as you can, seems the guano has hit the rotating mechanism somewhere.'

'Shit,' said Jon as he read the signal which told him no more than Helen had already told him. 'Right Brian, I'll get on the phone. You initiate full recall and then get yourself, SPLOT and the AEO into my office as soon as you can.'

An hour later, Jon stood on a packing case in the hangar, in front of the whole assembled squadron. The curious faces of all the aircrew and maintainers looked up at him, all wondering what was going on.

'Right everyone,' Jon announced in a loud voice so everyone would hear. 'As you know, something is up. I've just got off the phone from FOF3. You may remember on the news the other day there was a bomb at the British Embassy in Beirut. Well, it's been decided to evacuate all remaining British nationals from the country. It's deemed unlikely that commercial or RAF fixed wing aircraft will be able to land and even if they could, most of the people we are after are spread all over the country. So, we have been tasked to get them out. The other two squadrons are committed elsewhere and anyway we already have the three cabs of A Flight deployed on Fearless so the rest of us are going to join them. We are all going, that's the three Mark Fours and the two Mark Twos. When we arrive, the Mark Two's will deploy to the two RFAs, Olna and Tidespring, who will be there. There is already one Mark Two from 826 on Olna so that means we will have a total of nine aircraft. Here's the fun bit. We will transit out and then operate from a converted RFA called Arapaho. She wasn't meant to be ready quite yet but they have accelerated her completion. We can stow five cabs on deck and then when the Mark Two's deploy to the RFAs we will operate from her. We will treat this as an operational deployment to the field so we take all our stores Fly Away Packs and support equipment with us. COMAW with be out there as well and in overall command. I'm sorry, I know you were all looking forward to summer leave after all the preparation work we've been doing but that's life in a blue suit I'm afraid. We need to start getting ready now and I want to be able to get the stores down to Plymouth starting tomorrow. We will embark the aircraft off Plymouth Sound in two days time. I know this is a big ask but I also know we are up to it. There are several thousand British people who will be depending on us. Let's get to it.'

He stepped down to a quiet hush as everyone digested the news. The reverie was broken by the stentorian voice of the Senior Maintenance Rating. 'Right you bloody shambles, you heard the boss, time to show the bloody rag heads a thing or two once again. Don't just bloody stand there. Get on with it, you know what to do.'

Jon smiled as his men rapidly dispersed, confident that in two days' time they would indeed be sailing away from England once again.

Chapter 11

The dry dusty wind ruffled the cloth of the tent making a slapping noise. No one inside took the slightest notice. It was the background to their lives. That and the ever present stink of unwashed humanity. Marie Jubert put the emaciated, dying infant back in its cot. Her only hope was drugs and she didn't have any, not even the simple antibiotic and rehydration drinks she needed. The baby was one of several lying in cots in the tent. Attended by their mothers, she knew there was little hope for many of them. She had been working here for almost a year now as part of the Médecins Sans Frontières organisation and supported by the Red Cross. The drive and vocation she had felt when she had started was slowly turning to despair. The camps were meant to be for the poor and displaced persons of the region but were slowly turning into armed camps for the angry and displaced who wanted to fight back. Although she had sympathy with them, they didn't actually seem to know who to fight against and she felt strongly that they were being used by puppet masters far away from the dust and the blood. And of course, in all this it was the babies that suffered the most.

Her husband Jean came in and saw the tired look on her strained face. He went up behind and put his arms around her. 'Good news darling, they say a convoy should be through this evening and there are our supplies on board.'

Marie shrugged. She had heard it all before. 'I will believe it when I see it. And what about these stories of the fighting getting closer?'

'Yes, that seems true as well. I have also heard that there may be an evacuation soon. The British are definitely coming to take out their people and I'm sure we could go too. There are only ten of us and five are British anyway. Could we really carry on with half the staff?'

'But that would mean leaving everyone we've been caring for, for so long, all these children,' she said with anguish, looking around the crowded tent. 'I'm not sure I could do that.'

'I know, I feel the same but what can we do if the Syrians attack?'

'Treat the wounded?'

'But what with? We can barely keep up with the normal problems of the refugees here. We have nothing to help wounded fighters, no morphine, no capacity for real surgery. And you know that most of the ordinary people will leave as soon as any fighting starts. We will just be caught in the middle.'

'I suppose so but there again will they even let us go? If things are getting so desperate, you know what they're like.'

They worked all afternoon doing what they could for their patients and to Marie's surprise, a convoy of battered trucks did arrive that evening. On board the last one were their cases of medical supplies.

As the back of the truck was opened up, she looked at the cases of medicine with dismay. All the boxes had been ripped open and there was mess everywhere. With a sinking heart, she knew why. Sure enough, when she started checking the contents, all the morphine had been stolen. Rounding on the hapless driver had been no consolation. He denied all knowledge of anyone looting the contents but Marie knew he was lying and also that there was absolutely nothing she could do about it. At least her other medicines were there and she should be able to treat the babies for the dysentery that was killing them but she knew it was only a temporary reprieve. That night she cried herself to sleep in Jean's arms.

The anonymous, narrow, dusty street had avoided the ravages of the war, being well away from the fighting areas and like many of its kind had small doors opening onto the airy open houses hidden behind them. This particular house wasn't big but was well appointed and had clearly had money lavished on it.

Karim sat in the light, well tended garden and looked in satisfaction at the wad of money he had just been given. It was not quite as much as he had hoped for. Morphine was in short supply but not as much as recent years. The Red Cross had been very active. Khalid joined him and grunted acknowledgement as he took a seat next to his brother.

'I could always go and retrieve our merchandise brother. Then we could sell it again.'

Karim looked at his twin. The years had been relatively kind. Behind the beard, his eyes were still hard and bright and the scar across his face still clear. Karim expected he looked much the same but without the scar of course. He also knew that his brother actually meant what he had just said. It was the thing that marked them as different.

'Don't be so bloody silly Khalid, why do you always have to take the most aggressive line. We still have to trade in this city and alienating our customers is not a good idea.'

If Khalid was worried by his brother's tone it didn't appear on his expression. 'So, a good operation then? Not many more of those likely. We'd better start looking for other ideas. It looks like the PLO and Syrians will be starting their own private war soon.'

'Agreed brother, you know I've been thinking, we've a fair amount in our bank accounts now, maybe it's time for a little holiday away from this benighted country. Maybe even shift our activities away permanently.'

Khalid thought for a moment. 'Not a bad idea, I've never really thought of that, what with things being so lucrative here but with even the country side becoming a battle zone maybe you're right. Where were you thinking of?'

'Oh, I don't know. We can afford anywhere. How about the South of France?'

'What about travel documents and identities?'

'That shouldn't be a problem. I can set that up in a matter of weeks, even days.'

Khalid looked thoughtful. 'We've never really looked to the future much have we? Maybe you're right. We have plenty of money now. In fact, now I consider it, I wonder we have stayed so long.'

Karim laughed. 'Because the pickings have been so easy, that's why. But if you are in agreement then I'll set the wheels in motion.'

Khalid nodded his assent. 'Meanwhile, there is a rumour that some of the western countries are finally getting cold feet and will be pulling all their people out. I do wonder if there might be a final opportunity for us when they come.'

'Have you had an idea then?'

Khalid explained to his brother what he had been thinking. They talked well into the night and agreed to one last operation.

Chapter 12

The long low swell was generated by the shoaling waters of the Bay of Biscay. Atlantic waves that had travelled over three thousand miles over water thousands of metres deep suddenly found themselves in less than two hundred metres. They piled up on the continental shelf and caused the RFA Arapaho, as she was now called, to roll in a slow ponderous manner. On her large flight deck was one of the Sea Kings they were transporting and right forward, three others were stowed in the hangar which had been constructed out of two rows of cargo containers with a roof stretching between them. The flight deck was made up of prefabricated squares all designed to fit standard container ship strong points.

The aircraft swayed to the motion of the ship on their oleos but were tightly held down to the deck by chain lashings. They were ranged to free up one deck landing spot at the rear of the flight deck. Once the ship reached the Mediterranean, the two blue painted Mark 2s would be disembarked and the deck would be capable of operating the remaining three machines in relative freedom. It was now dark and the weather was unusually calm for the notorious Bay, more noted for its gales and ship-breaking seas. The RFA was being followed by a long streak of silver caused by the phosphorescent plankton in the sea but no one was taking any notice.

Jon and Toby Jones, the Senior Pilot, were standing in companionable but tense silence to one side of the bridge overlooking the deck. The area was dedicated to aircraft control and known as Flyco. It controlled all air operations around the ship and on deck. Lieutenant Bill Smithers, who was the ships aircraft controller, sat in a swivel chair in front of a bank of switches and microphones. They were all waiting for the radio to inform them of the return of their fifth aircraft which had flown ashore to Corunna in northern Spain that afternoon to collect stores and a couple of passengers. A signal had been received but was scant on detail as to who the passengers were. The aircraft was late.

Toby leaned over, 'Bill, just give the radar room another call will you? See if they have anything at all.'

Arapaho

Jon looked at his deputy knowing that the radar controller would have told them as soon as he had any contact but also sympathising, the wait was getting to him as well.

A negative answer was soon forthcoming and Toby turned to Jon. 'I think we should be getting worried Boss. I know it's a long transit and they may have been held up ashore but they should have launched some time ago and we should have heard from them on the HF radio by now. I think we ought to get the other cab ready, just in case.'

Jon shared Toby's concerns but also knew that GG and Brian who were crewing the aircraft, knew what they were doing. 'In this case Toby, I'm thinking that no news is good news. If they had had a problem we would have heard either from them or the Spanish Coast Guard by now and we haven't. It wouldn't surprise me that their HF has gone tits up. You know how unreliable it is.' However, it wasn't that bad an idea and he was about to tell Toby to at least get the duty crew ready when the VHF radio burst into life.

'Mike Charlie this is Whiskey Bravo do you read over?'

An air of relief washed around the room and Bill reached for the radio microphone. Whiskey Bravo I read you loud and clear, stand by.' The radar room was calling for his attention as they also had finally found their target. After a brief exchange, he got back on the radio. 'Whiskey Charlie, believe we have you contact at one seven five range twenty eight miles, request you chirp for indent.'

The radar room came straight back and confirmed that the aircraft's transponder had 'chirped' the correct signal and they had the contact identified.

Before Bill could radio back, the aircraft got in first. 'Mike Charlie, sorry we're late, our HF does not appear to be working so we were not able to establish comms. However, be advised that we suffered a birdstrike a while ago. We were marginal on fuel to turn around so we continued but we have shut down the number two engine as a precaution as it started running hot. Request at least twenty five knots of wind over the deck if possible for a single engine landing.'

Toby leant over Bill. 'Ask if they could use the damaged engine in an emergency in case we have trouble with that much wind, it's going to be tight.'

Arapaho

The dialogue continued for several minutes. Once the aircraft had closed to within ten miles, the ship turned into the wind and went to maximum revolutions. Being an ex-container ship, Arapaho wasn't designed for high speed but even in the prevailing calm conditions, she was just about able to generate the required relative wind. GG confirmed that the damaged engine would be restarted at the last moment in case it was needed but felt confident it wouldn't.

In a few minutes, the aircraft's red and green navigation lights could be seen approaching from astern. The flight deck flood lights were turned on and they all held their breath as the massive machine slowed to land.

'Whiskey Charlie you are cleared to land. The relative wind is red two zero at twenty four knots.'

A terse 'roger' acknowledged the radio call showing that GG was working harder than his earlier laconic radio calls had indicated. The aircraft didn't actually stop in the hover alongside the ship as it usually would but continued at angle in directly to the spot. The Flight Deck Officer waved his illuminated bats, providing further guidance, as the aircraft made a direct descent to landing spot on the deck where it thumped down firmly, the oleos compressing with the impact. The flight deck crew ran in and attached four nylon lashings to the helicopter and then ran clear as the remaining engine was shut down and the rotors slowed to a stop. Jon thanked Bill and made his way down the ladder to the flight deck. There was enough light from the flight deck flood lights and the moon for him to see feathery remains around the intake of the starboard engine. The forward personnel door and stairs clanked open and GG clambered down and joined him.

'Nice one GG, looks like at least half a duck has gone down the intake.'

GG looked up at the mess. 'That'll teach him to get in my way. Have we got a spare engine Boss? Because I don't think that one's going to be of much use any more.'

'Yes, several in fact. Now, did you get all the stores we needed? And who were these passengers we were told to expect?'

GG grinned. 'Ah yes Boss, there's some bloke who says he knows you and also someone who I have to say I wasn't expecting. Oh, here they are.'

Arapaho

Coming around the side of the aircraft were two people who Jon recognised at once and with a great deal of surprise. The first was a face he hadn't seen for several years. The other he had seen only a few days ago.

Jon's old friend from the Falklands War and other adventures, Rupert Thomas, held out his hand in greeting. 'Jon we always seem to be bumping into each other. I have to say I was glad to hear you would be in charge of this little exercise.'

Jon shook his hand with warmth. They hadn't seen each other since his foray into the Arctic some years ago but there remained the bond of shared perils and also a large degree of mutual admiration and respect. 'Oh shit, if MI6 are in on this, does this mean more trouble? It usually does.'

'Probably I'm afraid but isn't that what we're paid for? And thank you for the usual thrilling helicopter ride. That's the second time I've landed on one bloody engine.'

'Oops sorry about that but you shouldn't have joined if you can't take a joke.'

Jon quickly turned to his other visitor. 'Helen, well, you said you wanted to go to sea. Seems you've got your chance for whatever reason. Look let's all go up to my cabin and you can tell me what this is all about.' He also spotted Brian clambering out of the Sea King and called over to him to join them and grab SPLOT as well.

Half an hour later they were all seated in Jon's palatial cabin. Unlike a warship, it was a suite with a separate bedroom and a large living room. Rupert looked around with admiration. 'Bloody hell Jon, this is a little better than Prometheus in the Falklands.'

'Well, Arapaho was built as a commercial ship, so some of us get the perks. There are mess decks for the lads in the new areas, I'll show you later. Anyway, this is all a bit mysterious, the signal didn't say who was coming or why in any detail, so how about telling me the reason you and my Staff Officer are here. I assume it's for the same purpose?'

Rupert suddenly looked serious. 'Yes, let's cover the key points. You probably remember that my job when we last met was head of the Scandinavian division. Well someone decided I needed some more field experience. For the last year I have been head of section for the Lebanon, based in the Embassy in Beirut. And before you ask, I was in the Embassy when that bloody bomb went off. It was my recommendation to the Ambassador that was finally acted upon. There are still too many British subjects in the country and its time to get them out and that's going to be your job Jon. As you know there is a Multi-National Force deployed there as well and it's quite possible our troops will need evacuation as well. Frankly, the whole country's a mess and the politicians are at last realising that our presence there might actually be counter-productive. I've got detailed briefing material and all the information you should need. We can go through it together on the way into the Med and then brief your people so we can plan the operation.'

Jon leant back in his chair. He wasn't surprised but was very glad that it was Rupert who he would be dealing with as he knew they worked well together. That still left one unanswered question. 'So Helen, why are you here?'

Helen looked a little abashed and was about to speak but Rupert got in first. 'Blame me Jon. I needed someone to accompany me with some Cryptographic Key material for the special communications gear that we've brought. When I heard that it was your outfit I would be working with, I asked for a squadron officer to accompany me. I didn't realise that all the men had already embarked but Helen is cleared to the right levels to handle the stuff and she was quite persuasive.'

Jon looked queryingly at the girl who was blushing slightly. 'Well Boss, I do have Positive Vetting clearance, it was necessary for a short job I did before joining the squadron and one of the things I specialised in was secure communications and cryptographic material. So it seemed a good idea and this is an RFA so I can be here and FOF3 staff cleared it.' She finished slightly lamely.

Jon laughed. 'Well done Helen, it seems you were needed so that's fine. Now, I'm sure we can find you both adequate accommodation. You've both had a long day and probably want to get sorted out. We'll have plenty of time to cover all the detail in the next few days, so Toby here will find you some cabins and let's meet up in the bar in an hour or so. If you think the cabins are palatial just wait until you see the bar.'

Chapter 13

'Bloody Met men,' Toby Jones muttered as Arapaho's bows slammed once again into a massive Mediterranean wave. He was standing with Jon on the spacious bridge and although they were far above the flight deck, the occasional blast of spray rattled against the glass windows like hail.

'To be fair, he did warn us that the Med could be unpredictable this time of year.' Jon countered.

Toby snorted. 'That's a good way of getting a get out of jail free card if ever I heard one.'

Just then Dave Southgate the Squadron Air Engineer Officer, otherwise known as 'Engines' and Robin Michaels who had stayed on as the ship's Air Engineer came in through the bridge wing door, shaking water from their foul weather clothing.

'All snugged down Engines?' Toby asked. 'We won't be flying in this for a while.'

'Actually, we have a problem,' the AEO replied. 'Robin and I have discovered one or two bijou designette issues with the setup. I think you'd better come down and see for yourselves.'

The four officers made their way carefully down several ladders until they were on the flight deck. Two Sea Kings were just visible in the hangar and the other three had been pushed as far forward as possible to get as much protection from the weather as the hangar complex could afford. Jon immediately noted that the deck was regularly awash with water being thrown up by the bows. With the wind howling, he kept his counsel until they were past the deck parked aircraft and into the relative peace of the hangar. He then realised what the problem was.

'Shit Dave, isn't an aircraft hangar meant to offer some protection from the bloody weather?' The floor was as awash as the flight deck and it was clear that the front row of containers stretching across the ship was offering little or nothing in the way of protection from the spray being thrown up by the ship's bows.

The AEO grimaced. 'In this case Boss, it's not stopping the sodding water it's merely slowing it down a little. All I can say is that it's bloody good she wasn't sent down south before we found this out. A little Mediterranean blow like this is nothing compared to the weather down there.'

'And the aircraft? Is it going to harm them?' Toby asked.

'Not in the short term SPLOT,' the AEO replied. 'As soon as this blows out we'll wash them down with fresh water. I wouldn't want to repeat this too often though. Oh and there's another problem you ought to know about.'

'Go on.'

'Tyres, we're shagging them out for a pastime on this rough deck the Yanks have given us. We've already used up nearly all our spares. I've got more on demand and they should meet us in Cyprus but we're going to have to be bloody careful.'

Jon shrugged. He knew that Arapaho was very much a concept at this stage. 'We shouldn't be surprised, putting something together like this at short notice was always going to throw up issues. I guess the key question is whether it will affect our mission once we get to the Lebanon?'

'No Boss,' Dave responded. 'None of this should stop us doing the job.'

Jon was about to reply when they all felt the deck shudder below them as they slammed over a larger wave than normal. It was followed by a large cracking noise and a shaft of weak sunlight suddenly poured in from the port side of the hangar.

'Oh fuck,' shouted Robin. 'That's the Met Shack, its broken free.'

They could all see that the container on the top row at the front of the port side of the hangar had moved and a large gap had opened up as a consequence.

'Is there anyone in there,' asked Jon anxiously.

'Its manned twenty four hours a day,' Toby responded looking worried. 'Let's get up there and see what we can do.'

With Jon in the lead, the four of them ran over to the port side and climbed the ladder to the second level. A balcony ran around the whole hangar at that height but it had sheared away when the container of the Met shack had moved. Jon realised that it was the cracking of the metal grating that had alerted them in the first place.

The door to the shack opened and a frightened face appeared.

'For Christ's sake don't come out,' Jon shouted as the man looked towards him. 'Look, the catwalk has failed.'

Just then there was another lurch and the shack moved even further outboard. Jon turned to the hangar floor alerted by a shout. Robin was holding up one of the chain lashings used to secure the helicopters in rough weather.

'Can you reach the bottom corner of the shack? There should be a ring there and you can clip this on,' Robin shouted up.

Jon looked where Robin had indicated and saw the ring but it was going to be hard to reach it even if the whole thing didn't move any further and there was no guarantee of that. He turned to Toby behind him and told him to reach down for the end of the lashing and pass it up to him. With the large metal fitting in his hand, he leaned forward towards the ring but he was several feet short. He didn't dare go any further as the remains of the catwalk he was standing on was bending alarmingly already.

'Toby, grab my belt and take my weight, get Engines to help support you and then I will lean forward. I should be able to reach'

'Be bloody careful Boss,' Toby responded. 'That thing could go overboard any moment.'

'Tell me about it.' replied Jon through clenched teeth as he leant forward with the two men behind him taking his weight. He soon realised he would need two hands. Not only did he have to get the claws of the lashing onto the ring but he then needed to twist the collar at the end to get them to close firmly. It took three attempts. The first two were far off the mark and then another lurch made the container slip back towards him. It made the job much easier but he suddenly realised that if it happened again he could be crushed between it and the next one. Suddenly the claws were on the ring and he was twisting the securing collar tight.

'It's on,' he called. 'For God's sake pull me clear.'

He felt himself being pulled backwards and was suddenly standing safely again. On the hangar floor, Robin and several of the aircraft maintainers were securing the chain lashing to a deck ring and tightening it. The container of the Met Shack was secure at least temporarily until they could make a better job of it. Someone got a ladder up to the door and helped the shaken Met Officer down as more chain lashings were being readied.

'Come on guys,' said Jon. 'Let's leave the experts to it. I really think a trip to the bar is in order.'

'Yes and Boss you're going to have to explain to the boys why you took so many risks just to rescue the bloody Met man,' Toby responded with a laugh.

The uneven skyline of the ridge along the top of the rock of Gibraltar formed the dramatic backdrop to the patio outside the restaurant. All the squadron officers and a few guests had mustered for a run ashore while the ship made its unplanned stop having returned to the naval base for repairs. Jon knew it would be their last chance to let their hair down before operations started in earnest. A few 'looseners' in the bar on board had started the party spirit going and things were livening up.

He turned to Brian who was sitting beside him. 'The only problem Brian is that I'm the bloody Boss now. When this all goes pear shaped, as it almost certainly will, it'll be me in the shit. I never used to worry about that when I was a squadron shag.'

'Don't worry Jon, Toby and I have got it covered, you just relax for once.'

Jon snorted with derision. 'Yeah right, I've been on runs ashore with you before, you seem to forget. Remember Hamburg? Or hang on, how about Fort Lauderdale, or even Newcastle for that matter?'

'Never happened,' his friend replied with a grin. 'Anyway, honestly, don't worry, part of being the boss is delegation and we'll keep this lot out of the poo until we sail.'

Jon nodded and looked around at his guys. They all seemed to be enjoying themselves. The main course of Paella had just been served and suddenly the conversation was subdued as they all started to eat. Jon suddenly felt a glow of enormous satisfaction. This was his squadron and these were his people. Not only that but there was a real job waiting for them at the end of the Mediterranean, not some endless NATO exercise but a real task that would make a difference. His eye was caught by the one odd person out, sitting in the middle of the table to his right. Helen was in a simple summer dress and for once had let her hair down. Not for the first time, Jon realised what a stunner she was, especially when she was out of the rather drab WRNS uniform. Her blonde hair had a slight curl to it as it fell in cascades down her back and her startling deep blue eyes were enhanced by the clearness of her skin. Her dress did little to conceal the figure underneath it. With a start, he realised he had been staring

Arapaho

and she looked up and caught his eye just as he was about to look away. She smiled. Jon smiled back and then paid serious attention to his meal hoping that she wouldn't see his blush from where she was sitting.

When the meal finished and the usual bun fight about how to pay for it had been sorted out, the talk turned to where to go next. Various suggestions were made but Gibraltar was a fairly limited place having been cut off from the mainland by the Spanish for many years now. In the end, the inevitable proposal was made and by unanimous consent, they all agreed to head for the Casino. It had a bar that stayed open later than most and everyone suddenly felt lucky.

The doorman grinned as several dozen, fairly lively naval officers signed themselves in and dispersed to the various tables. They all knew that the drinks were half price if you were playing.

Jon had a weakness for Black Jack. He very rarely went into Casinos but when he did he always preferred the cards. He also won quite often.

Just as he took a seat at a fairly empty table, he was alerted to the presence of someone else by the waft of perfume that accompanied them.

'So Boss, are you going to teach me how this works? I've never been in a Casino before.'

He turned and looked straight into Helen's eyes. With a coolness he didn't feel, he offered her the chair next to him. 'Sure Helen, it's like Pontoon except the odds aren't quite so good.' He went on to explain the simple rules and then they started to play. For some reason, the cards didn't go his way and very shortly he had spent all his fifty pounds worth of chips, the most he ever allowed himself. Helen, on the other hand, seemed to have the luck of the gods and the pile of chips in front of her was growing almost magically.

'Sorry Helen, I'm cleaned out but don't let me stop you, you seem to be on a roll. Are you sure you've never played before?'

She laughed. 'I never said I haven't played, merely that I haven't been in a Casino before. When you grow up with three brothers you learn quite a lot on the way.'

Jon grinned ruefully. 'Well I'll leave you to it, I think I'll head back to the ship now, goodnight.'

Helen looked slightly surprised, even disappointed but Jon knew that if he didn't bail out now he would regret it in the morning in possibly more ways than one and anyway there was something he wanted to do. He quickly sought out Brian who was at a roulette table.

'Heading home now Brian, I'll trust you to keep this lot in order. No, don't worry I know my own way back and I feel like a bit of a walk anyway.'

As he made his way back to the dockyard gate on his own, he stopped at the little overgrown garden by the side of the road. He had discovered the place on his first visit to Gibraltar as a Cadet when in the Dartmouth Training Squadron and always made an effort to pay his respects. Slightly maudlin with all the booze he had consumed, he felt a great wash of melancholy as he looked at the gravestones of some of the survivors of the Battle of Trafalgar. One in particular always took his attention. He reached over and pulled some leaves away so he could read the inscription clearly. He often wondered if in some way they were related. The inscription was quite simple and that made it even more poignant, it gave the date and then simply said 'Joshua Hunt, Fourteen years, Powder Monkey, HMS Victory.'

Chapter 14

Eight O'clock the next morning, the squadron had its usual 'shareholders' meeting. Jon felt quite smug as although he felt a little jaded, it appeared to be nothing compared to the state of some his aircrew. They all stood up for him as he entered with SPLOT and SOBS and he waved to them all to sit down. The meeting started with the usual met brief. It appeared that the weather was due to settle down now and it should be good from here to the eastern Mediterranean. There were several muttered comments about the Met guys arranging it so they wouldn't end up going over the side with the met shack until SPLOT shushed the culprits.

Robin then gave a brief on the state of the repairs which were now complete. 'They should hold up with the weather we expect from now on,' he explained. 'But a serious rethink is going to be needed if this ship ever goes down south. However, we are still likely to get some water coming in if it gets rough, so we will just have to muddle through as best we can.'

Jon thanked everyone and then stood and took centre stage. 'Listen up you bunch of drunks, that's our last run ashore for a while. We get serious from here on in. We sail at midday and the flypro starts as soon as we are clear of the Rock. It's only a few days until we're on station and I want us all to be really well up to speed with day and night operations. We still don't know the details of the tasking and exactly what to expect. However, one thing I do expect is that we are all in the best possible shape to deal with whatever comes our way. Any questions?'

There were none and so everyone dispersed, some to start flying, some to nurse their hangovers elsewhere. Jon asked Toby to join him in his cabin for a more detailed chat.

As the room quickly emptied, Helen found herself seated at the back and suddenly realised there was nothing for her to do. All the squadron paperwork was up to date. Most of it had been left behind at Yeovilton anyway. She had been doing some work compiling intelligence with Rupert Thomas but he had disappeared at Gibraltar. The few days on board had apparently been sufficient and the lure of getting back to Beirut faster by aircraft had been too much to resist.

At one point, she had considered asking to go with him but the opportunity to suggest it had never arisen.

She remembered back to the arguments she had had with her parents when she had announced that she was going to join the WRNS. Although her father had been a Lieutenant Commander in the navy during the war, for some reason he was dead set against any of his offspring following in his footsteps. He never spoke about what he did or experienced during his time in the navy but it was clear something had happened. She knew he had been in the battle of the Atlantic and also the Arctic convoys but that was as far as it went. Any attempt to question him brought only silence or an immediate change of subject. Her mother didn't help either. She always seemed to agree with him and offered nothing in the way of support. But growing up as the fourth child in a household of boys, she was always trying to prove herself. She did the law degree to keep dad happy but the more she saw about the life, the less she was attracted to the idea of dusty offices or drab courtrooms. The day she announced to the family that she had, in fact, joined up was etched in her brain. At first, dad had been silent. Her two brothers, who were at home at the time, actually looked at her with something approaching respect but when her mother burst into tears it all kicked off. Harsh words were exchanged. Her father pointed out that she wasn't even joining the real navy, as WRNS Officers weren't subject to the Naval Discipline Act and couldn't serve at sea or in any of the fighting units. She had to smile at the recollection. Here she was at sea as part of a Naval Air Squadron about to go into a real operation. Then she sighed to herself, of course, she couldn't fly one of the helicopters or go ashore to maintain them. So maybe dad was right. However, there were rumours starting to circulate that girls might be allowed to serve properly soon. It had happened in several other countries already. She had no doubt she would be at the head of the queue if it ever happened here.

And life on the squadron was so much fun, even better than she had imagined. Yes, she had had to fend off nearly all the males in the crewroom at one time or another, even a couple of the married ones but that was something she had had to deal with all her life. She was well aware of the effect she had on the male of the species. In fact, several of them were quite tempting. She had even surprised herself when she turned them down. It was starting to get a habit she realised. But just being involved in a fighting unit with so much get up and go let alone testosterone was exhilarating. And then there was the Boss.

Her thoughts were interrupted when Brian put his head around the door. 'Ah, there you are Helen, got a moment?'

'Of course SOBS, plenty of them in fact.'

'Not for much longer I'm afraid. We've got a little job for you and you're going to need a little extra military training to go with it.'

Intrigued she got up and followed Brian out of the door.

'Let's go to my cabin first,' he said as they made their way back over the flight deck as one of the Sea Kings was being manned up by two of the pilots. Brian didn't offer any more information until they were seated in his cabin in the superstructure.

'Now Helen, you probably realise we could have sent you home from Gib?'

She had wondered why that hadn't been proposed but didn't want to ask in case it triggered just the event she wanted to avoid.

'Yes SOBS but you didn't expect me to ask why while we were there did you?'

He laughed. 'Good girl, well Jon and I have decided that you could be really useful if we have to do a large evacuation. We've checked with the powers that be and as this is not classified as a war zone as such, then we can continue to use you unless actual hostilities break out. Is that alright with you?'

'Of course but I would like to know what it is you're suggesting.'

'Put simply, I need a deputy. Almost certainly, we will be putting a Forward Operating Base ashore. You probably know that it's unusual to have Observers appointed to a Commando squadron. But as we have the additional MCT task, I got the job. However, for this operation, the Boss wants me on the ground to coordinate the evacuation as an Operations officer and I need someone to coordinate and control the evacuees. We're talking about logging who we take out, collating information about where others might be that sort of thing. There's not a lot of normal staff work for you to do here so, think you're up to it?'

Helen's eyes were positively gleaming. 'Try and stop me.'

'Ah, there is one thing though. If you go ashore you will need to carry weapons for self-defence and also understand the basics of military organisation and operations. We normally train the aircrew in all this at the same time that they are learning to fly the Sea King and it takes months, culminating in a ten day field exercise. For you, we've got five days. If you say yes and you don't have to, as you well know, Sergeant Smithers one of our tame Royals is going take you under his wing and give you the concentrated version. Still up for it?'

'Where do I sign SOBS?'

Five days later, Helen was wondering whether she had done the right thing. The first day had been quite easy. She had been issued with combat clothing and various other paraphernalia. Getting some of the right size hadn't been easy as the ship carried limited stock but those that didn't fit she had been able to modify with her sewing skills. Then Sergeant Smithers got stuck in. Fitness training seemed to intersperse all the other activities, like how to erect tents and use the various domestic equipment that was needed to keep life and soul together. Then there was weapon training. It was limited to the use of the Nine Millimetre pistol and the SLR rifle. Helen had no problem with the pistol and was soon able to strip it down, clean it and reassemble it in minutes as well as fire it at targets at the end of the flight deck with reasonable accuracy. The rifle was a different matter. Stripping and cleaning was straightforward but firing the damn thing was altogether another issue. It kicked like a mule and the sights were rudimentary to say the least. After the first twenty rounds, it felt like she had been kicked in the shoulder by an angry horse and none of her shots had got near the target being towed behind the ship at only about fifty yards. The only consolation was that she wasn't the only one. For the rifle firing, after her first instruction, the rest of the squadron joined in. She wasn't the only member of the squadron, who to quote the Sergeant, 'couldn't hit a fucking barn door if it jumped right out in front of them.' Her sex was no protection and she found herself, along with several other of the aircrew, spending several more sessions firing over the stern of the ship until eventually, she started to get the hang of it. Her shoulder was going to hurt for weeks afterwards but at least she felt that the barn door might not stand quite so much of a chance as the Sergeant had so graphically suggested. One thing she and most of the rest of the squadron did notice was that the Boss and SOBS had no problems with the rifles. The Boss in particular even out-shot the

Sergeant. The rifle almost seemed an extension of his body. One of the pilots told her that there were rumours that a couple of years ago he and Brian had been involved in some sort of skirmish up in the Arctic and his shooting skills had been put to the real test. No one could find out what had really happened but there was no doubt that it had been important.

Then, there was the physical training. She didn't really see the point but the Sergeant was adamant. Initially, she thought he was just a bloody minded misogynist but soon realised that he had his reasons, especially when she discovered just how unfit she really was. Five days wasn't enough to remedy very much but at least she would understand her limitations as he was at pains to point out. She was also privately amused when more and more of the squadron joined in the sessions. She was damned sure that part of it was to watch her get sweaty but also some of the men realised that if she could do some of the things the Sergeant demanded of her then they had better be able to do so too.

The last part of her indoctrination was specialist training in operating the Clansman radios that they would be using. This bit she loved, it came naturally, both using the equipment and also talking and controlling radio nets. The female voice, for some reason, was always clearer over the radio and she used it to good effect when they set up a nominal communications network on the ship.

On the sixth day, they arrived off the coast of the Lebanon. HMS Fearless and several other RFAs were already anchored a few miles offshore. The hot wind was blowing off the land. It was the first time she had experienced a wind that actually felt hot and wondered what conditions must be like ashore if it was this stifling out to sea.

SOBS came up behind her and looked in the direction she had been gazing. 'Well Helen, do you feel ready to go ashore there and do your bit?'

She turned to him. 'Yes SOBS, I can't wait.'

He grunted in acknowledgement. 'Don't be too enthusiastic, the reality is never as you expect and this could get pretty bloody, very quickly.'

His words cut through her euphoria. 'And you and the Boss have had your share of that before so I hear,' she blurted out before she could help herself.

'Don't believe everything you hear Helen but yes we've seen our share of blood.' His tone was scarily sincere.

She found she had no answer to that.

Chapter 15

Karim was getting increasingly worried about his brother. Yes, they had both agreed to leave the Lebanon as soon as they had their papers. However, while Karim was becoming more and more inclined to look on it as an opportunity to change their way of life, Khalid simply refused to accept that it meant anything more than a change of venue. Neither of them had travelled outside the Middle East and Khalid seemed to think other countries were simply another place where they could continue their activities unhindered. Not only that but Khalid seemed to be getting more and more inclined to violence. Ever since the fateful day that he had received the wound to his head, he had always been the one prone to hit out first and ask questions afterwards. However, in the last few months, he seemed to be on a roller coaster of hate. In the current climate of Beirut that wasn't necessarily a problem. What really worried Karim was how he would cope in a more civilised country, where settling an argument with a knife, fist or gun would quickly lead to more trouble than they would be able to handle, especially being foreigners.

The last time they had discussed their future and Karim had tried to explain some of the differences it had ended in an explosive argument and Khalid had stormed out. Karim hadn't seen him since although the grapevine had allowed him to keep track of his brother. He seemed to moving around the locality quite a deal and Karim was pretty sure that he was scouting out the last operation he seemed so keen to undertake.

It was late afternoon and he was sitting in the shaded garden wondering what to do for the evening. Suddenly, the door banged open and a grinning Khalid appeared just as if he had only been away for hours rather than over a week.

He plonked himself down, unconcerned with the expression of anger on his twin's face. 'So brother, have I got a set up for us? It's just as we talked about and this could be bigger than anything we've done before. The timing is perfect for us to pull it off before we leave for good.'

'Go on,' said Karim still not responding to Khalid's bonhomie.

'The Syrians and the PLO are already at each other's throats as you know. It means that all the refugee camps are going to be in chaos very soon.'

'How does that give us an advantage?'

Khalid was just about to respond when there was a loud roaring noise and a large green helicopter flew low overhead. Its outline could briefly be seen before it disappeared behind the wall of the garden compound. Looking at its shape Karim realised what it was.

'Well, that's the first one of those I've seen. It must be from one of those warships that are anchored out off the coast. It's probably heading for the British Embassy.'

Khalid grimaced. 'Damned westerners, they think they can just come in and operate here whenever they like but look Karim it gives us a deadline and also an enormous increase in the value of the operation.'

With a sigh, Karim looked at his brother. 'Tell me then.'

Jean Jubert ducked as he heard the tell-tale whistle and rumble of a supersonic artillery shell overhead. Although he knew that if he could hear its note decrease, it was already past him, it didn't stop him cringing. He stood up straight again and ran the last few feet to the medical tents. His amazing wife was carrying on inside as if nothing untoward was happening. It was only when he saw the signs of strain on her face and in her eyes that he realised that she was suffering as well. She seemed to have aged years in the last months and he suspected that if he looked carefully in a mirror, he would see the same lines of grief and fear written there too.

'It's happening more and more,' he said helplessly as they heard the distant crump of the shell exploding.

Marie looked up at him. 'At least they're avoiding shelling the camp directly, just the perimeter defences.'

'And how long do you think that will last?' Jean responded.

Marie shrugged. 'At least most of the women and children have escaped.' She gestured around the tent. Most of the beds now were full of men. Of the lines of sick children, there was now little evidence.

'Escaped to where?'

She shrugged. She knew she should care but there was only so much compassion a human being could generate before it just simply ran out.

Jean saw the look on her face and walked forward and took her into his arms. As he hugged her, he also realised how thin she had become. This simple fact suddenly made up his mind for him. They had been here long enough. They had done as much as they could. It was now time for them to look after themselves.

He pushed her away slightly so he could look into her fatigued eyes. 'We're leaving, we've done enough.'

He expected an argument but was surprised when she slumped against him and started to sob. 'Oh Jean, we had such high hopes, such moral certitude but yes I don't think I can take much more of this. But will they let us go? They will want us to look after their fighting casualties won't they?'

'I've just been talking to Mike the British nurse. He has been contacted by the Embassy, to see if the British staff want to be evacuated. However, it sounded more like an order to me. He refused to answer until I had spoken to you. He says the British staff won't accept any help unless it is for us all, all the nationalities and he wants to know what you want. You're the boss you know. It's a measure of how well they think of you.' He smiled at her with pride in his face.

'How on earth did they contact him?'

'Apparently, he has a radio, it's his hobby or it was until things got dangerous here. Now, it's our lifeline.'

She sniffed and wiped her eyes. 'Yes Jean, we have to go but I still worry about the PLO maniacs. They have guns and we don't.'

'It seems the evacuation will be by helicopter some time in the next week and the Embassy will arrange some sort of safe passage. We will just have to hope for the best.'

Chapter 16

The assault operations room of HMS Fearless was hot sweaty and crowded. Jon was almost the last to arrive as he had flown into the city to the Embassy to pick up Rupert Thomas. The flight had been an eye opener. Parts of the city looked like they had been blasted by a nuclear explosion, yet other parts, mainly in the suburbs looked eerily intact. Rupert had shared the spare front seat of the Sea King on the way out to the ship and had been able to give Jon a detailed briefing as they flew over the devastated areas. They hadn't been able to get too close as anything in the sky was fair game to one or more of the many factions hiding in the rubble. Luckily, the most sophisticated anti-aircraft weapon was probably going to be the Russian Rocket Propelled Grenade or RPG and that had very limited range. However, Jon wasn't prepared to bet on it and they stayed at a circumspect distance.

Once on Fearless, Rupert disappeared into the superstructure escorted by one of the ship's officers while Jon shut down the helicopter.

James Arthur, Commodore Amphibious Warfare, COMAW was the last to enter the Ops room. A tall, surprisingly young looking, sandy haired officer, wearing the broad stripe of his rank on his shoulder boards, his presence immediately quietened the room. Jon looked carefully at the man, he was well known in the navy as a 'high flyer'. Promoted to both Commander and Captain at 'first shot' he had a reputation for an incisive mind and fiery temper. He was also a submariner and Jon and many others felt he was absolutely the wrong man for the current job. Their lordships clearly thought differently and the rumour on the streets was that he had been given the appointment to broaden his experience for future greatness. Jon hated him on sight. He knew it was foolish but with absolutely no aviation experience this man was going to run this operation and it seemed, from earlier discussions that he had had with some of the staff that he was not one to always listen to advice.

COMAW started by welcoming everyone, which included the Commanding Officers of all the ships present, two Frigates and Destroyers, as well as his own operations staff. Finally, Jon got a mention almost as an afterthought and as Jon commanded the assets that would actually conduct the operation, it almost seemed like a snub. He smothered a grunt of annoyance but it wasn't lost on Brian sitting next to him who knew of his friend's feelings about COMAW.

'Give the man a chance Jon, he's hardly uttered a word yet,' he whispered into his ear. Another muted snort was the only response.

Oblivious to the feelings he was generating, the Commodore continued with a short introduction to the situation and the assets they now had gathered off the coast before turning to Rupert to provide an up to date situation report.

Rupert took centre stage. 'Gentlemen, you are heartily welcome. There are many people ashore who are looking forward to your efforts, believe me. Now, in the last few days, things have got even worse if that's possible. The three main refugee camps out in the countryside have come under attack by Syrian forces. Their excuse is that the camps are run by the PLO and as such, are actually training grounds for the terrorists. The Lebanese Government, or what is left of it, are unable to do anything about it except make noises in the UN and meanwhile a tragedy is occurring under our noses. We have two problems. The first, which will take most of your time, is to get the two thousand or so British subjects still in the Lebanon out to the ships. We have prepared designated muster points for them and hopefully these are in safe areas. This task should be relatively straightforward. However, the second one won't be that easy. The refugee camps all have European volunteers working in them, mainly medical staff. They are from several nations, mainly British, French and Spanish and we have just received diplomatic clearance to evacuate them all. That is if we can get to them and that is if the leadership in the camps is prepared to let them go. We are working on that last point as we speak but if we do get the agreement of the leadership and can go and get them it could still get hairy, very quickly.'

There was a murmur around the room and the Commodore stood. 'Mr Thomas, thank you for that. The news about the camps is not unexpected but we will have to look at the situation carefully. However, let's take a quick look at the overall operation and how I intend to conduct it.' He spoke for a few minutes outlining the use of Fearless and Arapaho as receiving ships and the onward distribution of refugees using the other ships as transports to take them to Cyprus for repatriation to the UK. It all seemed logical except for one major issue which Jon was dismayed to realise had not been taken into account. He had proposed the idea to COMAW's Operations officer the previous day and was astounded to find it had been completely left out.

He raised his hand as the Commodore wound up but was seemingly ignored. Brian tugged at his elbow. 'Leave it Jon. We can sort it out afterwards.'

'Bollocks to that,' replied Jon. 'Who's the bloody aviation expert here? Sir,' he called loudly, finally getting noticed.

The Commodore didn't look too pleased at being interrupted. 'Yes Lieutenant Commander, what is it?'

'Sir, there's been no mention of setting up a Forward Operating Base ashore. I've got all the equipment we need loaded in Arapaho, including refuelling bowsers and if we can get into the field we will decrease our turn around time enormously. It will also give us much greater flexibility should any contingencies arise.'

'Thank you Lieutenant Commander Hunt. I did consider the idea but on balance I didn't see the advantages outweighing the risks of having a large number of my assets deployed away from the ships in such a dangerous area. Thank you for your input,' and then seeing that Jon was about to object. 'That will be all, I have made my decision.'

Jon subsided fuming inwardly but trying to maintain at least some outward sign of acceptance. The man was far more senior than him after all. Just then Rupert leaned over and said something to the Commodore who immediately looked sourly back at Jon and nodded distractedly before making an unheard reply.

The meeting wound up quickly after that with a few more general administration points being discussed before everyone was invited to the wardroom for lunch. Just as Jon was about to leave, one of COMAW's staff, another Lieutenant Commander approached him. 'Sorry old chap but the Commodore would like a word in private in his cabin, now please. And a word of advice, he doesn't like being contradicted in public so I'd stand by for a rocket if I was you.'

Jon looked at the man, his anger mounting. 'And I don't like being ignored by people ignorant of the facts of life, whatever rank they might have, thank you very much.'

The two of them continued in stony silence up two ladders until they reached a closed door. Jon knocked and the word 'enter' was heard from the other side. With a grimace of sympathy, Jon's guide left him to his fate.

Jon entered and shut the door behind him without being asked. The Commodore was sitting in an arm chair and looked relaxed. Jon suspected it was just a gambit but refused to be intimidated.

'You asked to see me Sir?'

'Lieutenant Commander Hunt. Jonathon, please take a seat,' and the great man indicated the other leather studded chair. Jon sat and looked at him enquiringly.

'Now, I've been apprised of your somewhat unique career to date Jonathon and I have to say I'm impressed. Not the least because large parts of it are classified beyond levels even I'm cleared to.'

Jon said nothing. This was definitely one of those occasions when saying as little as possible was going to be the best tactic.

The Commodore frowned for a second and then continued. 'But young man, I do not take kindly to being contradicted at my own operational briefing. Is that clear?' His hard blue eyes bored into Jon's as he said it and his face was suddenly devoid of any signs of his previous bonhomie.

'Yes Sir but I'm sure you also wouldn't want your operation to be marred by accusations of incompetence.' Jon mentally braced himself but he had chosen his words carefully and deliberately.

The Commodore flinched at the final word and then started to look really angry. Before he could say anything, Jon ploughed on. 'Sir, I can't do my job from a ship several miles offshore. I need to be on the ground, the whole concept of operations of our unit is to operate in the field. Not only that but operating from sea will double our sortie times as well as our fuel consumption. Mr Thomas, who I am sure you know has worked with me before on several operations, specifically asked for us to be based ashore near the Embassy compound when he visited Arapaho last week. He wants the short notice flexibility of having aircraft to hand. We don't need all the aircraft, just four out of the nine. All these points were made to your Operations officer and I am at a loss as to why they weren't made to you, as clearly they weren't.'

Arapaho

The Commodore looked at Jon for several seconds and then stood and went over to the ships internal phone on his desk. He lifted the receiver, 'tell Ops to come here at once.'

He seated himself back in his chair and looked at Jon with an unreadable expression. Nothing was said for almost a minute when there was a knock at the door and a short round Commander let himself in. He took one look at the tableau in front of him and a worried expression fleeted across his face.

The Commodore did not invite Ops to sit. 'Ops, you advised me not to put any aircraft ashore, maybe you could explain your reasoning again?'

Ops looked discomfited and then a determined look crossed his face. 'Two reasons Sir, one is there is no need, the aircraft can fly from our decks just as easily as from ashore and secondly we would lose a large amount of command and control if we deployed them away from our vicinity.'

The Commodore looked at Jon and raised an eyebrow.

Jon thought for a second and turned to the new man. 'Sir, are you a pilot and have you ever served with a Commando helicopter squadron?'

Looking taken aback, he replied. 'No, I did undertake flying training but I decided to go back to the main branch. And my reasons remain sound.' He ended, almost defiantly.

Jon turned to the Commodore. 'Sir, it's quite simple, you can take my advice or that of your Ops officer but I've been flying for many years, I've been involved in several major operations and your Ops officer hasn't.' He looked hard at the man.

The Commodore looked thoughtful. 'Ops, did you choose to leave flying training or did you, in fact, fail the course?'

'Sir, that's irrelevant.'

'I'm not so sure it is. Now, what's the answer?'

'Yes Sir I was chopped as they call it but that doesn't affect the advice I provided you.'

Jon asked, 'did you know that the Embassy had specifically asked for some of the aircraft to be based ashore?'

The question hit home and the Ops officer was suddenly at a loss for words. The Commodore waited.

Eventually, the silence forced Ops to speak. 'Yes, I did know of the request but still made the judgement that it would be better to have the aircraft under close control rather than let you lot loose without proper oversight.'

'Thank you Commander, may I remind you that I make the decisions around here. You may leave us now,' the Commodore was obviously angry and Ops clearly decided that being somewhere else was a good idea. He left without saying another word.

'Right Jonathon, give me the details of what you require to set up ashore and pass it to my people.'

'Yes Sir, do I continue to liaise with Ops?'

'Indeed you do but not that particular officer. He will be on the next trip to Cyprus. You will be informed who his relief will be as soon as I have decided.'

Jon blanched inwardly. This man clearly didn't take any prisoners. He suddenly realised the risk he had taken when confronting him earlier. 'Aye, aye Sir.'

'And Jonathon?'

'Yes Sir.'

'Never, ever, oppose me in public again.'

Chapter 17

Helen was tired, sweaty and dirty. She had thought she might have become accustomed to the heat after five days but now she realised that was just a dream. The drab olive tent she was hiding from the sun underneath seemed to make it even hotter. Unfortunately, the squadron had no others and at least it kept the raw sun off her head. Her military clothing didn't help either, also being olive drab and being in a total state of sweat soaked discomfort was starting to seem almost normal. She sighed to herself as she looked at the wooden trestle table in front of her. The long lists she had compiled had been taken back to the ships this morning and after five days of manic chaos, things at last, seemed to be settling down. Give it another hour and she would sneak back to the Embassy which was just off to one side of their impromptu airfield and she would be able to have a shower. That is if the water was running again. The supply regularly failed. She also dreaded the walk, although it wasn't so bad now that she covered herself up with her military garb and a naval beret. On her first day here, her blonde hair had caused something of a stir as the local men realised she was female. It seemed that any girl uncovered was fair game for crude remarks and gestures.

A shadow fell across her desk and she looked up to see Rupert Thomas approaching. She had quickly decided she liked the man. He had worked tirelessly by her side as the stream of refugees passed through the processing point that she had been running. She and SOBS had worked shifts but Rupert had no one to help him and even though he was clearly more acclimatised to the weather, she was amazed by his capacity to work long hours in the heat. His job had been to screen the people and ensure only British and other approved nationals were ferried out to sea by a constant stream of Jon's Sea Kings. It had almost broken Helen's heart on several occasions when families claiming to be British had been turned away. Rupert had been quite firm, pointing out that if he let them go then others would follow and they could end up being swamped. Her head understood but her heart had more than a little trouble.

'Good morning Helen,' Rupert smiled at her. 'Just heard on the radio that we've one more Sea King's worth on the way in and then that's about it.'

'Really? Have we actually got everyone out?'

Rupert grimaced. 'Well no, that's never going to happen. There are quite a few who won't leave and that's their prerogative but we know who most of them are. Then there are about one hundred and fifty who may have left by other means recently. We are chasing them up but again we know most of those as well.'

She could tell by the look on his face that that wasn't all.

'And so that really just leaves those in the camps.'

'How are the negotiations going?' she asked

'Its good and its bad. Two of the camps are virtually empty now and so we are hoping to go in this afternoon. However, the third one is holding out. We have virtually no political clout and no military leverage. These guys are armed to the teeth. However, one of the medical staff has a radio, so I need to talk to Jon but I think we are going to have to do some sort of rescue with or without the camp's approval.'

'But won't you need COMAW's go ahead for an operation like that? God knows how long it will take to explain it and get a plan approved.'

Rupert grinned. 'Maybe but maybe I'll give Jon an operational imperative that will allow him to just get on with it.'

'That will be interesting when the great man finally gets to hear about it.'

Rupert was about to reply when the growling noise of an approaching helicopter was heard and shortly afterwards the massive shape of a green Sea King appeared and landed in a swirling cloud of dust and sand. Rupert and Helen went out to meet it as the engines and rotor blades slowed to a stop. The large door on the starboard side was already open with an aircrewman peering out and Helen could see that most of the seats were occupied by civilians. Putting all thought of future operations out of her mind, she and Rupert slipped into their well rehearsed routine of shepherding the bemused refugees into the tents for processing onwards.

An hour later and the Sea King took off once more, to ferry the civilians out to sea. According to Rupert, they were all bona fide cases and Helen was glad she hadn't been subjected to another scene of misery by having to turn people away. The Sea King was also carrying a message from Rupert to Jon who was currently out on Arapaho to come ashore as soon as he could.

Later that afternoon, a recently showered Helen gathered in the Embassy with Rupert, Jon and Brian. Three Sea Kings were being quickly serviced on the landing site outside.

Rupert outlined the situation and then they all poured over the maps that were laid out on the table in the centre of the room.

'So, these two camps should be simple pick ups?' Jon looked at Rupert who looked back with a grim smile.

'As we both know Jon, nothing is ever simple but yes they should be. We've been in touch with our nationals and it's all arranged.'

'OK, I'll send GG and one of our more senior guys in to do the trips straight after the briefing. That said, they will be instructed to bug out if there's any sign of trouble. Our aircraft are unarmed and very vulnerable as you well know. We don't even have armoured seats, apparently looking after the aircrew is all too expensive.' Jon added with a touch of annoyed cynicism in his voice.

'I have to agree with your sentiments Jon,' Rupert replied. 'All of them and yes, tell your people to get the hell out at any sign of trouble. Now, about the third camp, that's going to be a little more tricky. I'd love to be able to bounce this up the chain and get COMAW involved but I'm afraid our latest intelligence indicates that we won't have time for that and we need to go now or not at all.' He looked at Jon with a straight face.

Jon looked back. 'I understand Rupert and I'm sure that you will explain that to the man if he asks.'

'Right, we've been in touch with one of the medical staff by radio. As we understand it, the PLO types won't let them leave. They've taken quite a few casualties recently and want the doctors and nurses to look after them. However, there has been a lull for a few days and apparently no new cases brought in so our man says he thinks they can sneak clear if you can get to them quickly.'

Jon looked at the map thoughtfully. 'Where do they think they can get to?'

Rupert indicated a point south of the camp. 'This is a dried up river bed. It will give them cover to get away and they say it's wide enough to land a helicopter in.'

'I wonder if they know just how big a Sea King is.' Brian commented. 'Dried up river beds tend to be narrow.'

'Apparently our man was a paramedic with the Search and Rescue lot at Lee on Solent in the past and has flown in the S61 variant of the Sea King so hopefully he has a good idea on that score.'

Jon looked relieved. 'That sounds good then. How about timing?'

They are suggesting while the camp is at sunset prayers. Which today, will be at about nineteen hundred. Most of the camp will be occupied for quite a while and they say that if they can get past the perimeter, they should be in position within fifteen minutes so you need to be making your approach at nineteen fifteen.'

'That sounds feasible it will be just after sunset but it stays light enough for at least half an hour afterwards. We'll take night vision goggles as well just in case. What sort of radio does this guy have? Will we be able to talk to him?'

'It's a civilian VHF you have those don't you?'

'Yes, tell him we'll use 121.5, the distress frequency. We'll hold clear until we hear from him and then do a fast run in and stop. But we can only afford to do this once and if we come under fire or they are not there then we get out and don't come back.'

'I'll make that absolutely clear Jon.'

'Right, we want minimum crew on this one so I'll fly it with PO Aircrewman Jones.'

Brian looked discomforted. 'Come on Jon, we always do the dodgy stuff together. I should be coming not Jones.'

'It's not far Brian and you're needed here. I want you here as coordinator of all three trips.' And seeing the look on his friend's face. 'Look we go in, they're either there or they're not. If they are we pick them up, if not we get the hell out. You know me, I don't take silly risks and anyway it's a simple job, what could go wrong?'

Chapter 18

Karim sat under a large, sun blasted rock. He may have been born to this climate but it didn't stop him sweating. Khalid was sneaking about checking the ground, along with the two goons they had hired. There were several more hours to go and he just wished the whole thing was over and they could be on their way out of the county, to somewhere cooler and more civilised.

A sudden rattle of stones alerted him to someone sliding down the gully behind the rock. He cocked his AK47 and pointed it towards the noise.

Khalid appeared, dusty and dishevelled. 'Hey brother, don't point that thing at me. Who did you think it was?'

Karim just grunted and moved slightly so his twin could sit next to him in the small patch of shade provided by the overhanging rock.

'Well?' he asked. 'Is it as you expected?'

Khalid grinned. 'Better, the medical facility is nearer to the edge of the camp than we thought, in four large tents. Two of them are the hospital and two are for the staff accommodation. We saw several of the targets moving around. Once it's dark, we should be able to move in with little fear of being observed.'

'And sentries?'

'We've paid them enough to look the other way. I made contact with one of ours and he confirmed that he and the ones we've bought will definitely be the ones on duty.'

'And what about our two guys, where are they?'

'Watching the route in to make sure nothing untoward happens.'

'And to get caught rather than us if it does?'

Khalid chuckled. 'As we planned it. Hey brother, it's just like that day we climbed down that shit tunnel and pulled off our first job.'

Karim had to laugh. 'Yes but without the shit.'

'And we stand to make a lot more money don't forget that. So, now we sit tight until it's dark and then make our move.'

Marie Jubert was getting more and more nervous as the deadline approached. Mike, the British nurse had confirmed earlier in the day that the British were sending a helicopter to get them out just as evening prayers were in full swing. All they had to do was sneak out the back of one of the tents and creep down into the old river bed behind them. Jean had done some checking and reckoned there was a large blind spot behind the first accommodation tent that should allow them to get below the skyline before any of the sentries saw them. Not only that, it was down sun and meant that they should be hard to see as they would be silhouetted against a dark background. There would be no moon until much later.

Jean opened the flap of the tent and saw Marie. He went up and put his arms around her. 'Not long now and we will be in modern hotel with a bath and room service.'

She leant into him. 'I can't wait, please let it all go to plan.'

'Why shouldn't it? I spoke to the head man this afternoon and we are all invited to his tent for a meal this evening. It seems he wants to show us his gratitude for what we've done. So he clearly doesn't suspect anything. I hope he won't be too surprised when we don't turn up.'

'I just hope we're far away by then. It's just the waiting now that's wearing me down.'

'Not long now,' said Jean looking at his watch.

The sun was setting and the evening was at last starting to cool down. Karim nudged his brother who had started snoring. 'Wake up brother. You're making enough noise to alert the whole city.'

Khalid looked disoriented for a second and then angry before realising who was talking to him. 'Sorry brother, was I snoring again?'

'What do you think? Anyway no more dozing off, it's almost time.' Suddenly another trickle of stones alerted them and Ahmed, one of their men appeared.

'Khalid, something odd is going on. We've just spotted the whole medical team sneaking out of the back of one of the tents. They're heading this way.'

'Did they see you?' asked Karim urgently.

'No, it looks to me as though they're heading for the river bed to get away from the camp.'

'It'll be a very long walk. They must be mad,' observed Khalid grimly. 'I think we should offer them a lift.'

Arapaho

Even Karim was grinning at this turn of luck. Although something didn't seem quite right, it was an opportunity too good to miss.

Khalid took charge. 'Can we get ahead of them?'

'No, not now but once they are on the flat river bed we can easily catch up.'

'In that case, lead us to where you saw them.'

Marie was starting to relax. Getting away had been a complete anti-climax. No one noticed them and there was no sign of alarm. As soon as they reached the river bed, Mike the nurse had called the helicopter and it answered straight away. They were all sitting looking to the west and spotted it almost immediately. Very soon they could also hear it and in what seemed like moments, it was landing in front of them in a swirling cloud of choking dust. As the dust cleared a man in the large cabin door started to signal at them and they ran in under the thundering rotors and started to clamber on board. Jean pushed Marie in ahead of him and was the last one in. Immediately, the machine started to lift and transition away.

Khalid stopped dumbstruck when he saw the helicopter appear. Karim immediately realised what was happening.

'They weren't running. It's a bloody pick up by the British. Shit, we've lost the lot.'

The helicopter had already loaded its passengers and was starting to fly away. Khalid dropped to one knee, aimed his AK47 and started firing. The other two hired thugs did the same. Karim just stared, knowing it was too late. The helicopter was already clear.

Only one AK 47 round actually hit the helicopter but it hit the magnesium casing of the tail rotor gearbox. Magnesium is immensely strong for its weight but is very brittle. The gearbox casing also acted as the mounting for the flying controls for the tail rotor. When the gearbox broke up with the impact of the bullet, two things happened. Firstly, the drive to the tail rotor was lost and secondly, the controls ceased to function. Either failure would have caused the pilot to lose control. Jon didn't stand a chance. The first thing he knew that something was wrong was when the nose of the aircraft violently yawed to the left. He automatically pushed full rudder pedal in to compensate but with a sick feeling realised it was having no effect. Had the aircraft been hovering he might have had a chance to slam it back on the ground but he was already travelling at over fifty knots and was one hundred feet up. He did the only thing he could and reached up and slammed the two engine levers to shut off and when the ground was close pulled the collective lever up as hard as he could.

The world went black.

Khalid whooped with delight when he saw the helicopter start to spin and then drop dramatically to the ground only a few hundred yards ahead of them. Karim once again was thinking ahead. 'Get down and take cover you idiots. There's going to be debris flying everywhere.'

It took Khalid several seconds to realise what his brother was shouting about. But when the ground shook at the same time that the dreadful thud of the crashing machine was heard, he realised what his brother meant and joined him flat on the ground. Ahmed wasn't so quick and a large piece of rotor blade that had been shed from the wreck that was thrashing itself to death in front of them neatly severed his head. The torso, spraying blood from the neck, stood for a second almost as if it had a life of its own and then crumpled to the ground.

Amazingly, it was suddenly quiet. Once again Karim acted first. 'Quick, let's see if anyone survived because the camp will have heard that and be here pretty soon.'

The three remaining men ran towards the shattered wreck. Privately Karim didn't hold out much hope, the machine seemed to be smashed to pieces but they would have to go past it to reach their truck anyway, so they might as well look.

Chapter 19

Brian made a decision. Jon should have been back at least ten minutes ago. The last they had heard on the radio was him calling confirmation of the pickup and that he was running in and then nothing. The camp wasn't that far away by air. There was no way he should be this delayed without them hearing something on the radio.

Rupert, Helen and GG were with him in the command tent. 'GG get airborne as fast as you can and see what has happened. Meanwhile, I'll alert COMAW of a possible problem.'

GG simply nodded and sprinted for the remaining Sea King that had returned earlier from the other camps as the other was already out to sea with the refugees.

Rupert turned to Brian. 'I should go as well. If there's a problem on the ground I speak the language and will have some understanding of the political situation.'

Brian thought for a second and nodded. 'Get a flying helmet and go. Tell GG it's with my approval.'

Rupert ran from the tent. A few minutes later the sound of the helicopter engaging its rotors and then lifting off was heard.

As soon as the noise died down, Brian turned to Helen. 'Helen, see if you can raise Fearless on the radio. Tell them we have a possible down bird and have sent another Sea King to investigate. If they ask for more information, tell them we don't know, only that an aircraft is overdue but should have confirmation within a few minutes. I need to find our Royal Marine Sergeant and get some contingency sorted out.'

Helen nodded and reached for the radio as Brian left the tent calling for the Royal Marines to muster. He had a horrible premonition they might be needed. As soon as he had alerted the platoon of marines to get their fighting order ready, he headed back to the command tent.

Helen turned to him, 'I've told the ship they didn't seem too concerned. It's not the first time we've had an aircraft overdue or with radio problems after all.'

'Just wait till they find out what he was up to,' Brian responded grimly. 'Then it'll hit the fan.'

'But Rupert gave us a deadline. We had to act.'

Arapaho

'Let's hope Wonder Boy sees it that way.' He was about to say something else when the radio came to life.'

'Bravo this is Victor Foxtrot. We have a crashed Sea King at the pickup site. It's a wreck, it's on its side, the tail is broken off and it looks like it speared in hard. There are soldiers all around it. Rupert wants me to land him so he can speak to those on the ground.'

Brian realised he had to trust Rupert's judgement. He grabbed the microphone. 'Victor Foxtrot affirmative. Do as requested. However, suggest to him that you immediately return to base and collect our troop of marines to give him some back up.'

There was a moment's silence and then the aircraft replied. 'Agreed, he will try to start negotiating while I return.'

Brian knew there was little more he could do but a dreadful feeling stole over him. This was bad on all fronts. A diplomatic incident was just the start, more importantly, his friend could be dead or injured.

Brian briefed the nine marines on what they were getting into and ordered Helen to man the Command Post to act as their relay to sea and the Embassy. He then spent a few minutes on the telephone to the Ambassador but was interrupted by the noise of the returning aircraft. As soon as it landed they all jumped in. Brian made his way up to the cockpit and slipped into the spare seat.

He plugged his helmet in and looked at GG. 'Right let's get back. What happened when you landed with Rupert?'

'There wasn't too much of a problem. They let us land and Rupert spoke to them for a few minutes and then waved for me to take off. So I'm hoping talking is all that's going on.'

'Any sign of survivors?'

'Yes, there were several people being helped out of the wreck but there were clearly a few bodies as well. Brian, that Sea King went in hard, something catastrophic must have happened.'

'Yes, well, let's get on the ground and worry about people first.'

'You mean the Boss don't you?'

'What do you think?'

They flew in tense silence for ten minutes and then Brian could make out the crash site despite the fact that darkness was rapidly falling. A massive field of tents could still be seen stretching away into the distance and just this side of them was the dried up river. The watercourse could clearly be made out even though it hadn't seen water for years. The crash site was a maze of lights. GG made a direct approach to the river bed just short of the wreck and the soldiers on the ground scattered as he put the machine down in its own little storm of sand.

'Shut her down GG but be ready to flash up straight away. I'll keep the marines on board as well for the moment until I've got a better idea about what's going on.'

He jumped out after speaking to the Sergeant and made his way through a crowd of armed men too scruffy to call soldiers but deadly looking nevertheless. He saw Rupert in the distance talking to a middle aged man in green denims and Arab headscarf.

Rupert turned to him. 'Brian, this is the head man here. He is very angry that we were trying to steal his medical staff as he puts it. However, I've pointed out that I have a very strong force at my command. He is quite aware of how many ships we have deployed off shore. He's no fool but doesn't want to lose face.'

'I've got nine Royal Marines on board do you want me to deploy them?'

'Hang on,' Rupert turned to the other man and a heated exchange took place with lots of hand waving and angry gestures. Brian was desperate to know about survivors but realised that without the acquiescence of these people they would get nowhere.

Eventually, Rupert finished talking and turned to Brian. 'Get the marines out and cordon off the wreck. For the moment I've got them to accept that this is our problem. I've also got him to agree that we can repatriate any survivors but we need to be quick, this could all turn ugly, very quickly.'

Half an hour later, they had secured the site. Most of the marines had formed a perimeter much to the annoyance of some the PLO soldiers but a fragile truce seemed to be holding. The remainder were helping the survivors, who were sitting next to the wreck. As soon as he could, Brian had turned to looking for one particular survivor. The cockpit of the aircraft seemed to relatively intact but as the aircraft was lying on its port side with its nose buried in a heap of sand and debris, it was initially hard to see inside. He called urgently and Rupert and GG joined him. Although he had told him to stay with the other aircraft Brian could understand why GG had ignored the order and he decided to say nothing, not the least because of the help he needed to get into the cockpit. With an effort, he was finally able to clamber up the hull and onto the starboard side of the aircraft. What he saw dismayed him but puzzled him as well. The cockpit was empty. The aircraft must have impacted with forward speed as the nose was crushed but where Jon's seat should have been was an empty space and the cockpit instrument panel and windscreen in front of it were ripped clear as well.

He managed to clamber back down. 'He's not there,' he said breathlessly. 'The fucking cockpit's empty, even his seat's been ripped out.'

GG immediately looked ahead of the aircraft. 'I've heard of this happening before, a Lynx hit the sea at high speed a couple of years ago and both the guys in the front were flung through the windscreen, still in their seats and they both survived.'

'Right, let's look around,' said Brian. 'If the aircraft was spinning he may not be where we expect him to be.'

They searched for some minutes but to their puzzlement, nothing was found. Then one of the PLO soldiers shouted to them and pointed to something in the distant darkness. They ran over and sure enough, it was a Sea King seat in remarkably good condition apart from its feet which were still attached to ripped out sections of floor. But it was empty. The straps were there but undone. There was no sign of Jon.

'What the bloody hell?' exclaimed Rupert looking around. 'He must be here somewhere. Did he unstrap and then just wander off?'

They continued searching but there was no sign of him. By now it was getting very dark and their torches were proving fairly useless but it was GG who spotted it first.

'Hey guys,' he called. 'Look at the ground here.'

He shone his torch onto the sand near the seat. There were footprints everywhere. 'These can't all be ours and look here.' There were two grooves in the sand with footprints either side and they led away to a point where they stopped but they could see quite clearly in the torches beam the prints of a vehicle's tyres.

The next morning Brian was back in Fearless talking to the Commodore. 'Sir, there were ten refugees in the aircraft and two crew; the Aircrewman and Lieutenant Commander Hunt. Three of the refugees are dead and two are in hospital in a critical condition.

The others all have minor injuries. The aircrewman is also beaten up but in surprisingly good health. However, we have two missing persons. One of the Doctors, a lady called Marie Jubert and the pilot, Lieutenant Commander Hunt. We've searched extensively and even had the cooperation of some of the PLO soldiers but they're nowhere to be found.'

The Commodore's face didn't betray any feelings but the angry tone of his voice did. 'Is that all? I realise that there is still an immediate search to make but in due course I would like to know why these flights weren't cleared with me. Evacuating these camps was always going to be a tricky operation. Mr Thomas made that clear right from the start.'

Brian had the distinct feeling that the Commodore was more annoyed in case the whole situation reflected badly on him but was far too concerned about the fate of his friend to care.

'Mr Thomas is the man who gave us the problem Sir and it needed immediate action. The window of opportunity was so small. I suggest you talk to him and Lieutenant Commander Hunt when we have found him.' Brian's tone dripped acid.

The Commodore didn't react except to stare at Brian even more intently. 'Yes, well, this will have to be looked at more carefully in due course. I will talk to the Ambassador presently. Now, what is happening ashore?'

'As I said Sir, two people are missing, which is extremely unusual and there is some evidence of an unidentified vehicle in the vicinity.'

'You think they may have been rescued by a passer by?'

'That's a possibility Sir but why then didn't they stay to help the others?'

'What are you suggesting?'

'Actually, I'm not suggesting anything Sir but Mr Thomas is. He thinks they may have been taken hostage.'

Chapter 20

Jon slowly drifted into consciousness. The first thing he felt was a light headedness that didn't make sense as his flying helmet should have weighed him down. He realised that he wasn't wearing it. That wasn't good as they were very expensive and they would charge him for losing it. His thoughts swirled in a muddle for what seemed like ages and then he became aware of some light filtering through his eyelids and decided that opening his eyes would probably be a good idea. The first thing he saw was a whitewashed ceiling of rough plaster and it was very hot. He realised he was lying down so he must be on some form of bed. When he tried to move his right hand up to wipe his eyes he heard a clinking noise and found that something was restraining his wrist. But none of it seemed to matter.

Suddenly, a face swam into his vision. A dark, hawk nosed man, with piercing cruel eyes. 'He's awake doctor, check him over.'

'Ah,' thought Jon. 'I must have had an accident and I'm in some sort of hospital.'

The man's face was replaced by a concerned looking woman. She seemed to be in her thirties but looked very strained and concerned at the same time. She lifted his head and shone a light into his eyes. He then felt her hands pulling and twisting various limbs. At one point he screamed in pain when she lifted his left leg but none of it really seemed that real anyway and he drifted off to oblivion again.

The next time he woke it was dark and he had a raging thirst. The room he was in was quite large with another bed on the far side. Without thinking, he sat up and wished he hadn't. It felt like someone had kicked his head like a rugby ball. Points of light flashed before his eyes and he was suddenly violently sick, luckily on the floor rather than over himself. He also realised his right hand was secured to the bed frame with something.

The noise must have alerted someone because a man immediately appeared. Jon recognised him but couldn't remember from where. The light was turned on and he blinked in its glare as the man said something in a language Jon almost understood and then went over to the other bed. There was a clinking noise. Jon leant back feeling exhausted. The man came over escorting the woman he knew was the doctor. He then did something strange. The woman's wrist had a chain around it and the man proceeded to fasten the other end around the bed at the same point that Jon's wrist was secured.

The woman ignored the man and spoke to Jon in a strange accent. 'Do you know who you are?'

'What a silly question,' he thought but when he tried to reply it came out as a croak. The woman turned to the man and said something angrily in the foreign language and he left and came back with a large glass of water which he passed to the woman. Jon tried to grab it but she pulled it away. 'Slowly or you will spill it or be sick again.'

He did as he was told and the relief as the liquid slipped down his throat was wonderful. He soon finished the glass and asked croakily for another. The man took it and went away. When he returned with another, he made another remark to the woman, closed the door and left.

She turned to Jon again. 'Do you know who you are?'

'Jonathon Hunt, I'm a pilot in the Royal Navy,' this time it came out quite clearly.

'And do you remember what happened to you?'

Suddenly it all came back, the late evening pick up and then flying away, something had gone horribly wrong with the aircraft and the last thing he could remember was the ground rushing up towards him.

'Yes, I crashed the helicopter but where are we? Is this a hospital? You are a doctor aren't you?'

'Slowly, you've had a bad concussion and your left leg has a large wound. Luckily,p the bone is not broken. And no, we aren't in a hospital, although I am a doctor.'

'Hang on, you're French, are you one of the people I was picking up?'

She smiled. 'Yes, I am Marie Jubert. I was the head doctor of the team you were rescuing Jonathon.'

'Call me Jon, I hate Jonathon. So, where are we? What on earth is going on?'

'As far as I can make out, that man you saw rescued us from the wreck but has kidnapped us. I have been chained to my bed like you except when he ordered me to attend to you. I tried once to protest but he hit me to the ground and then kicked me. So I'm sorry but I've done everything he's asked.'

Jon sat back as the reality of the situation hit him. He suddenly felt weak and very scared and not because of the bang on the head or his aching leg.

'I suppose they know who we are then?'

'Well in your case, you are wearing a British flying uniform so it wasn't exactly hard to work out and I'm afraid I told him everything he asked me.'

Jon realised he was still in his flying overalls although he could see his name badge had been ripped off and his left trouser leg cut away. A bloody bandage was wrapped around his lower leg.

'Has he said what he wants?'

'Not in so many words but my expectation is that we are hostages for ransom. It's a common form of business around here.'

'Shit, well my government never negotiates.'

Marie smiled wanly. 'Mine does, maybe I can get you cut in on the deal.'

Jon barked out a laugh. 'Oh God we're really up the creek aren't we?' He saw the look of incomprehension on her face. 'Sorry a British saying, I meant we are in real trouble.'

She looked back at him. 'Completely fucked.'

The room had one small, barred window high up and well away from their reach. As the light was now left permanently on, they even had difficulty knowing if it was night or day. Their watches along with all their personal possessions had been taken, although they were able to make some estimate of the time by the changes in temperature with what little they could see from the window. The hawk faced man came at irregular intervals with water and basic food, bread and a tough stew which Marie identified as goat. He didn't speak, no matter how much they tried to get his attention. So they talked. Marie told him all about her time in the camp and her previous life. Jon told her about his life and career, including some of his experiences in the navy including the Falklands which seemed to fascinate her. But all the time they talked, he was remembering the words of that American Naval Officer and his experience in Vietnam. If they were going to get away they had to do it as soon as they could. Unfortunately, he immediately found that his leg wouldn't take his weight. Not only that but he was dog tired nearly all the time which Marie said was due to his concussion. Luckily, it was clear that their captor wanted them alive and well. When Marie asked for antibiotics and fresh dressings for Jon's leg they were supplied even though the man never answered her directly.

The first time Jon saw the gash, he realised how lucky he had been. His calf had been cut almost to the bone. Marie had been able to stitch it up but was of the opinion it would be weeks before he could walk without crutches. Marie explained that she had been flung out of the door by the impact of the spinning helicopter and by enormous luck had landed in soft sand. She also told Jon that he had actually been found still in his seat some distance away from the wreck. He was even more amazed at his luck when she told him, although he had heard of the same thing happening before. But none of this helped as he wracked his brains to come up with some plan to get them free.

'We must still be in Beirut or nearby,' he said to Marie. 'There's nowhere else to go.' He spent some time with a glass listening at all the wall he could reach with his tethered wrist as did Marie. He was sure he could hear occasional traffic but it was so faint he wasn't sure it was just wishful thinking. But every idea they came up with failed at the first hurdle. Jon was partially immobile, they were chained to metal beds with strong handcuffs and the beds were cemented into the floors. There was only one strong door and they had no idea what or who was on the other side. Toilet facilities consisted of a bucket for each of them which their captor changed daily. As time passed, despite Jon knowing that it was happening, they both started slipping into an apathetic lethargy.

Chapter 21

The meeting room in the Embassy was blessedly cool. For once the power was on and the air conditioning was working well. The Ambassador sat at the head of the table and was flanked by the Commodore and Rupert. Brian as acting CO of the squadron and Helen were the only others present. Helen's task was to take the minutes. Brian's task was to do all he could to find and rescue his friend. The Commodore was not making it easy. He was just winding up.

'So we have no real intelligence as to where our two missing people are and what condition they might be in. There has been no word from any hostage takers so we can't even start to negotiate. I'm terribly sorry to have to say this but I don't see what the Royal Navy can do in such a situation. It seems to me to be in the province of Special Forces and Diplomats now.'

Brian was about to speak and probably end up regretting his words when Rupert didn't give him the chance. 'That's not quite true Commodore. I'm afraid we are in the Middle East now and these things happen at a different pace. For one thing, I have high confidence that Jon and Marie are still alive.'

Brian noticed how Rupert named the two victims. It gave the whole situation a personal touch that the Commodore seemed to want to avoid.

'How do you conclude that?'

'Simple, we have clear evidence that they were abducted from the crash site. Why would you do that unless you wanted them for some purpose? The PLO soldiers arrived on site very fast otherwise we might have had more people missing. Also, we haven't found any bodies. If they were abducted to be made an example of we would have found them by now and it wouldn't have been very pretty believe me. Now, I have word out with my contacts, there are several organisations who might have done this but strangely, as the PLO were employing them at the time, it actually narrows down the field. My best guess is that it is criminal rather than sectarian or political and if that's so, it narrows the field down even more.'

'So if it's a criminal operation how will they benefit?' Brian asked.

'Very soon there will be a notice on the grapevine that certain goods will be auctioned. Then they will be sold to the highest bidder.'

'Oh my God that's so brutal.' The words were out of Helen's mouth before she realised she had said them.

'Welcome to my world,' said Rupert, tight lipped. 'And Her Majesties Government never, I repeat never, gets involved in that sort of thing, as I'm sure you know.'

The Ambassador spoke. 'Yes Rupert but the French do. Have you spoken to your counterpart in their Embassy?'

'Yes Ambassador I have and they may well cough up but only if the situation becomes public knowledge and as you know we've managed to keep it under wraps so far.'

'So why keep it secret?' Brian asked.

'Come on Brian, you know why. We never let the bad guys get publicity. It's what they want in the first place.'

'Not if they're criminals and only after money. And what if another politically motivated group come up with the winning bid? What will happen to them then?'

'Several possibilities and none of them good I'm afraid.'

'So we've got to find them and get them out.'

The Commodore sighed. 'Lieutenant Commander Pearce, we are not playing out a scene from a James Bond film here. We don't know where they are and we are not equipped to do anything practical even if we did. My orders are to withdraw to Cyprus as soon as the evacuation is complete, which it almost is. So, unless something comes up in the next two days that is what we will be doing. Do I make myself clear?'

Rupert looked hard at the Commodore. 'You could, of course, argue that the evacuation isn't over until everyone is out and that would of course, include the French doctor and your pilot.'

'What are you trying to say?'

'Commodore, you are probably aware that I have been involved in several operations with Jon Hunt and Brian. I know just how capable they both are. If we are going to hear anything from the kidnappers it will probably be within the next few days. They won't want to hold them for too long. Could I suggest that a small troop of Royal Marines and at least one Sea King are left here ashore to act as a quick reaction force if we get sufficient intelligence to act?'

'You're asking me to do exactly what caused this foul up in the first place when I left them ashore without sufficient command and control oversight? I don't think so.'

Rupert looked at the Ambassador who nodded slightly. 'Commodore the operation you refer to was set up by me, not Lieutenant Commander Hunt. It was my responsibility and my estimate of the situation that drove the timing and I have to say that your people did an exemplary job. As you are well aware, the conclusions of the engineers on site are that the aircraft was brought down by lucky rifle fire and we know from the testimony of the survivors that it wasn't the PLO soldiers so it was hardly something that could have been foreseen. Do you really want it to be known that you are prepared to abandon one of your own people without even providing a token effort to try to help?'

The Commodore was looking embarrassed and angry at the same time but when he glanced over at the Ambassador and saw the same look on his face he knew he was beaten.

'Fair enough but I need to be kept in the loop this time.'

Brian had a brainwave. 'Why not stay here yourself Sir, maybe with some of your staff? Little will be happening in Cyprus that will need your personal attention.'

The Commodore looked hard at Brian then turned his attention to Rupert. 'Is there room for say half a dozen of us and are you willing to have us under your coat tails?'

The Ambassador answered for him. 'Of course Commodore, I would be delighted to offer you our somewhat erratic hospitality, especially if it will aid in getting these people released.'

Sometime later, after the meeting had broken up, Helen managed to get a quiet word with Brian. 'SOBS, was that a good idea, suggesting the Commodore stays with us? He'll be breathing down the back of our necks all time.'

Brian just smiled. 'Haven't you heard the phrase 'keep your friends close but your enemies even closer?' A certain Mr Machiavelli was a clever guy.'

Karim looked over his shoulder from the stove where he was preparing yet another large pot of stew as Khalid came in through the front door.

'Is the word out then?' he asked as he continued to stir the glutinous mass.

'Pretty much,' his twin answered. 'I've let it be known what merchandise we have and that we will accept offers with a deadline of Friday midday. We can't wait any longer than that as on Saturday we are out of here.'

'What do we do if no one bites?'

'Dispose of them in a way that looks like it wasn't us and then just leave.'

'And here's me always accused of being the ruthless one. How are they by the way?'

'The French woman is no trouble but that pilot seems to have fully recovered and he could be a problem. We will have to keep a closer eye on him now.' Karim looked grim.

'Do you think they've worked it out yet?' Khalid asked with a grin.

'Well, no one else ever has, which is why it gives us such an advantage when we return them. No one ever thinks to look for two people when they've only ever seen one. Just make sure you keep that scar covered.'

'Don't I always? Do you want me to take them the food, now that you've burnt it so successfully?'

Karim cursed and turned to the stew which was definitely burning at the bottom of the pot now. 'Oh well, I never claimed to be a cook. Yes, take them some. I'm sure they'll enjoy the extra flavour.'

Khalid spooned two bowls full and tucked two bottles of water under his arm before Karim carefully opened the door so that it screened him as his brother entered.

Both the prisoners looked up as he entered and Khalid could immediately see what his brother meant. The woman was sitting on her bed and barely lifted her eyes but the English pilot locked eyes with him. His malignant stare could even have been menacing if wasn't for the fact that he was securely chained to his bed. Even so, Khalid was not expecting what happened next. As he bent slightly to give the Englishman his bowl, the man grabbed it and flung the contents into his face. The almost boiling stew caused Khalid to shut his eyes for a second and the man was onto him. He had definitely recovered. He had his arm around Khalid's throat before he thought it possible and started to choke the life out of him. Khalid struggled but the surprise as well as the scalding pain to his face gave his adversary an advantage that was rapidly increasing as his strength waned. He kicked savagely at the ground and then there was a dull thud and suddenly the pressure relaxed. Staggering back and finally able to clear his eyes, he saw Karim about to take another swing at the Englishman with the baseball bat he held before he suddenly stopped when he realised that the man was unconscious and slumping to the ground. Taking his brother by the arm, Karim snarled at the Frenchwoman. 'You better use your doctor skills on him again and when you have, tell him he gets no food and water until he learns to behave.'

The two left the room and Khalid got a wet cloth from the sink and wiped his face. The pain was receding. He looked at his brother. 'Well, they'll have worked it out now won't they brother.'

Karim sat down looking shaken. 'I suppose it doesn't really matter. We'll be gone in three days.'

Jon came to with a throbbing head for the second time in a week. Once again Marie's concerned face was the first thing he saw. However, this time he had no trouble recalling the past events.

'Almost got the bastard, didn't I?' He managed, despite the throbbing in his temples.

'And what good would it have done us?' Marie asked with a note of asperity.

'If I could have strangled the bastard we might have been able to get away.'

'And do you think he would have had the keys to the cuffs on him? I would be very surprised and then we would have been chained here and no one would ever find us.'

'Shit, I didn't think of that,' said Jon as he took the wet cloth from Marie and held it to his head as he sat up and then wished he hadn't.

She looked strangely at him. 'Did you see who hit you?'

'No, I was too busy trying to break that bastard's neck.'

'Well, you should have looked because it was the same man.'

'Eh, what do you mean?'

'It was another man, identical to the one you were trying to strangle.'

'Ah, that answers how one man was able to oversee us for so long. So there's two of the buggers. Not sure if that's of any real consequence though.'

'Well, it could curb your enthusiasm for mayhem.'

'Marie, look. We get training in this sort of thing. Not enough, as I'm rapidly discovering but at least enough to give us some idea of what to expect. And one of the key things is not to get into a frame of mind where you start accepting your fate. For the first few days here I was getting over the crash and a concussion. But once I was thinking straight, I started looking for any way to get an edge, even if it's just a psychological one. By having a go at that shit, I don't know about you, but by God it's made me feel better. They're not going to grind me down.' He looked at her with a challenge in his eye.

She laughed for the first time and Jon saw that his point had told. 'And it's more than that. It's very easy to get into a frame of mind where any action seems futile. The Germans were able to exterminate whole villages in the last war using only a few soldiers. If the victims had turned on them, they would have been overwhelmed but they didn't. I'm not going to be like that and I have a temper, I know that and I've been feeding it. Every time one of those bastards comes in here I'm going to get angry and if there is the slightest chance to take one out I will take it. Whatever they have in mind for us won't be good and I'd rather die trying to take one of them with me than just lie down and roll over.'

Jon saw a look of hope bloom on Marie's face. 'Jon that hits home. I've been in that state of mind for days now but do you have any concrete ideas?'

'Maybe one or two.'

Chapter 22

Rupert sat at a run down roadside café. There were still a few about even in the war torn city. He was drinking coffee and waiting. Dressed in scruffy jeans and T shirt with several day's stubble, he didn't look out of place even being a Westerner. The population of the city was even more cosmopolitan these days with all sorts of riff raff attracted to the violence and the chance of a quick buck. As he sipped at the bitter brew he kept a careful eye in both directions. He had chosen this particular venue because there were only two practical ways to approach it and he could see them clearly. His man was late but that was nothing unusual in this part of the world. Resisting the urge to keep glancing at his watch, he was just about to order some food to allay any suspicion as to why he was there so long when his target appeared.

The short, swarthy man was wearing his usual dirty white suit and strolled past Rupert without any sign of recognition. When he reached the end of the road to Rupert's right, he turned right at the T junction. Rupert sighed with relief, had he turned left it would have meant that the meeting was compromised in some way and Rupert really needed to talk to this man urgently.

Waiting another few minutes, he left some change on the table and casually strolled in the same direction as his quarry. When he turned into the small street, he looked for the doorway he had been told to go through. At first, he couldn't see it and a slight feeling of panic started to gnaw at him. However, in a few yards, he spotted it. He had been told to look for a blue door. In fact, it was almost white with scraps of blue paint peeling from its sun bleached wood but he was confident this was the place. Trying hard to look nonchalant, he did his best to make sure no one was looking and went up to the door and knocked. Three raps followed by a gap and then two more. It immediately opened and the man beckoned him in.

'You weren't followed?'

'No Ahmed, I wasn't and I hope this place is safe?'

'As safe as anywhere in this city. It belongs to my cousin who is away at the moment.' He gestured to Rupert to sit at a dilapidated old table in the courtyard to the small house that overlooked them.

'Do you have the money?' he asked with a gleam of avarice in his eyes.

'Half of it and the balance if the information is good.'

'That is not what we agreed.'

'Ahmed, do you take me for a fool?' Rupert handed over the envelope and Ahmed grabbed it and started counting.

Amused at his greed, Rupert knew that the promise of the same amount again would be enough to get him what he wanted even if that hadn't been the original deal. And if the information was suspect or wrong then he would have saved his country a reasonable sum of money.

'So what do you know?'

'The twins.'

'Is that it? I could have guessed that myself. They're top of the criminal kidnap industry around here.'

'Ah but there's more.'

'There had better be.'

Ahmed clearly came to a decision. The money in his hand was having the desired effect.

'The story on the streets is that they are about to leave the Lebanon. Over the last few weeks, they have been arranging false papers. That can only mean one thing. They were setting up for one last operation but it seems to have gone wrong in some way. However, they are holding an auction for the merchandise they have and bids have to be in by tomorrow at noon.'

'And what is the merchandise?'

'Surely you already know that?'

'Enlighten me. Pretend I don't know.'

'Two people, a French doctor and one of your pilots, one that has been flying those helicopters around for the last few weeks.'

'And why would anyone be interested in paying for them?'

Ahmed snorted in amusement. 'Come on, you know half the crazies here would love to get their hands on them for political leverage or old fashioned blackmail and the doctor could even be used in her profession.'

'So how would I bid?'

'What? I thought your government never paid ransoms.'

'Just humour me.'

Arapaho

Ahmed looked smug 'Simple, tell me what you are prepared to pay and I will ensure the right people get to hear of it.'

'And how is payment to be made.'

'If your offer is accepted, then a bank account number will be provided. Once the money is transferred, you will be given a location.'

Rupert sat back and studied the man. It all sounded reasonable. The twins were notorious in the criminal underworld but as they had never acted against British security interests they had only been of peripheral concern. Clearly, that had now changed. He came to a decision.

'Ahmed you are correct. The British Government never negotiate with terrorists but in this case, of course, we are dealing with criminals, which might be considered different. Also, the Doctor is a French national and we may be able to do something there. However, is there anything apart from money that might make our approach more attractive?'

'I can't answer that but I will ask for you.'

Rupert nodded and handed over the second envelope which was grabbed greedily. 'I need to hear today.'

'I will contact you in the usual way by this evening, now you must go.'

Rupert stood and left via the gate without saying anything more and walked quickly away down the street. As he did, he reached up and scratched his left ear forcefully and then continued on his way.

That morning the argument had raged in the Embassy. The meeting with the Commodore had once again proved difficult. Rupert's security people had already left, the whole Embassy was due to be shut in only another two days. If there was any hope of finding the hostages location before they were passed on elsewhere then Rupert needed extra eyes. His contacts had passed on the message that Jon and the Doctor were being offered for sale the day before and that had given him some ideas about who was behind the operation but was of no help in finding them. Ahmed was a man he had used occasionally and as soon as he had made contact, it was clear that he was in the loop in some way. Normally, Rupert would have taken his time and used trained staff. He had neither and knew he would have to rely on what he had to hand. His first port of call when heard the news was to Brian and Helen. He was honest with them about what he knew and what he thought the chances were of actually finding the hostages in time.

'And if we don't get to them before the deadline we are in a whole world of extra trouble. They could be taken anywhere. Frankly, I wouldn't rate their chances highly. There are just too many of these fanatical organisations that would love to conduct a public execution and send the tape to a TV station.'

Helen looked sick. 'What can we do?'

'Well, negotiation has been ruled out as I'm sure you understand. I've already been on to London and with such a short deadline there is little help they can provide in the next few days. They're going to get me some people as soon as they can be flown in but that means into Cyprus and onwards by ship and helicopter, three days or more. So I'm going to make contact and see what the deal is. What I could really do with is someone to tail the contact after the meeting and try and see where he goes and what he does.'

Before anyone else could say anything Helen spoke up. 'Me, I can do that and never be noticed.'

Brian and Rupert looked at her questioningly. So she told them her idea.

When they put it to the Commodore he went ballistic. 'Absolutely not. You, young lady, shouldn't be here at all, you're not trained for this sort of operation and there is no way I'm going to authorise such a risky thing.'

'Actually Sir, you can't stop me,' she said determinedly.

'I beg your pardon. You may have noticed that I outrank you just a little.'

Brian looked over at Rupert and nodded slightly. This was going to be interesting.

'Sir, I am a member of the Women's Royal Naval Service. I am not a commissioned Naval Officer and I am not subject to the Naval Discipline Act as I'm sure you well know. In addition, until military assets are required, this operation is under the control of the British Intelligence Service, in other words Mr Thomas. So if I volunteer my services to him, firstly you have no authority to stop me and secondly if he accepts me, that is his decision.'

The Commodore looked angry but turned to his secretary who was standing to one side.

The thin faced Lieutenant Commander replied. 'Technically she's correct Sir, although you could of course report her once we are back in the UK. I'm sure her superiors will take a dim view of such behaviour.'

The Commodore turned to Rupert. 'And you've said you will accept her help in this way?'

'I'm sorry Commodore I have, we've talked it over in detail and I have to say I see it as a low risk option that might just work. As an experiment we tried it out before we came here. Frankly she became invisible.'

The Commodore sighed. 'I'm sure you all think I object to all this on some sort of principle. I don't, I'm just trying to balance the risks. Yes, we've lost a key member of my team and a valuable French national but what happens if we lose Miss Barratt here as well? How is that going to look?'

Rupert nodded. 'Commodore, yes there are risks but I intend to trail Helen at the same time that she is following my man. This will give me enough separation to be unobserved. Believe me, if I see anything untoward I will intervene.'

Helen saw Rupert leave through the old gate. She was quite far away down the end of the alley but his signal was quite clear. She waited and watched him disappear and then moments later the man in the crumpled white suit came out. He looked carefully both ways and started walking towards her. She continued to squat on her haunches at the side of the road and as expected, he completely ignored her and walked determinedly past. She gave him a few moments then stood up and started walking behind him, about a hundred yards clear.

The sweat was trickling down her face because of the heavy clothing although it wasn't as hot as she expected. Her hair was tied back, well clear so that it wouldn't be seen and she had coloured her eyebrows black. The biggest problem was her limited field of vision. The Burka she was wearing made her anonymous but also made her feel very claustrophobic. The eye slit above the veil was small and made it quite difficult to see. The idea had come to her after her experience with the Arab males she first encountered when they had deployed ashore. There seemed to be little inhibition to their behaviour when confronted with a blonde western woman, who was dressed completely immodestly in their view. However, the more she disguised her sex, the less she was bothered and she had noticed how veiled women were universally ignored. And so it was now. She almost felt like the invisible woman. She had to take care to walk in a sort of shuffle and keep her head bowed but it was like magic. No one was taking the slightest notice even when she had stopped and squatted against the wall while she waited for Rupert to appear.

Keeping the man in view and praying that Rupert had doubled back to tail her, she followed him down several alleys and into a more prosperous part of town where the numbers of people increased. She quickly realised that he was being careful to check behind him but his eyes just slid off her. At one point, he stopped and looked into a small shop's interior and she was forced to keep going past him but was able to slow down and let him overtake a few minutes later. He actually hadn't gone that far before he stopped at one of the few working public telephone boxes and fumbled in his pocket for some change. With her heart in her mouth, she kept walking and tried desperately to see what number he was dialling. Once again her disguise worked perfectly, she stopped several yards behind him where she could see his hand and the dial of the telephone. Just as he stopped dialling he turned around but she had already started walking again and once again was ignored.

Chapter 23

'Damn, bugger and damnation,' Rupert was sitting at his desk back in the Embassy. Helen and Brian were with him. 'How sure are you that those were the numbers he dialled?'

'Rupert, I'm certain, those old fashioned dials are slow and so I was able to see each number.' Helen looked upset but also firmly convinced she was correct.

'Well, I've checked the phone books, all of them. The first part would have been an area code if the call was away from the city but it wasn't. There aren't enough digits for a start. That means it's somewhere within the confines of this city area,' and he indicated the map on his desk. 'But there is no record of that number. Also, I called the local exchange and asked them to do a check and they say it doesn't exist.'

'So we ought to try ringing it and see who answers.' Brian suggested.

Rupert grimaced. 'Maybe as a last resort but we need to think this through carefully. If it's the bad guys at the end of the line, the last thing we need to do is warn them and an anonymous call or one from people they don't know could be disastrous.'

While Rupert was talking Helen had been looking at his desk and his old fashioned rotary dial telephone. 'Hang on a second Rupert. Is that a standard Lebanese phone?'

'Yes, why?'

'Hold on,' and she grabbed a piece of paper. After a quick scribble, she passed it to Rupert who studied it briefly and then laughed. 'Of course, blame the bloody French.'

'Would someone like to tell me what the hell is going on?' Brian asked.

'Sorry Brian,' said Rupert looking relieved. 'The Beirut telephone system was designed by the French many years ago and as usual, they designed the hand sets differently from everyone else. In most of Europe, the first number is zero and the last is nine. Here the first is one and the last is the zero. Helen saw which hole our man put his fingers in but was off by one digit for each one. Let's see if we can trace this number.'

After a frantic few minutes with the phone book, he had to admit defeat again. However, he didn't give up and picked up his phone and after a few minutes of frantic Arabic put the receiver down with a grin of satisfaction on his face.

'Thought so, it was an ex-directory number. I've just been talking to my contact in the telephone company again and explained the urgency. I've got an address and I know where it is. We'd better go and see the Ambassador and the good Commodore.'

Half an hour later they were once again all together in the main conference room. Rupert summarised the operation and how they had found the location of the telephone that the man Ahmed had rung. He had hung a large scale map of the city on an easel.

'Right gentlemen, the house the phone belongs to is here.' And he pointed to the edge of the city to the north east. 'It's right on the edge of the city and is in an area that is sparsely populated. I've been through there several times over the last two years and the houses are quite large with extensive grounds. It's just the sort of place for the sort of privacy our guys need. In fact, it's better to call them compounds as they often contain several buildings behind high walls. This road has quite a few along its length but they are well spread out. What I suggest is that as soon as we can, we get airborne and fly over close to the place to take a look and get some photographs. The helicopters are a common sight and we won't actually overfly. Then we can decide on an approach.'

The Commodore looked thoughtful. 'It seems to me that you are already considering a military assault to be the only option. But there are going to be several issues are there not? Firstly what about the Lebanese Government? Won't they take exception to a foreign nation interfering with their internal affairs?'

The Ambassador laughed. 'Tell that to the Syrians or Israelis or any of the other smaller groups for that matter. Technically, you're right Commodore but don't worry, I'll square it with them. It won't be an issue.'

'And won't the local police want to be in on the act as well?'

Rupert answered. 'If we could trust them then you would be right Commodore. But involving them or even the local militia would be like holding up a bloody great sign saying we know where they are being held.'

'But do we know they are there?' The Commodore didn't look convinced. 'Just because they gave that number to your man doesn't mean that's where they're located.'

'Good point Commodore,' Rupert was forced to agree. 'But it's all we've got at the moment and the place looks just the sort of real estate you would need for this sort of operation. But that's why I want to scout the place as carefully as I can. As I said, I want to do an airborne recce and then if it looks possible, a raid in the small hours. The deadline is tomorrow at midday and therefore nothing will be happening tonight. If we move now it will take them by surprise. If we leave it any later we risk losing them. And if there's nothing there then we've also lost nothing.'

The Commodore looked at the Ambassador. 'If this is our best option then let's do it and then review the situation later this evening.'

Karim and Khalid were debating the day's events. 'Things are looking up. That's five organisations who have expressed an interest but I'm surprised the British even made contact. They never negotiate.' Karim looked puzzled.

'They wanted to know if there was anything else that would sway our decision, is there?' his brother asked.

Karim just chuckled. 'Sounds like a desperate question to me and no, money is all we want unless you can think of something.'

Khalid was about to reply when the telephone rang again. They waited for nine rings before Karim lifted the handset. He didn't say anything, just listened to the tinny voice at the end of the line before replacing the receiver with an odd look on his face.

'That moron Ahmed must have been followed by one of the British. Somehow they've got hold of this number. That was my man at the telephone company. I'll wring the silly bugger's neck when I see him again.'

'So they'll have traced it by now?'

'Almost certainly.'

'And know the address?'

'Of course.'

'So brother, should we be worried,' Khalid asked with a knowing grin.

Karim answered with another smile. 'No, not at all.'

Arapaho

Chapter 24

Jon was lying on his back looking at the ceiling. He knew every crack in it by now. Earlier that afternoon he had heard the distinctive sound of a Sea King flying not too far away. The familiar roar rammed home just how far away yet how tantalisingly close he was now from the life he knew.

'Marie, we've got do something and do it soon.'

They had been telling each other their life stories but even that topic was exhausted. In Jon's mind the mantra from his survival training of: Protection, Location, Water, Food, kept echoing around in his mind. It hardly fit the current situation. Protection was meant to be from the elements, which to all intents and purposes was not an issue. Water and food hadn't been an issue until he'd clobbered that guard. He was still getting water as Marie was giving him some of hers and food wouldn't be an issue for days yet. His leg was still throbbing but at last it was starting to heal. So the word 'Location' was all he had to chew on. For the thousandth time, he looked around the room. It was bare, with whitewashed walls. A single neon strip light was fixed to the centre of the ceiling and well beyond reach. A switch to operate it was by the door, once again well beyond reach. The beds were cemented into the floor.

With a curse, he slipped over onto the floor on his knees and pulled up the mattress.

'What are you doing Jon?' Marie's voice came from behind him as he pushed the mattress to one side.

'Bugger, bugger,' he replied in an angry tone. 'I suddenly thought that the bed base might have springs or wires I could use.' He then felt the mattress but it was clearly only full of some sort of straw. He sat back on his heels contemplating the bed. The mattress was supported by simple wooden slats nothing else. The frame was metal, welded together and the legs disappeared into the floor. He had already tried to shift one of the legs to no avail and knew they must be well cemented in. His handcuff was attached to a very strong chain which itself was wrapped around the bed frame and welded to the frame and back onto itself. Whoever had thought this out had been very thorough.

'What use would a wire or spring be?'

'God, I don't know Marie, maybe I could make a lever to twist the chain and snap it or a harpoon to throw at that guard.' He was sounding desperate now as his momentary burst of optimism drifted away.

Suddenly, it all changed. He reached for the base of the bed and pulled one of the slats. It didn't budge. When he looked carefully, he could see a cross-headed screw fixing it at each end to the metal frame.

'Marie can you throw me the fork from your food. They still haven't collected it yet.' There was a dull clatter and a simple metal fork hit his ankle. 'Thanks, now let's see if we can bodge this.'

Using one of the tines, he levered at the head of a screw. 'Thank God for a dry climate' he thought. The screw clearly hadn't rusted into the frame as it probably would have at home and even with makeshift leverage it turned quite easily. Within a matter of minutes, all but one screw was removed. This meant that all but one of the slats was free, he counted six of them.

He threw the fork back to Marie. 'Listen Marie, when they next come can you ask for some sticking plaster for my wound. Say that the bandages aren't necessary now and plaster will make me more mobile or some other medical bollocks OK?'

'Jon, what are you up to?'

So he told her.

Rupert had mustered five Toyota Land Cruisers. Battered and dusty, they would hardly draw any attention to themselves. They were parked up by the silent bulk of the remaining Sea King while the raiding team assembled in the Command Post tent. Sergeant Cummings had just finished covering the tactical brief and Rupert stood to sum up.

'We go in half an hour, it will take forty five minutes to get to the Initial Point where we all disembark. Sergeant Cumming and his boys will then disperse around the building. Once in position, we go in hard. From what we could see, there is a wall about ten feet high around the compound with a gate for vehicles and a door for people and no other access. It may be secure but it could also be a trap for anyone trying to get out. However, as the Sergeant has detailed, two marines will cover the rear which is all loose scrub and waste ground. In addition, there will be a Marine at each side. That leaves five, plus myself to go in the front and knock on the door. There is only one main building but there is also a small outhouse to one side and of course, that could be where they are being kept. We just don't know. So once inside we split. Two to the outhouse, the remaining three, plus myself to the main building. Brian, you and Helen stay with the vehicles and radios. This isn't your sort of fight.'

Brian nodded unhappily. He knew Rupert was right but desperately wanted to be involved in rescuing Jon. However, he was also a realist and someone needed to watch over Helen who, at this short notice, was the only qualified radio operator apart from the marines who were needed for the raid.

The meeting broke up. The marines dispersed to check their weapons and the Commodore who had been keeping a watching brief came up to Brian and Rupert.

'Gentlemen, I still have some misgivings about this but the bottom line is that I don't see we have any other option, so God speed. One last thing though, if this a wild goose chase, please do your best to extricate yourselves fast and leave little trace. We don't want a diplomatic incident if we can avoid it. Rescuing hostages is one thing. Attacking an innocent Lebanese family is another. Yes, I know there is no record of anyone living there but you never know. So take care.'

He held out his hand and Rupert and then Brian shook it before he left for the Embassy situation room.

Brian looked sour. 'Translated, that means don't fuck up and if you do, don't expect me to back you up.'

'Cynical, Brian, cynical but also probably true. Anyway, let's forget politics and go find Jon.'

Three o'clock in the morning. The favourite time for the attacker, when a person's energy is at its lowest ebb. Karim and Khalid were asleep in their room confident that their hostages were secure. Jon and Marie were definitely not. Nor were the Embassy team, as they parked their Land Cruisers a few minute's walk away from their objective. The marines went ahead and Brian and Helen stayed with their vehicle sitting clustered around the radio.

Rupert and the marines were dressed in black with military helmets fitted with night vision goggles. They had swapped their usual SLR rifles for short snub nosed machine guns. Everyone also carried stun and smoke grenades. As they approached the compound, they could see little in terms of lights, even with the goggles. The Sergeant signalled with his hands and the team of marines who were covering the rear and sides split off to take up their positions.

While they were walking, Rupert took one last look around. Nothing was moving and it was eerily quiet. Some of the other houses showed lights but nothing suspicious. The Sergeant looked at his watch and then at Rupert, giving him the thumbs up sign. Rupert nodded and they crept carefully towards the main door. If an alert were to be sounded, now would be the time but the silence continued. The Sergeant lifted the latch on the door and it opened. He and Rupert exchanged puzzled glances. They had fully expected to have to smash it down. One of the marines had a large sledgehammer for just that eventuality.

Silently, they filed in. Two marines went off to the small shed off to one side, while the rest ran towards the door of the house. It too was unlocked. Smelling a rat but not wishing to stop now, Rupert nodded again to the Sergeant and they ran into the house.

Half an hour later and all five Land Cruisers were parked inside the compound. The compound that was totally empty as was the house and outhouse. Not only was it empty of people but it was clear it hadn't been used for years. There was no furniture, not even any sign of footprints on the dusty floor. The only item of interest was a telephone. Rupert lifted it and got a dialling tone. He rang the Embassy and got through immediately and then asked them to ring the number that they had traced before putting the receiver down again. Within in seconds it rang. Rupert picked it up and confirmed they had the right number before putting it down again with an angry crash.

'Bastards, this must have been purely for safety, a cut out.'

'But why no footprints around the phone? These are all ours. And it looks as though it hasn't been used for years,' Brian observed grimly. 'Is there an extension somewhere?'

'Bloody good point,' Rupert responded and he detailed everyone to search for the phone lines and see if there was any sign of an extension anywhere. There wasn't. The only thing out of the ordinary was an extra wire from the junction box on the outside wall by the front door, disappearing into the ground.

Arapaho

'Bastards,' Rupert spat when he saw it. 'There is a bloody extension but it goes somewhere else. It could be any of these houses. Shit we can't search them all. We're going to have to abort, at least for now.'

Helen who had been standing at the back of the group and looking down the street, suddenly exclaimed, 'I think I know where he is, look.' And she pointed down the street to a house in the distance. In the upstairs window, a light was flashing on and off. Then it stopped.

'Come on Helen that was just someone going to the loo,' Brian admonished.

'Really, well I know a little Morse code and why would you flash SOS if you were just using the toilet.'

'Are you sure?' Rupert snapped.

'Absolutely,' she replied with her heart in her mouth. 'It may have stopped now but I watched it for a minute or so to be sure before I told you all.'

'Right, everyone, same plan different house. Move.' Rupert ordered, praying Helen was right.

Karim was jerked to wakefulness by the telephone ringing. It only rang twice and he almost thought it was the alarm rather than the phone. Fumbling through fogged sleep, he got up from his camp bed and picked it up. Before he could speak, he heard a voice at the other end. 'Yes it's the right number,' a strange voice said in English. 'Right, we're probably going have to abort. Should be back within the hour.' And then the buzz of the dialling tone started.

Karim's head was clearing fast. He gave Khalid a kick and when he was sitting up he told him what had happened.

'It sounds like the British have found the decoy house. It also sounded like they were giving up,' he said.

'Good, it's nice to see our little contingency plan has worked. Mind you, it's the first time anyone has even got that close. Thank God we're leaving in a few days. I guess I'd better check the merchandise.'

Khalid got up and unlocked the door to the prisoner's room. At first, what he saw totally confused him. The woman was sitting on her bed looking surprised. The man was sitting at the end of his bed looking like a child who had been caught stealing sweets. If it wasn't so serious it would have been almost comical. In his hand, he had a long piece of wood. It seemed to have been taped together with sticking plaster. The plaster they had got for the doctor this afternoon for the man's wounded leg. For the life of him he couldn't work out what was going on and he called for his brother.

When Karim joined him, he pointed to the pilot. Karim looked as puzzled as Khalid and then looked around the room. Suddenly, he saw that the plaster around the light switch was chipped and there were tell-tale flakes of plaster on the floor all around it. The penny dropped.

Karim went over to the man and wrenched the wooden baton away and back handed him across the face. 'You've been signalling with the light haven't you?'

The pilot's head slammed around and he fell back on the bed but there was no mistaking the look of triumph in his eyes.

'Shit, if they saw the light flashing they may well be one their way here. You'd better hope they are not,' Karim snarled at Jon. 'Because if they are, your dead body will be the first thing they find. Come on Khalid we need to check the perimeter.'

The door slammed shut on Jon and Marie.

With his ears still ringing from the blow, Jon called to Marie. 'Stage two Marie, the silly sods didn't take the wood.'

Karim made sure all the lights were out and stayed that way by pulling the master breaker on the house's fuse board. He and Khalid then went upstairs and looked carefully out of the windows towards the decoy house. Sure enough, in a matter of moments, they could see the ghostly shape of unwanted guests approaching.

'How many do you think?' Khalid asked.

'More than we can handle, these will be trained troops. We never envisaged a standing fight with soldiers. Time to get away.'

'And the merchandise?'

'Leave them, we don't have time.'

Khalid was getting angrier by the minute. This had been his idea. The money wasn't that important but he hated the idea that that bastard Englishman had ruined it all. Firstly, by flying his damned helicopter into their operation and then by betraying them like this.

'You go Karim,' he hissed. 'I will take care of the two hostages.'

'No, we don't have time we have to leave now. They will surround the house and could find the tunnel at any time.'

'No, you open the tunnel. I'm not going to leave them to tell them about us. They know who we are remember?'

Karim could hear the cold resolution in his brother's voice and knew he was wasting his breath. 'I'll see you in the cellar as soon as you're done.'

They both made their way down stairs. Karim continued to the cellar and started pulling the old sacks and other rubbish they had piled up against the entrance to their escape tunnel. They had built it years ago, never really expecting to ever need it. He thanked the stars for their forethought now. It led under the road and into the garage of the house opposite which they also owned and where they kept their car.

Khalid reached into the drawer in the kitchen outside the hostage's room and pulled out a nine millimetre pistol. Reaching further into the drawer, he found the silencer which he screwed to the barrel. It wouldn't be a good idea to make any noise now. With a feral grin, he pulled the bolts back on the door and pushed the handle down. The door wouldn't open. Something on the other side was jamming it. With a start, he realised that they hadn't taken the wood from the pilot. He must have jammed the door somehow. Snarling with anger, he slammed his shoulder against the door. But they had built it to be strong and it didn't give an inch. With rage almost blinding him, he raised the pistol and fired several shots. If they had any effect he didn't see it. What he didn't hear was his brother shouting for him to hurry, nor did he hear the sound of the window glass breaking and something thudding to the ground. What he did hear was the stun grenade explode.

The shock was mind numbingly loud, as intended. Despite the disorientation and the roaring in his ears, he dropped to his knees and started crawling towards the cellar door. Karim appeared beckoning him on, just as the first soldier slammed through the door. He looked like a devil from Khalid's worst nightmare, completely black with a head that looked like some creature from Hell. Khalid made the last mistake of his life and raised the pistol towards the macabre sight. A stream of nine millimetre bullets almost cut him in half. His body was still jerking with the impact as Karim disappeared back into the cellar.

Chapter 25

The bar of Arapaho was noisy and crowded. The squadron had decided to have a party to welcome the Boss back. When Jon had hobbled into the throng, leaning heavily on a stick, a great cheer went up quickly followed by various ribald and very rude comments about squadron CO's using walking sticks. Jon put up with all the banter, in fact he loved it. He was back in his world, with his men, something he thought would never happen only a day or was it a lifetime ago. Someone thrust a frosted glass into his hand and he took a large gulp before realising what the hell it was.

'Harvey Wallbanger Boss,' someone shouted as he almost choked but he suddenly felt the last of the anxiety melt away.

At first, when he and Marie had heard the stun grenade go off they weren't sure what was happening outside. They knew that their captors were trying to get into the room and luckily neither of them had been in front of the door when several bullets spat through it. However, even with the door in the way, the violence of the grenade was staggering. It took Jon several minutes to work out what was probably going on. They had heard machine gun fire and then voices but his hearing was still ringing so it was hard to make out what language they were using. As soon as he recognised English, he managed to kick his impromptu door wedge away. The first face he saw was Rupert's, grinning like an idiot, quickly followed by what seemed like a horde of marines. Shortly afterwards, Brian and Helen appeared. Brian grabbed him in a bearhug and then Helen hugged him as well. He knew which one he preferred.

Within what seemed like moments, they were bundled into a car and driven away. Rupert stayed behind with some of the marines to clear up. They were both taken to the Embassy where a doctor gave them the once over but Marie's ministrations seemed to pass muster with him and he congratulated her on her work. It was only a few minutes and suddenly Jon felt incredibly weary. Whether it was the privations of the last few days catching up with him or the pills the doctor had given him, he fell asleep almost instantly.

The next day, he insisted he was well enough to attend a de-brief with Rupert. He learned that they had discovered a makeshift tunnel in the house leading to a garage in the house opposite.

'So the other bastard got away then?' he asked grimly.

'Yes and before you ask Jon,' Rupert cut in. 'We are not even going to try to find him. He knows the city far better than we do and anyway, tomorrow we're all leaving. I have informed the local police but I don't expect them to do anything. They have the body now, so it's up to them.'

Jon shrugged, he wasn't surprised. 'And Marie, where is she?'

'You'll be glad to know she is with her husband who survived the crash as well. The French Navy finally arrived the other day. They are all safe and on their way back to France. She gave me this note for you.'

Jon took it. He would read it privately later. They talked for another hour, Jon providing all the detail he could and in turn, being appraised on how they had found him.

'Seems like Helen needs a bloody good chuck up,' Jon observed. 'If it wasn't for her I wouldn't be here.'

'Absolutely, that girl has got some gumption. She's back out on Arapaho now so you can thank her in person this afternoon when you fly back out.'

'Shit, I suppose life goes on, doesn't it. Have you any idea what's going to happen now?'

'Ah, well that's for the Commodore to tell you Jon. He's asked to see you privately when we've finished but from what I can gather, everyone is retiring to Cyprus to wait for further developments. I guess you'll all just be hanging around for a while now until the politicians decide what to do next.'

Jon decided that the interview with the Commodore was almost as nerve wracking as being held hostage, at least for the first few minutes. Rupert left the room before the great man arrived.

'No, don't get up Jon,' were the Commodore's first words when he came in. 'I know about the leg.' He then went and sat in a chair opposite Jon and looked him over.

'You know, I really don't know what to do about you, young man. On the one hand, you went off on an unauthorised operation and exactly the thing I was worried about came about. On the other hand, you and your people conducted themselves with all the courage and fighting spirit that I could ask for.'

Arapaho

Something in Jon changed at that moment. He had survived a major crash and been held prisoner in fear of his life for days on end. He suddenly realised, he had no fear of this man. The navy was incredibly good at instilling an almost God like respect for rank but that all disappeared in the instant.

'Sir, can we take the rank tabs off for a second. It's just you and me in here and I feel I need to say something without fear or favour.'

The Commodore nodded.

'Firstly, I am not a 'young man' as you put it. I am the Commanding Officer of a Naval Air Squadron. That's one hundred and twenty five sailors and seventeen aircrew, as well as my aircraft. Secondly, I have probably more operational experience than just about anyone in your task force, including yourself. As you rightly pointed out the other day, I can't tell you about some of it but believe me when I say it's extensive. So, Sir, when Mr Thomas put a short term operational problem to me, I used my judgement. A factor which no one could have foreseen then intervened and we lost the aircraft and several people. But if they had stayed in that camp another day they would all now be dead. Rupert told me what has been going on up there in the last week. I stand by my decision and would do exactly the same again if asked.' He looked defiantly at the Commodore waiting for a response.

The room was silent. The Commodore suddenly stood and looked out of the window, his back to Jon. His words came as a complete surprise. Jon was expecting a bollocking not that he particularly cared at the moment. 'I absolutely agree with you Jon and please accept my apologies for calling you 'young man' I realise that was patronising. You did exactly the right thing. Even if I'm pretty sure you avoided discussing it with me because you probably felt I would say no. I wouldn't have you know but I do also realise that your time window was very small. Your conduct when being held prisoner was also exemplary. Frankly, I'm not sure that many of us could have kept it together as well as you did in the circumstances.' He turned and looked Jon in the eye. 'So, well done. I will be recommending you for an award, not that you haven't got enough already.'

He held out his hand. Somewhat taken aback, Jon did stand this time and took the Commodore's hand. 'One other thing Sir, my Staff Officer. If it hadn't been for her I wouldn't be here. Is there any chance of something for her, she really deserves it.'

The Commodore looked thoughtful. 'Well, as that young lady was happy to tell me, she isn't actually a full blown member of the navy, so I'm not sure we can get her a military award. Maybe we can get her an MBE or something like that instead. I'll let you look into it and you can make me a recommendation.'

A hand pummelling his back brought Jon back to reality just as another Harvey Wallbanger was thrust into his hand. Suddenly, Helen was standing in front of him. Maybe it was because the only female he had seen for the last weeks had been Marie or maybe it was the booze or maybe it was just Helen but a wave of something strange overcame him. Maybe it was lust, maybe something more but she looked absolutely adorable. Taking a grip on himself, he forced himself to act normally and thanked her for her part in rescuing him all the while aware that she was making his stomach turn somersaults. He didn't tell her about a possible award as that would need careful research but he did manage to hold up a decent conversation until she was dragged away by one of the pilots who decided she had been monopolising the Boss for too long. Jon didn't know whether to be grateful or angry. What he did realise was that he was going to have to get his thoughts about the girl straightened out. He was her CO after all and that complicated matters far too much. What he did overhear however, was a conversation between two of the pilots.

'I see Spanners has been eyeing up the boss again.'

Mystified he managed to corner Brian a few moments later. 'Hey Brian, I've just heard a couple of the lads referring to Staffy as 'spanners'. What's that all about?'

Brian looked slightly embarrassed. 'Thought you would have caught on to that one already Boss.'

'Nope, come on, spill it, I know what sort of minds my guys have got.'

'Well it's not derogatory if that's what you're worried about. As you know most of the squadron is in love with her.'

'Spanners Brian, what does it mean?'

'Simple Jon, one look tightens the nuts.'

Jon almost spat out his drink and choked at the same time. Now he really knew he was home and then he also realised that there was far too much truth in the joke.

Chapter 26

Karim was numb. Things had all happened just too fast. He and his brother had always been the predators, not the prey. Being on the receiving end had been an enormous shock. But that was nothing compared to seeing his brother cut down by those bastard soldiers. Luckily for him, the blast of the stun grenade had been deadened by the stairwell so he had managed to get to the top of the stairs in time to see his brave brother try to face down the troops. He also quickly realised that if he didn't want to follow Khalid to hell he needed to get out. One of his problems now was the guilt he felt in making that decision. Straight away, he realised that if he had stayed he would almost certainly have been gunned down as well but that didn't stop him feeling he should have done something more.

His passage through the tunnel had been easy and the car was ready. He had a moment of panic when deciding whether to open the garage door or not. Images of black clad soldiers waiting outside pointing their weapons at him assailed his mind. But he knew they had chosen the layout well. The garage opened up on a parallel road. Even if the house was still surrounded, it was extremely unlikely that a cordon had been set up this far out. Sure enough, he was able to drive away quietly without his lights on until he was well clear. As he drove, his mind was in turmoil. For the first time in his life, he didn't know what to do or where to go. His brother's body would be identified and then they would come for him. It must have been the British who mounted the raid but they were sure to tell the police and even with the leverage he had, he suspected they would be forced to come for him. However, in the end, he went to their Beirut house. As a minimum, he would need some personal possessions and then he could go and get the forged papers that were waiting for them and slip out of the country. With a start, he had realised he was still thinking in the plural. He was on his own now and it was like a spike driven through his heart.

When he got home, he packed a bag but a strange listlessness was falling over him. There seemed to be a space in his mind that he had never noticed before but now that Khalid was gone he realised it was something he needed. He had heard of people losing a limb but still feeling the need to scratch. This was the same only a thousand times worse. He and his brother had done everything together. Yes, Khalid had been more impetuous and cruel and often went off to God knows where to get his pleasures but they had always been a team. It was always Khalid with the wild ideas but also the ruthlessness needed to carry them through but tempered by Karim's common sense. It was almost inconceivable that he wouldn't just walk in through the door with that quirky grin and start arguing about something or the other.

Karim's eye was caught by the whiskey bottle they kept for visitors. He rarely drank but this time maybe it would numb the pain. Half a bottle later he collapsed on the sofa.

He woke to the sound of the telephone. His head felt dreadful and his mouth was dry. The events of the previous day came crashing in and suddenly he was retching on the floor. The damned phone wouldn't stop ringing. Groggily, he went over and picked up the receiver. He vaguely recognised the voice at the other end. It was one of his tame policemen. 'Karim, get out of there, the police have your brother's body and are coming for you.' The line went dead.

Karim looked wildly around and spotted the bag he had packed. Pausing, only to wash his mouth out with a glass of water, he grabbed the bag and let himself out of the back. He could already hear sirens in the distance. He would have to get out of Beirut and get out soon.

Two days later, Mr Ahmed Karai was standing at the back of a ferry heading down the coast. Shortly Karim would be in Egypt and then he had a flight to Tunis in Tunisia. It was where he and Khalid had been planning to go. A good climate and somewhere where there wouldn't be too many questions asked but also an Arab country where they would still feel at home. However, all his plans were slowly centring on only one thing. As the days passed and the loss of his brother only seemed to get worse, the only thing he could focus on was revenge. They had done it before when they had murdered the family of the bastard Israeli who had bombed their home. His mind was continually turning over how to do it again. He had money, plenty of it and he had contacts. He would act slowly and with care. Just like the last time. He would find out who was responsible. He already had the name of the pilot they had as hostage. It would have been his people who rescued him so finding out more should be relatively easy. He would then act with care and deadly ruthlessness. Once again, he wouldn't take it out directly on the individuals responsible but on their loved ones so they had to live with the loss and guilt for the rest of their lives, just as he had when he had lost his parents and now his brother.

The next day the ferry docked in the bustling port of Alexandria. Karim stood at the rail studying the ships and people. The void in his soul was still there. He realised it would never go away. As he looked over the great port at the multitude of vessels from small dhows to cruise liners, an idea started to form in his mind. He would do something spectacular, something to make the world notice and a fitting tribute to Khalid. Moreover, he might just be able to combine it with something for his people. Because coming here to Egypt had suddenly reminded him of where he came from. This was his country and these were his people, as were all the Arabs in the Middle East. All the Arabs that were exploited or persecuted by others. All those years in Beirut suddenly came into sharp focus and with it the idea, now fully formed.

He would cancel his flight to Tunis, after all he probably knew more people here than elsewhere. He had the money and drive but he would need people. On top of that, a certain level of expertise would be required and he knew where to get it all.

'Time to get political,' he chuckled to himself. It was the first time he had smiled for days. 'Time to take up a cause.'

Chapter 27

Arapaho and several other warships swung around their anchors in the blue still waters off the British base in Cyprus. They had been there for weeks while the politicians dithered. Half of 844 had gone home in Fearless and the RFAs but there was still a multi-national force in the Lebanon and so a British presence was still required. While the situation remained unstable, Jon had elected to stay but most of the squadron had managed some leave at home. Those who decided not to, mainly the bachelors had managed to take some leave on the island and some families had even been able to fly out.

Jon had just landed from his first sortie since the doctor declared him fit to fly. He and GG had conducted a standard 'back in the saddle' trip. Flying was a perishable skill. It hadn't stopped them having some fun as well and the second half of the trip was spent zooming through some spectacular scenery in the mountains before Jon brought them back for a good old fashioned beat up of the ship.

Sweating from the heat and just a little adrenalin, GG turned to Jon. 'Well Boss, I don't think trashing one of our cabs seems to have affected your flying. I'm just going to look at the side of the ship to see how many marks our rotor blades made on that last low pass.'

'Cheeky bugger, in that case I'll check the top of the funnel, you did it first.' And they grinned at each other like two school boys.

They walked back into the hangar to return their safety equipment where Brian had just finished talking to a couple of the maintainers.

'I take it you're back into your old bad habits then Boss?'

'Ah, you noticed our arrival then?'

'Yes and just about the rest of the ship's company as well. Now, when are you going to take some leave?'

The question hit Jon cold and he realised he didn't have an answer. In truth, he had been so focused on getting fit to fly again as well as dealing with all the fallout from the Beirut operation, that he hadn't even considered it. He had moved heaven and earth to get the best deal for the squadron but realised he had completely neglected himself.

'Er, hadn't really thought about it Brian, sorry I've just been too busy.'

Arapaho

'Hah, well we haven't and Staffy and I have been doing some plotting behind your back. As you know Kathy and the two girls are coming out on Saturday so we've booked you into the same hotel as us for a week.'

'Hang on, you can't do that, there's still too much to do here.'

'Sorry Boss,' said Helen coming up behind the group. 'I've just got the booking confirmation. All squadron paperwork is up to date. SPLOT is back tomorrow and can look after things in your absence.'

Jon knew when he had been out manoeuvred and suddenly the thought of a few days lying by a hotel pool seemed incredibly attractive. 'Alright you mutinous dogs, I get the message. Hang on a second Helen, what about you? You haven't had any leave yet either, I should know.'

'Ah' said Brian. 'We've got Helen a room as well but don't worry, Kathy is an excellent chaperone.'

Saturday arrived all too soon and Jon was sitting at his desk just debating whether to do a little more work on some of his officer's confidential reports when the door opened and SPLOT and Helen marched in.

'Sorry Boss,' SPLOT announced. 'You are hereby relieved of duty. Helen here has your bag packed and there's a boat at the gangway waiting for you.'

Jon lifted an eyebrow as he looked at Helen. 'And how exactly did you know what to pack?'

'That was hardly difficult, T shirts, swimming trunks, shorts and that was about it, oh and I grabbed your washbag from your bathroom. Anything missing can be bought in the hotel.'

'So Boss, no excuses, go and have a good week off and don't worry, if anything comes up I know where to find you. But believe me, it won't.' SPLOT was clearly not taking no for an answer.'

'Right, I give up, I surrender. Just let me go to my cabin and get changed.'

Three hours later Jon was sitting on a sun lounger, in his swimming shorts, in a very up market hotel by the pool and surrounded by girls. Brian was there somewhere but his wife Kathy and his two daughters, Amy and June were monopolising his attention. Jon had known Kathy for years. A lively red headed Irish girl, where Brian was a steady hand, she was all mercury and fire. Brian was well over six feet and built like the rugby player he was.

Kathy was almost elfin and clearly hadn't let the birth of two children affect her figure. Whenever Jon saw them together he felt wistful and just prayed that one day he could find a partnership like Brian and Kathy's. The two little ones aged seven and five took after their mother and also knew Jon well and clearly decided that he was more interesting than their boring old dad. Luckily, Brian approached with a large beer for Jon and attempted to chase the girls off but in the end had to promise to take them off to get an ice cream which left Jon and Kathy to talk.

'Was it that bad Jon? Brian told me a little about what happened.' She asked with concern when they were alone.

Jon lay back not sure how to answer but knowing Kathy, anything other than the truth would have been seen through in an instant. 'Kathy the worst bit was the loss of hope. We had no idea where we were, who had captured us or what they wanted. I'm the sort of bloke who likes to be in charge and be the first to know what's going on. When that's taken away from you its bloody horrible. I guess I was lucky because I wasn't on my own but even so it was just so hard to motivate yourself to do anything. That may sound strange but take away hope and things just crumble.'

'But you managed to do something and luckily for you, your Staff Officer saw the signal. I hear she's quite a stunner by the way.'

Jon saw the look on Kathy's face. 'Now stop it Kathy. You've been trying to marry me off to half of Somerset for years, it won't work you know. Anyway, you should meet her soon she's staying here as well.'

Just as he said it, Helen appeared. She had a towel over her shoulder and was wearing a small blue bikini. As she walked, every male head turned and tracked her. Oblivious to it all, she saw Jon and Kathy, smiled, waved and walked over towards them. Kathy turned to Jon and saw the look on his face. 'Maybe I won't have to do any matchmaking after all,' she thought

That evening Jon, Brian and the two girls managed to escape the confines of the hotel. The little girls were asleep and the hotel had a baby sitting service. They had walked down a dusty lane and found a little taverna by the road. It wasn't much, just some garden furniture around some simple tables, a small building and some fairy lights scattered in the olive trees around it. However, the smells coming out of the kitchen were enough to stop them in their tracks and what was only going to be an evening stroll, turned into dinner.

As they sat down, the waiter appeared and they ordered some of the local wine while they considered the menu. 'Right, just a couple of ground rules, especially for you Helen.'

Helen looked slightly startled for a second but seeing the smile on Jon's face quickly realised that he wasn't being serious.

'We are now on leave, in a foreign port. Until we go back, none of us has any rank. My name isn't Boss or Sir, its Jon, alright. I know you might find that hard Kathy but you'll just have to get used to it.'

He got a sharp kick under the table from Kathy. Helen looked amused. 'I'll try Boss.'

'Last warning, Second Officer Barratt.'

He got another kick, although not anything like as hard.

'Oh and second rule, please, no shop. No talking about the last few weeks, or Sea Kings or Beirut or the bloody Royal Navy in general. All agreed?'

There were no dissenters. The evening passed in an atmosphere of laughter and friendship. Jon learned about Helen's past including her enigmatic father and her parent's reaction to her joining up. Jon spoke a little about his childhood and his burning ambition to fly that drove all his thinking as a teenager.

Brian who had gone to school with him wasn't having any of it. 'Yeah right and of course you were never interested in motor bikes, parties and girls.'

'Well apart from the motorbikes parties and girls of course,' Jon responded.

'And then there was that old car you patched up and immediately crashed and the time when we all went to that pub and got in even though we were under age.'

'Don't you bloody dare tell that story Brian, or I'll have to pull rank.'

'Ah, but you said there wasn't going to be any rank. But you're right, I seem to remember I was there too, so maybe we'll draw a veil over it all.'

This was a story that even Kathy hadn't heard and for the next ten minutes the girls tried to drag it out of both of them with no success.

Kathy gave up. 'I'll find out in the end Brian, you know I always do.'

Brian wasn't going to be drawn and just smiled enigmatically. Jon managed to change the subject at last.

In what seemed like a matter of minutes they were finishing their desserts and coffee. Jon realised he hadn't felt this happy in ages. The food had been simple but excellent, the wine was drinkable which was all you needed to say about it and there was a beautiful girl sitting opposite him. And that of course was the problem.

Later that evening Jon and Helen were alone. The other two had gone off to resume parental duties. They were sitting by the pool again which was lit by subtle underwater lights. Ahead of them, the sea was gently lapping at the sand and there was a full moon almost overhead. Jon had got them both drinks but for some reason the conversation had dried up. Jon was quite aware that Helen liked him. He was quite aware that he liked her and in any normal circumstances that would be great. But he took his responsibilities seriously, too seriously some would say but that was just the way he was. He decided to take the bull by the horns.

'Helen?'

'Yes Jon?'

'We need to get something straight and I'm finding this extremely difficult.'

She turned to look at him and the moonlight caught her features, it was almost as if she had a halo of light around her head. She was wearing a yellow, halter neck, summer dress that had been driving him mad all evening as it was obvious there was very little underneath. For some weird reason it only strengthened his resolution.

'Look, forgive me if I'm wrong but I strongly get the feeling that you like me rather a lot. And before you say anything, to be totally honest, I feel the same way too. And on top of that of course, if it wasn't for you I wouldn't even be here, so I owe you an enormous debt of gratitude. But we are both officers in a military unit and, oh shit I'm not putting this right. Look I'm your Commanding Officer. I can't be seen to be taking advantage of that.'

Helen didn't say anything for some time and Jon had the sense to keep silent. Eventually, she found her voice. 'So what was all that talk about no rank for the week?'

Jon sighed. 'If, for one moment, I thought that it would only be one week then that would be different. But,' and he looked her in the eye. 'It wouldn't be would it?'

She broke his gaze, stood up and silently walked away.

'Fuck.'

Chapter 28

The next morning, Helen came down to the hotel patio for breakfast and found Brian, Kathy and the children already there. The little girls were arguing and fighting as only sisters can and Kathy was half-heartedly berating them and managing to eat her breakfast at the same time, as only mothers can.

'Morning Helen,' said Brian cheerfully. 'Have a good night?'

'Yes fine,' she responded. 'The bed was certainly comfortable.'

Kathy was far more perceptive than her husband and immediately caught the undercurrent to Helen's words. 'Anything you want to talk about Helen?'

'No, not really.' And then after a pause. 'Well, it's Jon actually.'

'Eh, what's he done now?' asked Brian.

'Nothing, that's the point. Look, maybe I shouldn't be discussing this but we're all friends and I could do with some advice.'

Brian looked at Kathy then back at Helen. 'Let me guess, he's playing the martyr bit?'

Helen looked surprised. 'I suppose you could say that. Look you must have guessed that I quite like him and would like to know him more. Last night he admitted he felt the same but because he's my CO he felt it would be wrong to go any further.'

'He has got a point Helen,' Brian commented.

Kathy was having none of it. 'Don't be so bloody stiff necked Brian. Look Helen, we've both known Jon for years and he can get a bit funny with women. Last year he had a really bad experience, I'm not meant to know about it and Brian won't tell me all the detail but I do know that it hit him quite hard.'

Brian cut in, 'and there's something else you need to know about him. He's probably the most unambitious person I've ever met, yet most people in the navy have him marked down as a high flyer just like that pompous Commodore. The difference between them is that Jon is a bloody good naval officer naturally and doesn't have his eye on the main chance all the time. One of the reasons he's so good is that he loves the navy. You've heard the phrase 'swallowed the anchor'?'

Helen nodded.

'Well that's Jon and it sometimes clouds his thinking. Mind you, if I said that to him, he would just laugh it off. And of course, one of the things that means is that he tends to be a stickler for sticking to the letter of the law, at least as far as the command chain goes.'

'So what are the rules he's worried about breaking?' asked Kathy.

Brian thought for a moment. 'You know, I'm not sure there actually are any. As Helen has pointed out, as a Wren, she's not formally subject to the same rules as us. I suspect what Jon is worried about is giving the impression of abusing his authority. I don't suspect for a moment anyone on the squadron would think that but I know the way his mind works. Would you like me to have a word or two?'

'No, absolutely not Brian, thank you.' Helen replied. 'I'll have to work this one out myself but thank you for your advice.' She saw Brian's expression change as he looked over her shoulder just as Jon plonked himself down at the table.

'Morning campers, looks like I'm the last one out of bed, sorry about that. So, what are we going to do today?'

He didn't see the look exchanged between Kathy and Helen.

That afternoon, Jon and Helen were sitting at the top of the Greco-Roman theatre at Kourion. They had spent the last few hours sight seeing using a car that Brian had hired. Unfortunately, the attention span of a seven year old was not that long and Brian and Kathy had made their excuses and taken the kids to the beach, leaving the two of them together. Now they were on their own, the conversation had become fairly stilted as they both tried to avoid the consequences of the previous night.

Jon looked out over the serried ranks of stone seats. 'These guys knew a thing or two you know. The acoustics here are as good, if not better than any modern theatre. This island probably has more history in an acre of land than most places put together. It was conquered by Alexander the Great, occupied by Greece and Rome as well as the Ottomans. Even these days people are fighting over it.'

'You mean Greeks and the Turks?'

'Yes, I'm sure you know the recent history.'

'Of course, it seems such a shame to have such a beautiful place and then kill each other over it.'

They were sitting side by side but not close. Helen was in a pair of small white shorts and a blue lightweight blouse. Jon thought she looked delightful. He felt his resolve slipping. He stood up. 'Yes, over there is the temple to Apollo. Let's go and have a look.'

They walked over to the ruins that overlooked the bay. The sea was a sparkling blue in the distance and even though there wasn't a cloud in the sky the breeze kept things cool. Helen walked on ahead and Jon was able to admire her legs. His resolve dropped another notch. She turned towards him and looked into his eyes.

'Apollo was the son of Zeus you know, he was a Greek and a Roman God,' he realised he was burbling but couldn't stop. They were standing very close now. 'He was also a Sun God, at least that was what some believed.' He stopped talking because he realised she wasn't listening. He could see the tiny golden hairs on her top lip and her long eyelashes. So he kissed her. She kissed him back. He had absolutely no idea how long it lasted.

When eventually he pulled back, he looked into her deep blue eyes which were smiling at him. 'Bugger, I really shouldn't have done that.'

'Why?'

'You know why. This is going to get complicated.'

'No it's not. There is absolutely no reason why we shouldn't be together. When we are at work we can keep things as they were. And when we are not at work…' she grinned at him.

'Yes what about when we are not at work?'

'This.' And she kissed him again.

The week passed in a blur. That afternoon they went straight back to the hotel and went to bed but only just. Even with only a few clothes to shed, they nearly ended up on the floor. Jon realised he hadn't actually made love to a girl for over a year and had some serious catching up to do. Helen was as uninhibited in bed as Jon and also extremely inventive. They had fun. That evening they went down to dinner with Kathy and Brian. Two enormous grins appeared as they spotted them holding hands.

'Don't say a word, you rugby playing, smug git,' were Jon's first words to Brian.

'Me what would I say? Apart from about bloody time.'

'Hmm, was it that obvious?'

'Yup' replied Kathy. 'To everyone except you by the looks of it.'

Jon looked at Helen. 'Well, she did save my life after all.'

That remark got him yet another kick under the table from Helen. 'Ouch and you're quite cute too. Hey, I've got an idea, let's all drink too much and go out clubbing.'

It didn't happen as Brian knew it wouldn't. He knew his friend too well and had a quiet word with Helen at one point. Jon was famous for getting very bouncy just before falling fast asleep. Helen managed to get him up to his room before it happened and then kept him awake for some time longer.

They toured the island some more, spent time lying by the pool and at the beach. They ate out at various Tavernas. They also spent a great deal of time in bed. Helen was even more beautiful naked than when dressed as he repeatedly told her. She responded by saying he was just saying that to stop her putting on any clothes. He didn't argue. She didn't put on the clothes.

One afternoon they were walking hand in hand along the crowded beach. Kids were running around and building sand castles. Their parents were either joining in or trying to ignore them so that they could top up their tans.

'This is just like a corny scene from a film you know.' Jon said as he looked around.

'What do you mean?'

'Oh you know, the love interlude bit, lots of scenes of the lovers walking hand in hand while the schmaltzy music plays.'

Helen stopped and looked at Jon. 'Lovers?' was all she said.

He turned to her. 'Yes that's the word, isn't it? Lovers.'

She didn't say anything, just brushed his lips with hers.

It all came to a crashing end the day before they were due back at the ship. They were all enjoying yet another late breakfast together when a harassed looking policeman approached them.

'Lieutenant Commander Hunt?' he asked.

'That's me,' replied Jon standing up. 'What can I do for you?'

'I have been told to tell you that there is an emergency recall in force. You and any other members of your squadron are to report back to you ship straight away. I have a car outside if you will come with me.'

'Just give us a few moments to go to our rooms. Do you have any idea what's going on?'

The policeman just shrugged and said he hadn't heard anything more than there was some sort of security alert.

Ten minutes later, after a hasty packing, Jon met the others in the hotel lobby. Brian and Kathy were saying goodbye and Helen arrived at the same time as he did. Kathy agreed to sort out the bills as most had been prepaid and then they were climbing into the waiting police car. If there had been any doubt as to whether it was some sort of false alarm, it was dispelled by bright flash of light and climbing cloud of black smoke in the distance, followed seconds later by a booming crash. Then it happened again, this time from almost behind them. Jon suddenly felt sick, he had a pretty good idea what was in both directions and it wasn't good.

Chapter 29

Karim sat back in satisfaction. Both bombs had gone off within seconds of each other. He had heard them easily despite being several miles away. It showed that his new friends were keeping their word and that they really did have the drive to follow this through. Well, the die was cast now and one way or another he would have his revenge.

When he landed at Alexandria, he had immediately made his way to Cairo and started calling his contacts. Most of them thought he was mad when he told them what he wanted but persistence and not a little cash soon convinced them that he was serious. It had taken less than a week to set up a meeting which had taken place late one evening in an anonymous house in the suburbs. As soon as he arrived, he had been expertly frisked and escorted by two armed men into the house and told to sit and wait. He had been kept waiting for over an hour but didn't mind, the tactic was one he had used himself often enough in the past. Eventually, a man had come in. Lean and middle aged, he was dressed in a western business suit but Karim wasn't fooled. He knew who he was but for form's sake pretended no to.

'Mr Ahmed Karai or should I say Karim, my name is Abu Abas but I expect you already know that.' He looked shrewdly at his guest.

Karim knew that only total honesty was going to work with this man so he smiled openly back. 'Yes of course I know who you are and I expect you know a great deal about me. What you don't know is why I am here.'

'I might be able to guess but please continue.'

'Several weeks ago, my brother was killed by the British. Quite simply, I want revenge but I don't have the resources. You do. What I do have is a great deal of money and quite a lot of experience. On top of that, I have an idea which could be mutually beneficial to us both.'

At the mention of money, Karim saw the man's eyes narrow. These people were always short of cash. They were always very strong on idealism but that never paid the bills.

'Very well, I will listen but you must understand that the Palestine Liberation Front is a political organisation. We do not take part in acts of revenge unless they meet our political aims. From what I know of you, you are a simple criminal and have never been involved in the struggle.'

If he was attempting to insult Karim with his words, he failed. Karim knew exactly what to expect and was even a little surprised how quickly his bait was swallowed. He started to outline his idea and they talked for several hours.

In the end, they agreed to everything with the proviso that if the first part of the operation didn't have the desired results, then the rest would carry on as planned. They gave him a young man with a shock of curly dark hair, olive skin and an oddly manic glint in his eye. Karim only ever knew him as Mohammed. He had been trained in one of the many camps in the desert and was the veteran of several attacks already. Moreover, he probably hated Israel even more than Karim, as not only had he lost his parents to them but his wife and two children as well. They got on extremely well, especially when Mohammed was told the details of the operation.

They also gave him access to their intelligence which was surprisingly effective. He discovered who Lieutenant Commander Hunt actually was and even where he was. It seemed that the ships used in the evacuation had been recalled to Cyprus and would probably be there for some weeks to come. Karim started studying shipping movement forecasts until he found several candidates. He also got the PLF to get a man ashore in Cyprus and report on any British navy personnel. It seemed that quite a few of them were taking the opportunity to take leave on the island and some even had families with them. It was all looking better and better. He knew he would never know exactly which soldier had pulled the trigger on Khalid but making Hunt and his comrades suffer would be as good as he could get. Then he hit the jackpot, the timing would be tight but there staring at him out of the pages of a shipping brochure was the perfect target.

He went straight to the PLF and outlined his final plans. Getting the explosives to the island had been hard but Mohammed managed it somehow. What had been really difficult was getting on board as members of the crew. In the end, they had watched the ship carefully when she was docked in Alexandria and had simply captured two of the crew. They were now resting under the desert sand and would cause no further problems. The next day, Karim had simply walked up to the ship and asked if there were any crew vacancies, not surprisingly there were and two new stewards were signed up. No one queried the size of their personal baggage or asked to look inside. When they moored in Cyprus, Mohammed sent word ashore to the local agent. Everyone seemed to think Cyprus was safe. They would soon learn differently.

There were only two of them on board a ship with over a thousand passengers and crew but that would be enough. Karim now prayed that what he hoped would happen, would actually occur but even if it didn't the world would sit up and take notice one way or another.

Chapter 30

On board Arapaho, there was considerable confusion. As soon as Jon arrived, SPLOT greeted him. 'Sorry to drag you back a day early Boss but we had an alert early this morning and a general recall but no one seemed to know what it was about.'

'I guess they bloody well do now. You heard the explosions I take it?'

'Couldn't miss them, it seems one was at the military airfield and one was at the civilian one.'

'Yes, that was my guess too. Right, let's see who we've got back already and you can brief me on the state of the aircraft.'

Things settled down as the morning progressed. Most of the squadron staff on the island made it back to the ship and there were enough aircrew and ground crew to man the three remaining Sea Kings. Intelligence from ashore was hard to come by. In the end, it was the BBC World Service and local radio that gave them the best idea about what was going on. It seemed that the explosions had indeed been bombs. The first, at the civilian airport at Larnaka had been some sort of car bomb. A van had been left at the departure short stay area and exploded. Amazingly, no one was seriously hurt. The military attack had been different. Again, it was a car bomb but in this case someone had driven a car through the barbed wire at the far side of the base and ran for it. The results, although spectacular, had done very little damage apart from making a large crater in some scrubland.

Jon was sitting in the officer's mess with several others discussing the situation at lunch time. 'I can't get my head around what they were trying to achieve,' he said thoughtfully. 'Has anyone taken responsibility yet?'

Nobody seemed to know.

After lunch, Jon decided to see if he could make a phone call ashore. He got through to the Consulate and asked if Mr Thomas was available. After several minutes, Rupert came on the line.

'Rupert, it's Jon Hunt, sorry to bother you but is there anything going on that I need to know about or can help with? We've all been recalled but frankly what we're seeing makes little sense.'

'You're not the only one Jon. Obviously, I can't say much but we got a tip off that something might happen hence the recall and increase in alert levels. It was all too late I'm afraid as I'm sure you realise. Either we've been terribly lucky or they weren't that clever, whoever they were. Just sit tight while we try and find out what the hell is going on.'

'Fine, thanks Rupert, one thing though I've got several families here who were due to fly home tomorrow, what's the situation with commercial flights?'

'Sorry Jon, nothing is coming or going out, military or civil until we find out more and that could take some time I'm afraid. They will just have to stay on this lovely island and have extra holiday until we're sure it safe. And before you ask, that could be days or even weeks.'

'OK Rupert, thanks for that I'll let you go. I can imagine how busy you must be.'

'Cheers Jon, oh and one final thing, our intelligence suggests that this may not be the only thing planned so make sure your outfit is ready to go. You never know when you might be needed. Your lovely Commodore has gone home hasn't he?'

'Him and his staff in Fearless, they must be at Gib by now. And no military flights either you said, that's a shame.'

'I'm sure they'll be approved fairly soon that's what you lot are paid for after all but I suppose until he gets here you're the senior military officer afloat?'

'Bloody hell, hadn't looked at it like that. I guess you're right, the Frigates went with Fearless. Well, as Senior Naval Officer Cyprus or SNOC as I guess I now am, keep me in the picture old chap.'

'Right you are SNOC.'

Later that evening, sitting in his cabin, Jon was wrestling with a problem. He knew what he needed to do but was desperately trying to come up with an idea of how to implement it. Brian stuck his head around the door. 'Ah, there you are Jon, got a moment?'

'Yeah sure, come on in, what's up?'

'It's Kathy and the kids and some of the other families. It's the end of the school holidays and they all need to get home. Any news on when commercial flights might start again?'

'You know as much as me. I told you what Rupert said. It's going to be days at least. He knows quite a lot more than he's telling I'm sure.'

'No surprises there then. Look, if flying from here is out of the question, how about by sea? There must be ferries operating?'

'Nope, not for the moment, they are trying to quarantine the island so no one can leave, sorry.'

'Damn, but look there might be one other option. I don't know if you've noticed but anchored out on the far side of the bay is our old friend from the Falklands, Uganda, remember? She was the hospital ship.'

'Bloody hell, what's she doing here?'

'Well, she's back in her peacetime role. She does specialist cruises and in the summer holidays she takes parties of school kids from the UK on a Mediterranean cruise. The thing is, she only got in today and hasn't landed anyone. If she had some room, she could ferry our people to her next port of call and then they could get flights home.'

Jon looked at his friend shrewdly. 'You've already asked, haven't you?'

'Yup and she says she can take all our families. Next stop is Ancona in Italy. So how about seeing if the authorities will clear it? It would take a great weight off my mind and that of some of the other guys.'

'How many are we talking about?'

'Five families, that's five mums and seven kids, including mine.'

Jon's mind was whirling. This could also be the solution to his problem. 'Let me see if I can contact Rupert and see what he says.'

Jon managed to get hold of the Consulate again and explain the issue to Rupert who promised to talk to the Consul but in principle, it seemed a good idea. Brian also confirmed that Uganda was prepared to wait twenty four hours but no longer as she was adjusting her itinerary due to the inability to land any of her passengers in Cyprus. Taking a firm grip on his feelings he went and knocked on Helen's cabin door.

'Come in,' he heard and so went through the door smiling.

'Hi stranger,' she said, as soon as she saw who it was and got up to give him a hug.

'Now, is that any way to treat your Commanding Officer?' he queried, as her hand reached a certain part of his anatomy.

'Oh yes,' she breathed in his ear.

All Jon's good intentions fled, although he did at least have the presence of mind to lock the door before he got totally carried away.

Later, while lying in a tangle of sheets and Helen's legs, he reflected ruefully on his total lack of will power. This was a problem and he was going to have to grip it.

'Helen, we need to talk. I'm sorry but I need you to go home.'

She sat up on one elbow and looked down at him. He immediately focused on her right breast. It was quite beautiful, her skin was so flawless and the contrast with the erect pink nipple was wonderful. He tore his attention away.

'I was waiting for you to say that,' she said without rancour.

'What, how did you know?'

'We both know we shouldn't be doing this on board and knowing you, it will drive you to distraction. And anyway there's far too much paperwork piling up back at Yeovilton.'

'Oh thanks for that, any way you're right. But also I've got a job for you.'

'Oh really, what?'

'I want you to be the family's liaison officer and take the five mums and their kids back home. You know, someone to organise the tickets once you get to Italy, make sure they get on the plane that sort of thing. As far as I'm concerned, they are all my responsibility until they are safely home.'

'So, when will I have to go?'

'Hopefully, we will get approval tomorrow morning and get everyone over to Uganda tomorrow afternoon.'

'So, we've only got tonight together then?'

'I'm afraid so,' and he made a grab for the offending nipple while thanking the stars for such a lovely and understanding girl.

Chapter 31

The Educational Cruise Ship Uganda was noisy. There seemed to be children everywhere on the upper deck. Some were behaving, the older ones mainly but there seemed to be plenty who seemed to think that running around and shrieking was a great way to pass the time. Helen could understand. Instead of playing on the beach or seeing the sites they were cooped up here on this old ship.

The ship's Purser stood by her. A greying, overweight man, he seemed oblivious to the chaos around him. 'Yes, you're lucky my dear, this is our last cruise. I'm afraid the poor old girl is just about falling apart. You lot used her rather hard during the Falklands as the hospital ship and she's never really recovered.'

Helen looked about her. The ship was definitely shabby but from lack of maintenance by the look of it rather than any previous abuse. Still, they only needed to be on board for two days and then they could all fly home from Italy. She looked over the anchorage where the grey bulk of Arapaho was silhouetted and suddenly had a longing for Jon. She would probably see him in a few weeks but suddenly that seemed like years away. Getting a grip on herself, she followed the Purser down several decks to their accommodation.

They reached a rather scruffy corridor and he opened a door. 'I'm sorry but as you know, we are a schools boat so we don't have too much single accommodation. However, this room has bunk beds for ten so should be fine for the children and through the adjoining door there is another slightly smaller cabin for five. It's bunk beds again I'm afraid and the showers and toilet facilities are just down the corridor. We weren't fully booked this year otherwise even these cabins would be full.'

Helen was surprised at how clean everything was even it all looked as tired as the rest of the ship. 'That'll be fine, we really are extremely grateful you know, otherwise we could be stuck on the island for weeks. With the school holidays over in ten days or so, everyone is very keen to get home.'

'Well, we're going straight back to England as well for the same reason and you could do the whole trip if you wanted but I understand you already have your flights booked.'

'Yes and I've just realised something, there are six adults if you include me. Is there any other accommodation?'

The Purser looked crestfallen. 'Oh dear, yes you're right and no sorry this is the last. I'm afraid one of you will have to share one of the spare bunk beds with the children. Will that be a problem do you think?'

Helen thought for a second. 'No of course not, we'll work something out. After all its only for a couple of days. Now, the others will all be here in about an hour, is that alright?'

'Yes fine, we sail at seventeen hundred so you should all have plenty of time to settle in.'

The afternoon passed in a blur. Kathy with little Amy and June arrived along with the other children. In the end, Helen volunteered to sleep in the children's room, she could see how exhausted the parents were going to be by the end of the day. The combination of the novelty of being in a ship along with the presence of all the school kids kept all the children manic for the afternoon. She did take some time to have a look around the ship. There was a large communal eating area and several play and study areas for the children. Mercifully, she also found the teacher's lounge and after introducing herself, was invited in along with all the other parents. The room was an oasis of calm after the noise everywhere else in the ship and it had a bar.

At five that evening, right on time, they sailed and headed out. Once at sea and with nothing else to do, Helen joined Kathy putting the girls to bed. All the parents retreated to the bar once the children were asleep but by ten in the evening they had also succumbed to tiredness and were settling down for a good night's sleep. Helen found a spare top bunk and soon joined the children around her.

Karim looked at the dish washing machine with distaste. It was always going to be pot luck which jobs they got. Choosing their victims in Alexandria was always a matter of chance but working in the galley was not one he would have chosen. Luckily, it wouldn't be for long. The main meal of the evening was over now and so soon would be his rota of washing up. He knew they had sailed earlier on because of the announcement over the ship's loudspeakers. However, apart from some vibration from the ship's engines he would never have known. It must be flat calm outside he realised which was just what they wanted. Half an hour later, the head cook had nodded at him and told him to get an early night. His morning shift would start at five.

Leaving the galley, he went to look for Mohammed. He found him near the teacher's bar area having also just come off shift as a steward. They found a quiet area to talk on a small deck space near the stern.

Mohammed looked pleased. 'Well Karim, you are in luck, we took on some extra passengers this afternoon. I'm not sure exactly how many but it looked like several mothers and their children. I managed to sneak a look in the Pursers office and they are in two rooms on five deck, Juliet section, near the stern. I have to say I wasn't sure your idea would work but it seems you have been very lucky.'

Karim snorted in derision. 'Not luck but good planning my friend. Now we get the weapons and start the next phase.'

They went back to their mess deck, which luckily they shared and waited until after midnight. They then carefully retrieved their pistols and silencers. With weapons concealed, they made their way carefully up several decks until they were near the bridge.

'Now it is your turn. We need your knowledge Mohammed.' Karim whispered as they took cover behind a large ventilation outlet. Mohammed had been a merchant navy deck officer and had been at sea when his whole family had been wiped out. It was one of the reasons he had been given the assignment, that and his burning hatred of the western nations.

'The bridge has two open-air wings on either side, they may have lookouts on each one, we need to see. If they are there, we take one out before entering the bridge, if not we go straight in as planned. Understand?'

Karim nodded.

It was a dark night with no moon so it was not too difficult to climb the last ladder onto the starboard bridge wing and stay concealed. Mohammed put his head up above the top rung and looked around carefully. He then ducked down and made a negative shake of the head to Karim and then crept up onto the small open space. Karim followed. They stopped by the screen door that opened into the bridge and pulled out their two pistols from under their jackets. Carefully, they screwed the silencers into place.

They looked at each other. Karim nodded and Mohammed stood, opened the door and walked through. Karim followed.

For several seconds no one took any notice of them and it gave Karim time to quickly assess the situation. A man was standing by an old fashioned looking telegraph system and holding the ship's wheel. Another man, clearly an officer, was leaning against the glass of one of the bridge windows looking out and at the rear of the bridge, a pair of feet could be seen below a curtained off area. They levelled their weapons at the officer.

'This ship has been taken over by the Palestine Liberation Front. No one is to move or they will be shot.' Karim spoke as his English was much better than his companion's.

The stunned silence lasted for only a few seconds and then the man in the officer's uniform started to move. Mohammed trained his pistol on him and he froze.

'What do you want?' he managed to croak out.

'Call the Captain here.'

The man still looked confused.

'I said, call the Captain, don't say why you want him, just tell him he is needed urgently.'

The man nodded, clearly still in shock and pressed a button on a console. A man's voice instantly responded. 'Captain Sir, you're needed on the bridge.'

A terse acknowledgement was all that was heard. Mohammed kept his gun trained on the officer. Karim moved towards the only internal door to the bridge and stood to one side, just as it opened and a middle aged, rather overweight man, with greying hair, wearing uniform appeared.

'What is it Mike? I was just about to go to bed.' he sounded petulant but his words trailed off as firstly, he saw the weapon trained on his officer and then he felt the cold of a barrel pushed into the back of his neck.

'The ship has been taken over Captain.' Karim said into his ear. 'We are from the Palestine Liberation Front and we now command here. You are required to do as we say. Do you understand?'

The petrified Captain merely nodded.

'Now, go and join your officer there.'

The two men were pushed together by Karim who expertly secured their hands together with cable ties and then forced them to sit with their backs to the front bridge wall. The man on the wheel was next and Mohammed took control while he too was tied. All the time, Karim had been watching the feet of the man behind the curtained area out of the corner of his eye. They had been slowly sliding back from view. Clearly, the man, whoever he was didn't think he had been seen.

Karim turned to the Captain. 'And in case you think we don't mean what we say, here is a demonstration of our intent.' He levelled the pistol and fired several rounds into the curtain. The gun made a loud spitting sound and for a second nothing happened. Then, there was a gurgling noise and a body fell out pushing the curtains apart and spilling a bright white light into the bridge area. Karim saw with satisfaction that all his bullets had found their mark. The man's chest was a mass of blood. Even so, he was still breathing. A final bullet to the head solved that. He dragged the corpse away to one side and closed the curtains which covered the chart table, cutting off the light. Once the body was off to one side, he took the wheel himself and gestured to Mohammed who went in behind the curtain.

'You utter fucking bastard, that was one of my cadets, what had he done to you?' The Captain was starting to get his nerve back.

Karim looked at him. 'Nothing in particular, other than being a member of a race that has been exploiting and suppressing mine for centuries. Now shut up or you can join him.'

Mohammed came out and looked at Karim. 'One four zero, fifteen knots.' Karim nodded and Mohammed moved to the engine room telegraphs and consulted a table above them. He picked up a microphone. 'Revolutions two zero five,' he ordered. Then taking the wheel he very slowly altered course until the compass before him registered the new course.

Karim then moved the three men so that they were sitting around the base of the Captain's chair and secured their wrists to its base.

Karim grinned at the bound men. 'Now, we wait.'

They waited for four and a half hours. In that time the tally of bound men increased to six as the team due to take over at four o'clock arrived and were promptly immobilised and the body of the dead man was tipped unceremoniously over the side.

At the appointed rendezvous time they slowed the ship to a more sedate ten knots and started to scan the ocean ahead of them. It seemed to be empty but Mohammed had been keeping a watch on the ship's radar and picked up a small contact in the right place. Then with a rush of relief that made him realise just how tense he had become, Karim saw the light they were anticipating. He flashed the ships navigation lights in acknowledgement. Within minutes, a modern motor yacht was approaching their port side. Karim went aft to meet it. As it came close, a large pole with a hook at its top was clicked to the guard rails near the stern. Dangling from it was a rope ladder. In a matter of minutes, four black clad men were on board along with two large bags. Without speaking, they all filed back up to the bridge. Karim took a portable radio out of one of the bags, selected the correct frequency and repeated a code word three times. A curt acknowledgement was all he received but he knew that very soon the whole world would be taking notice.

Chapter 32

Jon stood at the guardrail at the stern of Arapaho and stared out at the calm anchorage. It was late and he really ought to be going to bed but he was already missing Helen. After the panic of the bomb attacks ashore nothing seemed to be happening and no one seemed to want to take responsibility or credit depending on their viewpoint. He had managed a more measured chat with Rupert that afternoon but it hadn't enlightened him anymore except that the consensus seemed to be that there could be more to come. He was grateful that he got Helen and the families out, so at least he could concentrate on the military issues without distraction. He felt rather than heard a presence next to him.

'Evening Boss,' Brian's familiar tone broke his reverie.

'Hi Brian, I was about to go to bed.'

'Me too but I saw you gazing gormlessly over the water and thought I'd join you. Missing Helen? I know I'm missing Kathy and the kids. It was a bloody good week wasn't it?'

'Yes, right up until the poo hit the rotor blades.'

'Well, that's what we're paid for.'

Jon looked out over the side. 'It isn't though really, is it? Since eighty two we've fought people who were our friends and sunk criminals. Yes, I know we had that little trip to the Arctic but when I joined up, the big threat was from the Soviets and it still is. Look at the size of their navy, just as one example. Sometimes I wonder where it's all going to end. There's this new guy in charge there, Gorbachev, who seems to be more liberal but who really knows? And here we are hanging around the Middle East acting as nursemaids.'

'Wow, you've really got the blues old chum. Look, this will all blow over soon and then we can head home. We've got a nice meaty NATO winter exercise to look forward to remember? We can play at killing Soviets to your heart's content then.'

Jon snorted in wry amusement. 'And probably get frostbite. Oh well, I'm for my pit, see you in the morning. Good night Brian.' And with a wave of his hand, he headed for his cabin leaving Brian to contemplate the night.

Helen couldn't sleep. It was a mixture of the narrow bunk and the slightly alien sounds made by the sleeping children as well as the ache of missing Jon. Eventually, the need to go to the toilet forced her out of bed. Wrapping herself in a dressing gown, she crept out and down the corridor to the toilets. When she came out, she noticed the door at the end of the corridor. Curious, she lifted the catches and found herself on a small half deck near the stern of the ship. The wake was streaming away behind the ship very close and riotously alive with silver phosphorescence. The sight was so entrancing that she found it hard to take her eyes away but when she lifted them up she saw the stars. It was a dark night with no moon and this far from land there was very little light pollution. The Milky Way was a clear pale arc from horizon to horizon, speckled with the twinkling lights of the closer stars and planets. She promised herself that one day she would make an effort to learn more of the constellations but still looked for the ones she knew. She soon had Orion and the big 'W' of Cassiopeia identified and then the Plough which always looked like a giant saucepan to her. Suddenly, her eye was caught by a green streak flying across her view. She had seen shooting stars before but never one this clear. As suddenly as it appeared, it disappeared in a flash far away on the horizon. She waited a few more minutes in case there were others but eventually the breeze of the ship's passage and the cool night air drove her back inside to the warmth of her bed. As she finally dozed off to sleep she realised that there was something odd. If they were heading westwards to Italy, the Plough should have been to starboard of the ship but it was behind them. She remembered seeing it and the wake of the ship together. The thought slipped from her mind as sleep took her. She would ask in the morning.

At five in the morning, just as a rather good dream was getting up steam, a hand shook Jon rudely awake. It was Derek, one his pilots who was the Duty Officer.

'Sir, you need to wake up and listen to the BBC.'

'Oh, what is it?' he asked still half asleep.

'Listen for yourself Sir.' And he turned on the speaker by Jon's desk that was broadcasting the BBC World Service as it did every morning.

The announcer's upper class accent was mixed with something else as he read the news. 'This is a repeat of our earlier headline.

Over half an hour ago, a message was sent to the British and Israeli Governments. It was also sent to several news agencies and international radio and television stations around the world. It stated that that the Palestine Liberation Front had successfully hijacked a British cruise ship in the eastern Mediterranean and were holding the passengers and crew hostage. They are demanding the release of a large number of Palestinian prisoners from Israel. The actual vessel wasn't named but other sources suggest that the only British registered vessel in the area is the Educational Cruise Ship Uganda. She currently has twelve hundred British school children and teachers on board as well as a crew of almost two hundred. A special hotline has been set up for anyone wanting to get in touch. The number will be read out at the end of this bulletin. More information will be broadcast when it becomes available. In other news…'

Jon reached over and turned the speaker off and sat down by his desk feeling sick.

'Who else has heard this?' he asked the Duty Officer.

'No one else Sir. I was up early and just caught it as I was leaving my cabin.'

'Right, get SOBS here as fast as you can and then get the whole squadron to stand to. I think we're going to be very busy, very soon.'

'Yes Sir.'

Jon didn't even hear him leave as a wave of ice cold dread and guilt washed over him. Not only had he put Helen in harm's way but his friend's family and the others too. It was his fault. He thought he was being so bloody clever. For the first time in his life he, hadn't a clue what to do. Not even how he was going to break the news to Brian and the other fathers and husbands.

Helen knew there was something wrong. It didn't help that she felt tired and irritable. She finally got to sleep and then after what only seemed like minutes she was woken by several of the children giggling. Despite her most tactful attempts to get them to go back to sleep, she quickly realised that she was fighting a losing battle. Resignedly, she had got up and managed a shower before anyone else and made her way up to the lounge in the hope that some of the crew were up and there was coffee available. Her hopes were dashed when she found that the doors were locked. Looking at her watch, she realised that it was not even six o'clock yet. With nowhere else to go, she went up to the main deck and sat down in one of the deck chairs there. The place was deserted so maybe she could nod off here in the early morning sunshine for a while. Suddenly, she remembered her concerns of the previous night. She looked up and saw that the sun was on the port side of the ship which meant that they were still heading south. Becoming more alert, she also realised that they had slowed down considerably. The ship's wake, far from being the frothing tumult of last night, was now barely a light stain of white on the clear blue sea. Why would they be heading south and so slowly? Her tiredness gone, she decided to go to the bridge and ask what was going on. Her only problem was that she didn't know how to get there. Then she remembered that there were diagrams of the ship's compartments on all the decks by the main staircases. She made her way to the nearest one and although it didn't show the bridge area in any detail, as it was off limits to the passengers, she was able to work out where to go. Then, before she could set off, she heard footsteps. Several people were coming up the main staircase ahead of her. Their heads appeared and for some inexplicable reason, she decided to step back so she couldn't be seen. One man was clearly a member of the crew but he was accompanied by two others wearing black balaclavas. Between them was a man who could only be the ship's Captain. As they came fully into view she saw that the men with the balaclavas were dressed fully in black and both carried some sort of machine pistol slung around their necks. They were in animated conversation and she was able to keep out of their sight as they were clearly making their way to the bridge. She suddenly realised how lucky she had been. Another few seconds and she would have met them head on. A cold shiver of fear ran down her spine as they disappeared from sight. What on earth was going on? But she also had a premonition that she knew. This must have something to do with the bombings in Cyprus. The question now was what could she do about it? Suddenly, her thoughts were interrupted by the ship's tannoy making a loud whooping noise followed by the verbal instructions for everyone to muster at their emergency stations. She immediately realised that this was all part of the same thing. Controlling her panic, she realised that there was only one thing she could do now and that was to disappear and fast.

Chapter 33

Helen held back as streams of concerned teachers shepherded their young charges to the muster points. They had all done this exercise the day they left Southampton and never expected to do it again. As there had been no further announcements on the ship's tannoy many of the adults were taking it seriously even if most of the children weren't. Although she and the others hadn't been at the earlier exercise they had all been briefed and Helen knew she was expected to go to the port boat deck. She also knew that the ship's Purser would be there to muster everyone. He had been the one to brief them yesterday when they came on board.

Frantically, she looked for him through the crowd. With a sigh of relief, she saw him making his way to the port side of the ship where she had taken cover behind some drinks machines. As soon as she could, she dashed out and grabbed him by the arm.

'Purser, can you tick me off your muster list when you get there please.'

Looking distracted, he shook her arm off. 'Don't be silly, just come with me it's just an exercise you know. We do these sometimes.'

'What? At this time of the morning and without your knowledge?'

He looked alarmed as her point sunk in. 'Yes well, I'm sure there will be an explanation now come on, Helen isn't it?'

'Yes but sorry, look, please just make sure that you say everyone has mustered. I can't explain right now. Please, just trust me.' And she slipped away before he could say anymore praying he would work it out in time. Looking for somewhere to hide, she suddenly saw the ladies toilets next to the ship's main lounge. It would have to do.

The Captain's voice came over the tannoy just as she had squatted on her heels on a toilet so her feet couldn't be seen under the door. 'Ladies, Gentlemen and crew, this is the Captain speaking. I have some grave news and I need your undivided attention. This morning the ship was boarded by brave soldiers of the Palestine Liberation Front who are now holding it as hostage for the release of illegally detained members of their organisation by the Israelis. I have been assured that no one will be harmed as long as we all do as we are told. Because of this everyone is to remain at their muster station. Food and water will be provided and the toilet facilities may be used. However, anyone found away from their station or the direct route to the toilets will be deemed to be an enemy and treated accordingly.' It was quite clear from the stilted way he was talking that he was reading from a script. He suddenly continued in a more normal but anguished voice. 'Believe me, the bastards have already killed one of my offi…..' The tannoy cut off and then the Captain's voice was replaced by another with a strong accent. 'My name is Mohammed, what the Captain has told you is true. My men and I have taken over this ship and will not accept any disobedience. You have been warned. My men will now attend to each of the muster stations and ensure that everyone is accounted for.'

Helen prayed that the Purser would now understand what she wanted. She also realised the risk she was taking. If one of the crew had already been killed then she was placing herself in grave danger but what else could she do? The toilet she had chosen was well away from any muster station but she decided the best thing to do was wait. Sure enough, she was left alone for several hours then the door opened and she heard someone come in. Clambering back onto the toilet with her heart in her mouth, she could only wait and pray. The footsteps slowly approached her cubicle but didn't stop. She caught a glimpse of black boots and then they were retreating. He must have just been looking under the doors she realised, thank God she had kept out of sight, had he tried the door it might have been different. Suddenly, she felt sick and only just managed to refrain from vomiting in the toilet bowl. 'Get a grip' she muttered to herself. But what could she do? One person on her own, there was no way she could take the hijackers on all by herself. She didn't even know how many there were. Presumably, they had issued some form of demand. With a sudden rush of hope, she realised that this was exactly what Jon's squadron was trained for. Maybe the outlook wasn't so bleak after all. It was after this thought that she realised she knew what she had to do. It was all about communication. That was how Jon had managed to signal his position when he had been held hostage. First, she needed the Purser.

With heart in mouth, she slowly opened the door and peered out. The ship was eerily quiet. She realised that the engines had been

Arapaho

stopped. The hum of the fans and the odd creaking noise was all she could hear. Carefully, she walked along the bulkhead by the toilet she had been hiding in. It was in a corridor that ran the length of the ship on the port side. At the far end she knew there was a ladder that led up two decks to the boat deck. It was one of the four muster points for the crew and passengers and where she should have been. She crept slowly to the first ladder and waited, listening carefully. She knew the Purser's office was on this deck at the next cross passage. She crept forward again and walked straight into him as he came around the corner.

'Jesus,' he exclaimed almost knocking her over. 'Oh my God, it's you.'

Gathering her wits, she looked around the corner to see if he was alone. 'Quickly, did you count me in on the muster?'

'Yes, I realised what you were up to when the Captain made his announcement. What are you planning?'

'I don't know yet but at least I have some freedom of movement. Why are you alone?'

'There are only six of them and they don't really need to escort me. Where would I go? So I was told to go to my office and get the master key for all the door locks.'

'Did you?'

'Oh yes,' he smiled. 'Actually, I've got both of them but they don't know that. Here, take one for whatever use it may be to you.'

She pocketed the large key. 'Look, what I really need is a radio, do you have any ideas?'

'The radio shack is up by the bridge but that's where they are operating from. The ship's radio officer is there and they are constantly monitoring him. Frankly, I can't see you getting in there.'

'Aren't there any other radios on the ship?'

'Not that I'm aware of. Hang on, there's a science classroom. Its down on two deck at the stern. There may well be something there. They've got all sorts of equipment. It's probably your best bet.'

'Have they set any deadlines yet?' she asked anxiously. 'I need to know how much time I've got.'

'They said noon tomorrow but that's all I've heard. Look, I've got to go or they will get suspicious. Good luck.'

Helen nodded. At least she had some hope and a timescale now. Knowing there were only six hijackers gave her a little more confidence that she could move around a little more safely, especially as she was going to the stern area away from the bridge. It almost proved her downfall. She was going down the stairs to get to two deck when she heard voices. Turning around she frantically shot back up and looked for somewhere to hide. With only moments to spare she was able to get behind a locker in a cross passage which blocked her from view. As she heard the men passing, she risked a peek around the corner of the locker. Three men were carrying large packages of bottled water. They must have been down in the ship's storerooms she realised. Two of the men were dressed in black but the third was one of the ship's stewards. With a shock of recognition, she realised his face was familiar. The mop of dark hair and large hooked nose were very striking but try as she might she couldn't place him. Maybe it was because she had seen him on the ship last night but for some reason she thought it might have been somewhere else. The men disappeared forward and she resumed her trip to the science classroom being far more cautious this time.

The Purser's pass key did the trick and she was able to let herself into the large room and then lock the door behind her. It looked just like a science lab in a school, with chairs tables and a large desk at the front. There were lots of pictures on the walls depicting Mediterranean archaeological scenes as well as diagrams and other scientific topics. Clearly, the room was used for teaching many diverse subjects. There was no sign of any equipment until she spotted the door at the rear. Inside, it was clearly the storeroom she wanted. There were racks and racks of scientific equipment all neatly labelled. Some she recognised from her schooldays but much was alien to her. Searching along the racks, she soon discovered one labelled 'radio'. With a sinking heart, she realised she couldn't make head or tail out of the jumble of equipment. Some seemed intact, some was clearly disassembled. How on earth was she going to make sense out of this mess? Then with a start, she suddenly remembered where she had seen the face of the steward she had spotted earlier. The reason she hadn't put two and two together was because the man she had seen was dead. He had been lying on the floor of the house that Jon had been held in. Jon had told her about the twin brother so this must be him. But what was he doing as part of the hijack? She couldn't work it out but it added another level of urgency to somehow being able to communicate with the outside world.

An hour later and she felt like screaming in frustration. She had never been good at science at school and physics completely dumbfounded her. It was quite clear that in the trays she had taken down was a working radio. However, some fiendish bastard had taken it to bits and she had to put it back together. There was a large board designed to take various modules but it was clearly an exercise designed to teach school children so a degree of radio knowledge was needed, knowledge she didn't have. She had even found the text book to go with all the bits and pieces so why was she finding the whole bloody thing so incomprehensible? For God's sake what the hell was an input transformer? With a sinking heart, she realised that this was probably beyond her. Looking around, she wondered if there was anything else she could do. At the rear of the room was another door clearly leading outside. It had the heavy securing clips of an upper deck door. Curious, she carefully opened it and looked out onto what she quickly realised was the ship's quarterdeck. There was a wake behind them again although quite a small one. They were only two decks above the waterline here and she could feel the gentle thrum of the propellers through the soles of her feet. The area was deserted and she carefully looked around. If anyone was going to get on board they would have to climb something. She knew that the marines had special techniques for this but maybe she could provide a little help. Her eye fell on a metal basket containing a fire hose. Yes, that might just do the trick.

Chapter 34

Jon's guilt and almost primordial sense of despair was buried beneath an avalanche of work. This sort of terrorist act was exactly what his squadron was designed to react to. More than half the squadron was now at home but there were enough Sea Kings on Arapaho to manage the task. He didn't have any radar fitted machines but there were ways around that. While he let the engineers and other aircrew get the hardware sorted out, he and Brian were dealing with the paperwork which in this case consisted of masses of signals.

The government committee, commonly called COBRA as it was held in Cabinet Office Briefing Room A, had already met and authorised the immediate despatch of the Comacchio Group of specialists. A C130 Hercules would be airborne very soon with them and their equipment. Meanwhile, Jon was working out how to cope without his radar equipped Mark Two Sea Kings which were now back at Yeovilton. As a stop gap, HMS Avenger had been sent back at top speed to rendezvous with Arapaho. Her Lynx helicopter would be able to provide the radar cover they needed, even if it wasn't Jon's first choice. The big problem was that the ship was twenty four hours away at best. However, the aircraft would soon be able to launch and refuel in Crete and should be able to reach Arapaho well before the ship. Jon was actually glad as this meant he wouldn't have to be subordinate to the Frigate's Captain until he arrived and by which time their plans would be set in concrete.

A number of signals arrived from various commands in the UK but luckily the command chain was quite clear in this sort of situation and Jon ignored most of them. It also didn't help that the RAF command ashore seemed to think that they should have an input as well and it took all of Brian's tact to keep them at arm's length.

Mid-morning, as the kerfuffle died down to a dull roar, Jon and Brian managed to sit back for a few minutes in the squadron briefing room which was doubling up as the operations centre and take stock over a very welcome cup of coffee.

'When do the grunts get here Jon?' Brian asked. 'That last signal had an ETA but I didn't actually get to see it.'

'Should be here this evening, landing at about 1800. So by the time they get out to the ship it will be getting dark.'

'Do you think we'll get a go ahead tonight?'

'No idea but Rupert is coming out at lunch time to brief us and he has been appointed as the negotiator. Shit, I'm so sorry Brian. This is all my bloody fault.'

'Jon, if you apologise to me once again, I might just forget that you're the Boss and lamp you one. You seem to forget that the original idea was mine. Yes, you did the spadework but I'm just as much to blame as anyone. So for fuck's sake stop beating yourself up over it. What's done is done.'

Jon looked at his friend. 'I suppose you're right but I never expected to have to do this sort of thing for real you know and never with such a personal interest. Actually, I'm surprised the powers that be haven't pulled us off it for just that reason.'

'And who else is there to do the job? Anyway, we've no idea what they intend, apart from their first demand. We haven't even heard of a deadline yet.'

An hour later, Brian's questions were answered. Rupert came on board and immediately asked to get together with all the squadron officers. As soon as everyone was present, he stood at the front of the briefing room. A large map of the eastern Mediterranean was pinned to the wall and he gave the Duty Officer a piece of paper with the current position of Uganda on it. The Duty Officer marked it up and sat down.

Rupert stood. 'Gentlemen, the situation so far. We can confirm that the ship has been hijacked and it definitely seems to be the work of the PLF. We don't know how many of them are on board and what weapons they have except for one thing, which I'll come to in a moment. Negotiations between the Israeli Government and ours are underway but you must remember that it is the British Government's policy not to negotiate with terrorists. I'm sorry for those of you who have family on the Uganda but that's the way it is.'

A hand went up from the back.

'Yes?'

'But what about the Israeli Government Sir? Haven't they done deals in the past?'

'Good question and I guess the final say will be theirs but the reality is we need to defuse this as soon as we can. You won't have heard it yet but they have issued some new demands and threats. They've got the ship's radio working and we are now in direct communication. They say that unless the first prisoners are released by noon tomorrow then they will start executing hostages. They have also said that a large quantity of explosives has been placed in the engine room and any attempt to attack them will result in them sinking the ship. With that many passengers and crew, you can imagine what that will do.'

A stunned silence greeted his last remark.

'Now, don't get too upset guys. I'm a trained negotiator and I'm sure I can buy us time. Personally, I suspect that this is an empty threat as it will almost certainly result in the hijackers own deaths. Every bit of previous experience of these incidents from the recent past says that these sort of people are not suicidal.'

Questions and answers went on for some time and included likely assault profiles but eventually Rupert called a halt as there was no point speculating until the Royal Marines joined them that evening. Jon stood up saying they would stop now for lunch and then scheduled another meeting for that evening as soon as the team from the UK were on board. However, as they were filing out, Rupert called Jon and Brian over for a private chat.

'I'm sorry guys. I wasn't totally honest with you there. I've more to tell and it's not good news but you need to know. The Cyprus bombs, they've now claimed credit for those and we have every reason to believe them. The problem is that we haven't a clue why. In fact, this whole operation doesn't seem to fit the normal profile for these people. Firstly, these things cost money and the PLF had never had much of that and secondly, we normally get good intelligence when they are planning something. These things take time to set up and we would expect to hear something in advance. This time there was nothing, which either means that their security has been tightened considerably or this was done very fast. It's got a lot of my seniors worried on top of everything else.'

'Well, the bombs shut down all traffic from the island. Was that what they wanted?' Brian asked.

'And we ended up putting some of our people on the ship that they've now hijacked. Could that have been a deliberate act?' Jon added.

'Seems pretty far-fetched Jon,' said Rupert. 'They could have discovered Uganda's itinerary quite easily but there's no way they could have known that we would put families on her. And anyway why would they want that? No, there's something else we don't fully understand yet and that's what I wanted to warn you about. This may not be as straightforward as we thought.'

'Frankly Rupert, I never expected it to be. We've all had enough experience to know that nothing is as it first seems,' Jon observed grimly.

The stubby, four engined Hercules C130 roared and shook with power as it accelerated down the runway at RAF Lyneham. Despite its weight of fuel, stores and equipment, it was airborne in less than half the length of the runway. As it climbed steeply away, it turned and took up a heading that would eventually take it to Cyprus.

Inside, the men from the Royal Marines Comacchio Group settled themselves into the cabin ready for the six hour flight to come. Veterans of many a Hercules trip, many had slung hammocks from the hooks in the ceiling. Others had made temporary beds on their stores pallets. Very few remained in the incredibly uncomfortable webbing seats provided for them once they had completed the take off. There had been a bit of a scramble to get the best location in the middle of the aircraft, the rear was always too cold and the front was always too hot but now they had settled in and most started thinking about the upcoming operation. The recall and briefing had taken place that morning. With such a worked up team, it was more a case of simply outlining the situation and then grabbing the necessary equipment. There would be time for a detailed tactical appreciation once they arrived in theatre. For most of them, despite the years of training, this was the first time they had been called on for real. Over half the team had fought in the Falklands five years previously but even these veterans knew that what they faced was a very different situation. It was one thing to march and fight a normal army. This time they didn't know what they were facing and civilians would be directly involved as well. No matter how tense a man can become, six hours in a noisy, bumpy and generally uncomfortable transport aircraft will dull even the keenest person's enthusiasm. So it was with a mixture of relief and anticipation that they all heard the engines throttle back and the aircraft start its descent.

The C130 they were flying in was the direct descendant of earlier models. Unlike nearly every other aircraft in current service, the Hercules had an odd history. The wings, central fuselage, nose and tail were actually separate units and when a machine was upgraded to the latest model it was done by replacing one of these units. At about the same time that the Hercules first entered service the British Comet airliner, which had revolutionised air travel was starting to suffer a number of unexplained crashes. The cause was eventually traced to a fatigue crack in one of the square shaped windows of the Comet's fuselage. Tragic though the accidents were and catastrophic to the British aircraft industry at the time, some good came of it all. A programme of full scale testing of all transport aircraft was instigated before they were certified to fly. The only aircraft that escaped was the Hercules because it was already flying. When later upgrades were added they were tested as units but never as a complete airframe. The Hercules that was carrying the Comacchio team was an old one. In fact, it had started life as a C model and had been extensively upgraded over a period of almost twenty years and was now a proud F model. If an aircraft could boast this one would have a lot to say. In particular, it was a veteran of the Falklands War, having made a number of thirteen hour round trips to the Islands and completing successful air to air refuelling, something it was never originally designed to do. Unfortunately, it was also starting to crack. Extremely hard to see, tiny fatigue cracks were slowly growing at the inner end of both wing spars. In fact, this was not unusual. Many aircraft get cracks as they age but the redundant strength of the original design was designed to cope. The Hercules was massively strong but continual increases in its engine power and take off weight were taking their toll.

The pilots had been warned to treat the military airfield on Cyprus as potentially hostile. This was the first aircraft allowed to land since the bombs exploded. Consequently, they were conducting a steep approach which would culminate in a short landing. It was designed to minimise the amount of time the large machine was a potential target to any bad guys on the ground. As the aircraft entered its dive the marines exchanged grins, they knew they were in for an exciting few minutes. They had been here before. As the aircraft approached the runway threshold, the pilots throttled back even more, lowered the undercarriage and fully deployed the flaps. As they pulled the nose up to skim the runway, the strain in the port wing root exceeded the ultimate tensile strength of the wing spar which was actually less than half its effective size due to the fatigue cracks in it. The wing snapped off.

No one in the aircraft lived for more than two seconds. The remaining wing which was still generating lift, immediately caused the massive machine to start to roll. As it rolled the nose dropped and slammed into the grass a hundred yards short of the runway threshold. Although the fuel tanks were fairly empty there was more than enough aviation fuel to start a catastrophic fire. Not that any of the passengers would have noticed, the violence of the impact either killed them outright or rendered them unconscious. Wreckage of the aircraft, stores and bodies cascaded onto the runway in a massive cloud of flame and smoke.

In the airfield control tower, the duty controller watched it happen. Without thinking, he hit the crash alarm and the airfield's well practised emergency response system swung into action. Sickened, he watched as the fire engines and other rescue vehicles sped to the scene of destruction. He knew there would be no survivors. He couldn't recognise a single part of the machine that only seconds ago was lining up to land. The only question in his mind and he knew it would be in many others as well, was what had caused the catastrophe. Was it an accident or yet more terrorist action?

Chapter 35

Later that afternoon, Karim was called to the bridge. Earlier on, he had helped distribute the water to the boat decks and then even managed a few hours sleep. Now dressed in more appropriate clothing, he was curious to know how the situation was developing.

Mohammed met him at the door. 'Karim, it's getting harder and harder to maintain order. The children just don't have the attention span and the teachers are getting more and more angry. We need to do something.'

'In that case, I think now is a good time to select my hostages,' he suggested.

Mohammed nodded. 'Alright, where will you take them?'

'Back to their accommodation, they can be kept there and there are toilet facilities they can use. It's easy to secure and right at the stern of the ship well clear of everyone else.'

'Alright, as we agreed then. I'll leave you to it. Let me know when you're finished and I'll lift restrictions on the rest of the passengers.'

Karim nodded and indicated to one of the other men to accompany him before heading off to the port boat deck where he knew the Purser would be. He found the man sitting with some of the parents and gestured to him to go with him. The Purser clambered to his feet and followed Karim who stopped when they were clear of the crowd.

'I require the list of all the extra passengers you took on board in Cyprus.'

The man blinked in incomprehension. 'Why do you want them?' he blurted.

Karim back handed him across the face. 'Don't ask me questions or you will join them. Now, where is the list?'

The Purser stepped back with a cry and a look of pain and horror on his face. He knew he would have to provide an answer, the look in this man's eyes told him he really meant business. 'In my office.'

'Go and get it then.'

The Purser shambled off, returned several minutes later and handed a sheet of paper to Karim. He glanced at it. He saw there were six adults and seven children. Then he noticed something

Arapaho

against one of the adult's names. Pointing to it, he asked the Purser to explain. 'What does WRNS mean?'

The Purser turned white, for a second he considered trying to make something up but nothing sprang to mind. Karim noticed his reaction. 'I won't ask again old man. What does it mean?'

'Women's Royal Naval Service,' he choked out.

'So, she is a military officer then?'

'I suppose so. She wasn't in uniform and was just travelling back to England with the other families.'

'Very well, now we will round up all these people,' and seeing the question form on the Pursers face, he continued. 'Why, is no business of yours. Just do as you're told.'

Karim let the Purser do the job. When the group of frightened looking mothers and children were ready he led them on below decks. The other soldier took up the rear. They soon arrived at their cabin area.

Karim turned to the group. 'You will want to know why you have been brought here. I will tell you. You are all families of the British military who were in Cyprus and the Lebanon before that. So, if there are any problems with our demands you will be the first to be sacrificed. Do you understand?'

There was a stunned silence until Kathy voiced their shared concerns. 'You can't mean the children as well. Surely you people aren't that uncivilised?'

Karim turned on her with a mad gleam in his eyes. 'So, it's alright if you people bomb and maim our children, even my own brother is it? And you call me uncivilised' He was about to carry on when something occurred to him. 'Purser, why are there only five adults here? where is the sixth one?'

The Purser looked stricken. 'She couldn't be found,' he stuttered.

'Is it the Barratt woman, the Naval Officer?'

The Purser could only nod.

'Right, you all go in now. that now includes you Purser.' And he swiftly left, shutting and locking the doors to the two rooms.

When he went back to the bridge and reported that the hostages were secure, Mohammed picked up the ships broadcast microphone. 'Ladies and Gentlemen you may all now return to your accommodation. You may carry on as normal. the ship's crew can return to their duties. But you must understand that not only do we hold the Captain as hostage to your good behaviour but we also have a number of you held securely. Any bad behaviour and they will suffer. You have been warned.'

Helen spent the rest of the day in the storeroom. It seemed as good a placed as any to hide. She continued to try to figure out the radio with no success. Suddenly, with a sudden surge of panic she heard the sound of footsteps in the main classroom. She ran to the door and crouched down on the inside. The door had a glass panel and she slowly raised her head and looked into the large space. At first, she couldn't see anything and then she spotted movement. It was a young boy of about fourteen. He had a shock of ginger hair and a large dose of puppy fat. Before she could react, he made straight for the door she was hiding behind and pushed it open. As soon as he was in, she stood and shut it turning to confront the boy.

He looked startled but not scared. 'What are you doing here Miss? I'm the science room monitor for the week. You shouldn't be here.'

Helen was taken aback for a second. 'Nor should you. Surely you know what's going on? Everyone is meant to stay at their muster stations.'

He looked unconcerned. 'Nah, they've said we can all carry on as normal now, didn't you hear them on the speakers? I take my duties seriously you know.' He added in a pompous, rather self-important manner.

'Oh, well, what's your name? Mine's Helen.'

'Oh yeah, I'm Robert, hey what are you doing with all the radio stuff? You shouldn't be playing with that.'

'Robert, I'm not playing,' she explained patiently. 'I need to get a message off the ship because of the hijack and I'm trying to make a radio to do it.'

'Well you won't do it like that,' he said with a condescending tone. 'Would you like me to make it work?'

'You know how to assemble this?'

'Oh yeah, Mr Spencer had us doing it last week. It's very simple. Each module connects up on that board. Look, bring it all into the classroom and I'll show you.'

'Can't we do it in here?'

'No, because we need to connect to the aerial and electric which are in there,' he said with the smug assurance of a teenager lecturing an adult.

They moved all the bits and pieces onto a bench in the classroom and much to Helen's chagrin, the lad then pushed her out of the way and started to plug in various bits of electronics into the large circuit board. She realised it was a very good teaching aid and clearly little Robert had been paying attention in class.

Within minutes, Robert finished and had plugged the whole thing into the mains socket. Various lights came on and a crackling noise came out of one of the modules.

'Look here,' he explained. 'Turn this knob to change frequency and you talk into this microphone. It works on High Frequency but you can't talk on it because you need a licence. Mr Spencer explained all that because he is a Ham.'

'A what?'

'Oh, it's a word to say that it's his hobby. He told us there are thousands of them around the world and they all talk to each other all the time.'

Helen vaguely remembered hearing about this. So maybe she could now get a message out. 'So how do we contact someone?'

Robert thought for a second. 'Mr Spencer said something about a schedule but I don't really know what he meant. If we turn this dial we can change frequencies and maybe hear people talking. He started to turn the dial very slowly. At first they only heard hissing but suddenly a voice was heard. Robert turned the dial back and suddenly they were listening to someone talking and seemingly getting no reply. Robert handed the microphone to Helen.

'Oh yes, I suppose I better do this, after all I did all that training for Beirut. Right,' she pressed the button on the microphone.

'Hello er Mayday, this is Helen Barratt calling from the cruise ship Uganda do you read me?'

They waited in tense silence and for several seconds nothing happened. Then a voice replied. 'Unknown station on this frequency what is your call sign?'

'I'm sorry I don't know what you mean.' Helen replied. 'Look, I'm calling from the hijacked ship, the Uganda. I need to get a message to the British authorities. It's really important.'

'Yeah lady and I'm Ronald Reagan. Now get off this frequency. You are not licenced to be here.'

Helen wasn't going to give up. 'Listen you idiot, this an emergency. You need to pass on to the British that there are only six hijackers on board but one is the surviving twin brother of the Beirut hijack. It's really important, six hijackers but one is the twin brother. Have you got that?'

'Right lady, that's enough. I don't know what you're talking about. We get fantasists like you quite regularly these days. Why don't you just go and bother someone else. This is Whiskey Charlie Three Bravo, signing off.' And the frequency went quiet.

Almost weeping with frustration, Helen was about to try again when she heard footsteps approaching. Quickly, she turned the radio off and shoved it to one side with a load of other apparatus. She was only just in time as the classroom door opened and she found herself staring down the barrel of a pistol held by the hawk nosed man.

Chapter 36

The squadron officers were all having an early meal in the officer's mess in anticipation of the arrival of the Royal Marine contingent and the good chance of a busy night to come. Jon, Brian and Rupert were sharing a table when the duty officer came in and asked Jon to talk to him privately. He handed Jon a signal with an odd look on his face. When Jon had finished reading, he looked pale and shocked. He came over to his table and banged hard on it to get silence.

'Gentlemen, fuck I don't know how to tell you this. Look, this afternoon at about seventeen thirty the Hercy Bird with the Comacchio Group guys was about to land and it seems to have crashed, no sorry, it bloody well did. There are no survivors. Apparently, it hit the threshold just short of the main runway and then broke up before it caught fire.'

A stunned silence greeted his announcement. Then suddenly there was a bedlam of questions. Jon held up his hand and called for silence. 'Look, I don't have any details. The signal simply states that the aircraft has been lost with all its passengers and crew.'

A lone voice summed up what everyone was thinking, 'Fuck me Boss, that's dreadful but what the hell are we going to do now about the hijacked ship?'

Jon simply stared at his men. 'Guys sorry, at this stage, I have absolutely no sodding idea.'

Rupert gave Jon a nudge. 'Jon, leave this with me for a moment, I'll get on to the Consulate and see what intelligence there is. Meanwhile, why don't you do an audit of exactly what assets we have on the ship and maybe ashore in the RAF base. The first problem I can see is that this could be more enemy action and if the plane was shot down then there won't be any more flights until we know. That means we're probably going to be on our own for a day or two at least.'

'Good thinking Rupert, get together in half an hour?'

'That should be enough. I'll see you in the main briefing room.'

The officer's mess emptied with half eaten meals on the table. No one felt like eating any more.

In fact, it took Rupert over an hour to get any sense out of the authorities ashore and in the meantime Jon, Brian and his team did their best to see what assets they could now call on. Jon also received a number of signals from the UK. COMAW, who was still technically Jon's superior ordered them all to standby but to take no further action until a decision was taken on the way forward. The RAF had a contingent of the RAF regiment ashore but none had been trained in Counter Terrorism operations. That didn't stop them volunteering but Jon had his reservations, he knew how important the specialist training was. On board, they had his three helicopters and also now the Lynx from HMS Avenger which had arrived that afternoon. There was only one RIB and that belonged to the ship as its sea boat so was currently painted bright orange. With the ships Master's permission, he directed some of the maintenance crew to find some paint and get stuck in turning it black. Unfortunately, it only had a small fifty horse power engine which would give it very little speed if loaded with any weight. Apart from the RIB, there were just the squadron's small arms of SLR rifles, nine millimetre sub machine guns and pistols. Luckily, they also had a small supply of stun grenades left over from Jon's rescue but that was about it. All the specialist equipment was with the marines and destroyed in the accident. They also had three Royal Marines as part of the squadron complement, a Sergeant and two marines. Luckily Sergeant Smithers was Counter Terrorism trained but that wasn't too much help without more marines and specialist equipment.

Jon called everyone together and he and Rupert took centre stage once again.

Rupert was first. 'The latest from ashore is that no one knows why the aircraft crashed. Some eye witnesses say they saw a wing break off but there is no confirmation of what caused it. The current betting is on more terrorist action. So I don't need to tell you what that means in terms of getting any more help in the near future.'

Jon joined in. 'That said, the marines are putting together a backup team as we speak. There are enough previous members of the unit plus some almost finishing training to make it worthwhile. But may I remind everyone that the deadline we are working to is noon tomorrow. Unless we can buy some time no one is going to reach us, so effectively we are on our own. Now the first thing that I propose is we get underway and close with the target. We will stay out of visual range but I see no point in hanging about around here. If shore support is forthcoming we can use the Sea Kings to fetch it. As the Uganda is now quite close to Egypt it will be much easier to fly the new team in there and for us to collect them.'

Rupert nodded. 'Good thinking Jon but won't you need permission from COMAW for that?'

Jon just grinned. 'Nope, we'll sail and then I'll tell him. I've no intention of being long screw-drivered by that man. There's no way he can get here in time anyway. He may have told me to wait further instructions but I'll quote Nelson back at him if he complains. You know the one where he said that no Captain can be criticised if he closes with the enemy, well something like that anyway. Rupert, you should be able to keep in contact with the government and any other authorities you need. The ship has good HF radios.'

'And the closer we get to the Uganda, the easier it will be to talk to them,' responded Rupert. 'So I'll back you up if anyone complains and I'll try to buy us time but we still need some sort of plan if things start to go wrong.'

'Well, it's about one hundred and fifty miles to their current position and this tub will do twenty knots maximum so if we sail within the hour we could be within range of them by three in the morning. That gives one night time window before the deadline.'

'I think we will have to hold fire at least until noon tomorrow Jon. It would be crazy to go in before the deadline and risk them sinking the ship or killing hostages, only to find that the Israelis were actually planning on releasing the prisoners.'

'Fair point Rupert,' and then he turned to the room at large. 'Listen up everyone, you all understand the situation as well as me. Now, I don't have a monopoly on good ideas and without our Comacchio chums we are on our own. So anyone with any clever thoughts, don't keep them to yourself. As things stand we are not going to be flying tonight so go and get some sleep but be prepared for an early shake.'

Most of the crew filtered out but Dave Southgate the AEO came over to Jon.

Jon looked up. 'Hi Dave, thanks for making sure the aircraft are all ready, although I'm not sure we will actually be able to use them.'

'Yes Boss but you asked for ideas and this may sound daft but I've had a thought.'

'Go on, any input is most welcome.'

'Well, we would normally try to get on board a hijacked ship, either by stealth or an airborne assault or both simultaneously right?'

'Correct, where's this going?'

'The key to me seems that we need to get close enough without arising suspicion.'

'Yes, that would help enormously but what are you suggesting?'

Dave explained his idea. When he finished Brian spoke first. 'Will there be time to do it?'

'If we limit it to one side of the ship, get everyone turned to and start work now. We might have to stay over the horizon until it's complete but if we turn all hands to it, then yes we can do it.'

Jon looked impressed. 'Dave I owe you a beer, big time, although I'm not sure making everyone lose their rack time will be that popular though. The only question I've got is, do we have enough paint?'

Chapter 37

John Chester left his car fuming. He had spent a great deal of time and money converting the old station wagon so that he could operate his Ham radio from the trunk. He always said, to anyone who asked, that it was the only thing that kept him sane during the working day. As an IT help desk operator, he felt he was on the front line of the stupidity wars. Not only that but he had to be polite to his enemy, the morons who thought it was always anyone else's fault than their own for not being able to read simple instructions. His work breaks, where he could mentally disappear across the world with the aid of his HF radio, were his safety valve. So the bloody woman who interrupted his morning search for a conversation across the planet only served to increase his frustration levels. He plonked himself down at his desk and reached for his telephone headset. Just as he was about to put it on, he looked up at the TV screen that was always on at the front of the office. Some management consultant or maybe it was a shrink, had decided that seeing a live TV feed would be good for the poor bloody operators at their desks. The screen was showing a white ship with smoke trickling out of the funnel. It looked like a rather old fashioned cruise ship. The CNN ticker tape at the bottom of the screen was giving details. His eye caught two words, 'Uganda' and 'Hijack' and his blood ran cold. 'Shit, that woman was for real.' He shot back down to the parking lot and got into his car despite his supervisor's angry stare as he ran out of the office. Turning on his radio he was met with static and no matter how much he called, the woman was gone. He sat back, grabbed a paper pad and wrote down as much as he could remember. What the hell was he going to do now?

Helen held Robert's hand tightly as they were escorted back into the ship. The man walked behind them with his pistol pointing at their backs. Before they left the classroom he quizzed them about why they were there. Helen managed to deflect his curiosity away from the science equipment and simply said she had found the classroom unlocked so was using it as a place to hide. Robert told the man that he was the Science Monitor for the week and had serious responsibilities. Helen noted that even the man had to smile at the lad's self-importance. However, it was clear that he was far from satisfied with Helen's answers. Before they left, Helen had been able to put her hand in her pocket and retrieve the pass key. Under the cover of stumbling, she managed to push it down inside her shoe. It was the best she could think of and she prayed they wouldn't search her that thoroughly. When they reached the boat deck, Karim told Robert to go back to his parents and to consider himself very lucky. Robert scampered off without a backward look. Helen was then taken to the bridge.

'I found her hiding in a classroom at the stern,' Karim reported to Mohammed.

'What was she doing there?'

'She says she was just hiding. I had a look around and couldn't see what else she could have been doing.' He turned to Helen. 'Why didn't you go with the other passengers?'

Helen decided the truth or at least as much as she could use would be the best approach. 'I was up early. I couldn't sleep and saw some of you with the Captain. I decided to hide and then when you sounded the alarm it seemed better to stay out of sight.'

Karim's eyes narrowed. 'You are in fact a British Naval Officer are you not?'

Helen blinked in surprise. 'Not really, I'm what they call a Wren. That means I work with the navy but I'm not commissioned. We mainly do administration work.'

'And you were with the Naval helicopter squadron that was operating in Beirut recently?'

'*How on earth did he know that?*' she thought furiously. 'I'm sorry I can't answer that.'

'No matter, I know you were,' Karim answered for her. 'We also have all the parents and children that were with the squadron as well so there is no use denying it.'

If that wasn't bad enough, he then said something that chilled Helen to the bone. 'Lieutenant Commander Hunt and the rest of his people will soon understand the meaning of vengeance.'

Karim noted that at the mention of the name the girl flinched. It clearly meant something to her. 'Ah, I see you know who I'm talking about, maybe he is your boyfriend?' he asked with a smirk. 'A pretty girl like you, it would be hard not to be attracted, no?'

Helen forced herself to look him in the eye. 'I have nothing to say to you, you bastard.'

Karim laughed. 'Your reaction gives you away but it is of no matter, except it will make my revenge even sweeter.' He looked over at Mohammed. 'We should use her as the first sacrifice?'

Mohammed nodded. 'That seems reasonable. Lock her in the Captain's cabin so she is readily accessible. Yes, she can be the first.'

Karim grabbed her roughly by the arm and with his pistol jammed into her side led her down the corridor behind the bridge. At the end, past the radio room, was a small cabin that the Captain slept in when at sea. He pushed her roughly inside. He took a large cable tie from his pocket and secured her hands behind her back. As he did so he felt her breasts pushing into his chest and just for a second considered punishing her in a more fundamental way. After all, she was clearly trouble and breaking her spirit would do no harm. Pushing her down onto the narrow bunk, he considered whether there would be time and whether Mohammed would object. She was extremely attractive. He had always like western women and her state of fear made her even more desirable. In the end, he forced himself to step back. There would be plenty of time once the deadline expired. His pleasure, the first stage in his revenge, could wait a little longer. He left without saying a word, slamming the door shut and locking it.

Helen lay still. She had seen the look in the man's eyes and was sure he intended something unpleasant. She was surprised when he left her but it seemed clear he would be back and the thought terrified her. He seemed utterly cold and ruthless. Rape would only be the start she was sure. She forced herself to calm down and think. There was clearly a lot more to this hijack than just a demand to release Palestinian prisoners. How on earth did that man know so much about her and the other passengers? She knew how he had escaped from the house in Beirut because they had found the escape tunnel. She also remembered Rupert saying that they had no idea where he had gone. Well, she now knew, she thought bitterly and he must have been integral to the whole plot. His talk of vengeance and sacrifices scared her to her core. Then she remembered the pass key in her shoe. It had seemed a good idea at the time as she was sure they would search her. That they hadn't was a surprise but knowing their attitude towards women maybe it was understandable. After a struggle, by sitting on the bed and leaning on her side, she managed to pull it out of her shoe and quickly hid it under the mattress.

As Karim left the bridge with the girl, Ahmed, one the soldiers turned to Mohammed. 'When are we going to tell him and what do you think he will do?'

Mohammed thought for a moment. 'Tomorrow, I want to hear the response to our deadline first. When we know how seriously we are being taken, then we will make the decision.'

The duty CIA officer in the New York office sighed in frustration as he put the phone down. Another fantasist on the line. He seemed to spend all his time dealing with cranks these days. Just then, his boss walked past his desk and noticed the look on his face.

'Something up Jim?'

'Oh, just another crank Boss. We seem to have an epidemic of them these days.'

'What was this one about?'

'You know the hijacking of the British cruise ship in the Mediterranean? Well, this guy claims to have talked on the radio to someone on board. I mean it must be four thousand miles from New York to there and the idiot expected me to believe him, sheesh.'

A strange look came over his boss's face. 'What did he say Jim?'

'Oh, that this girl had contacted him in some way. I can't remember exactly how and wanted to pass on some information about the hijack, as if.'

'Jim, think very carefully. Did he say the word Ham at all?'

Jim was starting to get a little worried. Why was his boss taking this crap seriously? 'Er maybe I wasn't really giving him my full attention to be honest.'

'Listen carefully Jim. There is a very good chance that this guy was on the level. If he was a radio Ham, they have sets that can work over thousands of miles, so it's quite possible he was telling the truth. And if he was, then he may have information that can save hundreds of lives. Now get back on to the switchboard and see if you can get a trace on that call. As soon as you've done that get a pen and paper and write down everything you can remember about what he said and I mean everything. You got that?'

Chapter 38

Dawn arrived as Arapaho closed with fifteen miles of the Uganda. Jon had decided they should stay over the horizon for the moment but if anyone on the Uganda was keeping a radar watch they would keep steaming past and then turn around when clear. They were also travelling slowly to minimise ship movement as there were quite a number of ship and squadron personnel hanging over the port side of the ship on paint stages. The ship's crane had been busy as had the engineering staff. Half of the hangar had been dismantled and the containers relocated down the port side of the flight deck. Any ship passing the port side would see a deck apparently covered in containers. Most of them had been repainted in a variety of colours instead of their drab naval grey as had large parts of the side of the ship. In particular, the large black letters A131 which identified the ship as a British Naval Fleet Auxiliary were no longer there and instead the name of a well known shipping line was apparent. At the stern, there was a Liberian flag. In fact, anyone seeing the ship would identify her as a commercial container ship which was exactly what was intended. Should the same observer see the starboard side they would be very confused as from that angle she was still an RFA.

Jon called a halt and gathered everyone together just as it was getting fully light. Like just about everyone else, he was splattered with paint and dog tired. 'Well done everyone,' he called, 'I've just got back from a quick trip in the RIB and we don't look like a military ship at all now, at least from one side. Hopefully, we can use this to good advantage to get close and see exactly what we are dealing with. Now, nothing will happen until the noon deadline. As you know we have our negotiator with us and hopefully he will be talking to the hijackers soon. So, until then, let's all get cleaned up, have a wash and a meal. The ship has arranged a suitably appropriate breakfast for us all in the main mess. I'll see you there in half an hour or so.'

As he was heading for his cabin, Brian approached. He looked as dishevelled as Jon felt but had a sense of urgency about him. 'Jon you need to get up to the Ops room. The hijackers have made contact again.'

Suddenly, all Jon's fatigue washed away in a rush of adrenalin and he shot up the ladder in the superstructure to the room next to the radio shack that they had converted to an adhoc operations room. Rupert was sitting at a desk with a radio microphone in his hand. He waved to Jon to sit down next to him as he continued to talk into the radio.

'Good morning Mohammed, my name is Rupert and I have been authorised by the British Government to liaise with you.'

A heavily accented voice responded. 'I do not care who you are. Are the prisoners going to be released as we instructed?'

'Mohammed, you have to understand that these things take time. The two governments need to talk. We can't just release them like that and arrangements have to be made.'

'So, you are saying that the prisoners will be released?'

'We are hopeful that we can come to some agreement Mohammed. Now, can I ask whether everyone on board is safe?'

'I will not answer anything until you tell me whether the prisoners are to be released.'

Rupert looked at Jon with a wry smile. 'Bloody single minded this chap,' he muttered and then he pressed the transmit switch again. 'Mohammed, as I said before, we will need more time. I'm sure you realise that these things just don't happen quickly.'

'And I have given you plenty of time. I remind you that the deadline is noon today. One minute after that the first hostage will die.'

Rupert flinched but kept doggedly on. 'Mohammed, if you do that the world will condemn you and the PLF, especially if we are in the process of doing as you ask. Can you not see that?'

There was silence for several minutes. Rupert and Jon waited expectantly. The voice returned. 'What are you proposing?'

'Give us another twenty four hours, please. I'm sure something can be worked out by then.'

There was another long silence before the reply came. 'We wonder whether you do this so that you can attack us. Be warned, the bomb in the engine room of this ship is very real and will sink her very quickly.'

'But then you will all die. Is that what you really want?' Rupert responded.

'What we want is our brothers and comrades to be released and the world to understand the real situation in Palestine. We will give you twenty four hours, no more. We will contact you again this evening for you to tell us of your progress. No military ships or aircraft are to come near us. We will take that as you breaking our agreement and act accordingly.'

Rupert tried to call back but this time there was no reply. When it was clear he wasn't going to get any further, he let out a long sigh and put the radio microphone down.

'Well, that was about as good as we could expect guys. At least we've extended the deadline and those comments about the world understanding the Palestinian situation give me a degree of hope that they aren't really suicidal. I need to get on to London and tell them what has happened. Do you want me to request that we sail past them now we don't look like a military ship?'

'Yes please Rupert, tell them what we've done and explain how important it is that we get a look at Uganda in daylight. Is there anything else we can do? Otherwise, I need a quick shower and a bacon sandwich.'

'No, that's fine, you do that, I know how hard everyone has been working. I'll let you know as soon as I get a response from London.'

On the bridge of Uganda, the atmosphere was tense. Karim and Mohammed had come out of the radio room and Karim was angry.

'Why did you extend the deadline another day?' he asked angrily. 'They will just use the time to make more preparations to move against us.'

'Maybe, my friend but we have to consider the end game. We always knew that we would be up against clever, well-resourced people and that we could only do this for a finite time. The longer the hijack goes on the more publicity the cause gets and the more intransigent the Israelis will appear in the eyes of the world.' As he spoke, he made eye contact with Ahmed and nodded very slightly.

Karim was in no mood to take notice. 'We told the world we would start to execute hostages at noon today. If we do not, we will just appear weak. No one will take us seriously.'

'Do we want the world to think of us as cold blooded murderers? We have the bomb in the engine room to keep them well away from us. There is no need to kill anyone yet, if at all.'

Karim said nothing but looked hard at his colleague. Mohammed reckoned he knew what was going through his mind and wasn't disappointed when Karim finally spoke through clenched teeth.

'You were never planning to take this that far were you? I bankrolled you and you all agreed to my terms but you are now going to betray me. You let me kill the officer so I would be incriminated but never intended to do anything more. I bet you planned to leave me behind to take the blame and you will all be seen in a better light.' He saw the truth in Mohammed's eyes. 'This whole thing is a sham.'

He pulled out his pistol and aimed it between Mohammed's eyes. 'Well let me tell you that this won't happen. I will have my revenge and nothing you can do will stop me.'

He heard the click of a weapon being cocked behind him. 'Do nothing you will regret. I will not hesitate to shoot Mohammed if I have to.'

Another weapon was cocked. It was if his words were simply being ignored. An overwhelming rage started to overcome him. He realised he could not survive a shoot-out. Apart from Mohammed, there were two others of the team behind him but he didn't care. Maybe the surprise of him shooting Mohammed would give him time to turn and take out the other two. With nothing to lose, he pulled the trigger. The pistol made an empty click as the slide went forward. Desperately, he pulled it back again and fired, again nothing happened.

'Do you think we were stupid enough to give a homicidal maniac like you a loaded gun Karim?' asked Mohammed looking quite unperturbed. 'We emptied the magazine hours ago.' He looked over Karim's shoulder and nodded.

Before Karim had time to even turn his head, the butt of an AK47 hit him in the temple and he fell stunned to the floor.

'Tie him and put him in the same room as that girl. That should keep him occupied.' Mohammed ordered. 'But handcuff him so he can't reach her. As he quite rightly surmised, we don't want any more killing.'

Helen had actually managed to get some sleep. The cabin had a small bathroom on one side and despite her hands being secured behind her, she had been able to use the facilities. However, her stomach was now beginning to rumble. She wondered whether she had been forgotten when she suddenly heard footsteps approaching and the sound of a key in the lock. The door shot open and to her surprise, her tormentor was pulled in by two of the other terrorists. He was barely conscious and they had trouble dragging him through the narrow door. She jumped to her feet as he was dumped unceremoniously on the bed. One of his captors took out a pair of handcuffs and cuffed his hands behind his back and around the frame of the bed. She tried to speak to them but they either didn't understand her or chose to ignore her. However, one did come over and cut the cable tie securing her hands. She rubbed her wrists in pain as the circulation was restored. One of the men said something in what she supposed was Arabic to the other and then turned to her with a malicious grin. 'You look after him now,' he said in heavily accented English and they left, locking the door again.

Chapter 39

John Chester had gone to bed frustrated as hell. The idiot at the CIA refused to believe him and he didn't know where else to turn. He had watched the news that evening and was more than ever convinced that the girl he had spoken to had been on that ship. He had tried several times to call her back but it seemed no one was listening any more. He resolved to go directly to the British Embassy the next morning, maybe they would listen to him. It was with some amazement and not a little fear when he heard someone banging hard on the front door to his flat.

'Mr Chester, this is the CIA, please let us in.' The voice carried even through the thick door.

Not wanting the neighbours to get the wrong idea, he leapt out of bed and hurriedly opened the door. As he did so, he realised it was only six in the morning. A leather wallet with some sort of ID was thrust into his face and two dark suited men pushed their way inside.

'Sorry to get you up so early Sir,' one of them said, clearly not sorry at all. 'Can you please confirm that it was you who contacted us yesterday with regards to the hijacked British ship?'

Still trying to get the fog of sleep from his brain he replied, 'Yes, that was me but you boneheads didn't want to listen. Why, has something else happened?'

'In a minute Sir, can you tell us why you used a public phone? It's taken us hours to track you down.'

'Because it was the nearest to where I work. I didn't want to talk to you guys on one of the office phones. I assumed a degree of privacy was in order. Of course it was a waste of time. You idiots didn't want to listen to me.'

'Yes Sir, well that's been taken care of. Would you please get dressed and come with us? We need to talk.'

Jon stood with Rupert, Brian and the ship's Master as Arapaho slowly steamed closer to the Uganda. They had received the go ahead from London half an hour previously and were now in the process of steaming past as close as they dared. All the crew and military staff were below decks and the three Sea Kings were well hidden in the remains of the hangar. Looking down on the deck, not for the first time, Jon wondered whether the ruse would work. From his vantage point this high up he could see everything. He knew that from the side the camouflage looked authentic but he prayed they hadn't missed anything.

Brian echoed his thoughts. 'Looks a bloody mess from up here. I just hope we don't get rumbled.'

'No, it looks fine from the side. Eyes out everyone and let's see what's what.' Jon picked up his binoculars as did everyone else on the bridge. 'You know, the last time I saw this ship, she had a big red cross on the side and was very scruffy. She seems in much better shape now.'

'Now that does surprise me,' observed Brian. 'There seem to be quite a few people about on the upper deck. Some even seem to be kids.'

'Well no matter how many hijackers there are there's no way they can completely control over a thousand passengers. I guess they have hostages and so don't feel the need.'

'Yes and that bomb they say they've got. Hang on, look at the stern Jon. Isn't that something tied to a guard rail and dangling into the wake?'

Every eye tracked to where Brian had indicated. They were over two miles away and it was quite hard to make out but there was a consensus that someone must have tied something over the stern. Jon caught a flash of light from the end where it was occasionally hitting the top of a wave. 'I'm pretty certain that that's a fire hose. Look, the end has a copper nozzle on it. Bloody hell, someone has a presence of mind over there. That could be our way on board.'

Sergeant Smithers was on the bridge and looking as well. 'Have you ever tried to climb something like that Sir? Oh and in the dark?'

'No Sergeant, I haven't,' Jon replied still staring through the binoculars. 'But I'm willing to bet some trained killer, kick ass, Royal Marine could.'

'I guess we'd best rig one up and try Sir. But you're right. It could make our problem so much easier.'

It took over half an hour to travel past the very slow moving liner. All the time, they listened for any call on the VHF or any sign that they had been rumbled. Nothing happened and the white liner slowly disappeared over the horizon behind them. As soon as they were clear Jon called them all down to the Ops room. Brian left them as he had been steadily taking photographs and took the films to be developed to the dark room that was part of the aviation facilities.

'So everyone, what do we think?' Jon asked waving everyone to their seats. Stuck to walls were large scale drawings of the internal compartments of the Uganda which had arrived by HF fax that morning. The discussion lasted over an hour. In the end, there was a consensus that the key to all their ideas was that fire hose. If they could use it to get on board covertly, then there was a strong consensus that something could be done. True to his word Sergeant Smithers offered to rig up a similar hose to the jib of the ship's crane and they could all see how difficult it would be to climb.

In the end, Jon summarised their thoughts. 'We reckon we could get on board tonight without being observed. That said, we don't know how many of the bad guys there are or how they're armed. We also know that there is meant to be a bomb somewhere in the engine room.'

Rupert continued. 'My and London's assessment is that whoever these guys are they are unlikely to use that bomb, if it even exists and probably won't even put up a serious fight. Most intelligence estimates are that they are not suicidal fanatics and would not want the adverse publicity.'

'That's easy for you to say Mister Thomas,' the Sergeant observed. 'You won't be the one to have to find out whether you're right or not.'

'Actually Sergeant, I will almost certainly be accompanying any boarding party so I'm sorry but I will be putting my neck on the line.'

The Sergeant looked slightly embarrassed and sat back in his chair.

Jon wound things up. 'Right gentlemen, we need to get this assessment back to London. COMAW actually approved our sailing, albeit after the event but what I'm proposing will be above even his pay grade. I am going to suggest a boarding tonight. The longer we leave it the more chance there will be of that fire hose being noticed. Yes Rupert, we know the deadline had been extended but if they are playing to the gallery then the quicker this is wrapped up the better and if they are really going to play hard ball, then going in tonight will be the last thing they will expect and let's face it, we are probably going to have to go in some time. I'm not convinced

London will agree but we must be ready. So, Sergeant Smithers and his two marines will lead, with Mr Thomas, myself, SOBS and a few more volunteers, probably another four so we have a reasonably sized team. I'm going because, in the end, this is my responsibility and SOBS has his family on board. Any other of my people who have family are welcome to volunteer. I have a couple of ideas for misdirection as well. What I suggest we do now is fall out for lunch and then meet on the flight deck in an hour for hose climbing practice.'

John Chester was almost screaming with frustration now. When he got back to the CIA headquarters in New York he told his story once again and was then left in a small office on his own for over an hour. He was then driven to their headquarters at Langley wasting even more time where he repeated himself yet again. At one point he had lost his temper and yelled at the idiots that didn't they realise that time was slipping by. Not one of his interrogators batted an eyelid, merely politely asking him to refrain from histrionics. Eventually, after more hours waiting, a man he hadn't seen before came in.

'Mr Chester, thank you for bearing with us,' he offered without any attempt to introduce himself. 'We've been checking out your story and can see no reason not believe that it isn't authentic. To be honest we've also been checking you out and once again you seem to be exactly who and what you say you are. So, on behalf of the CIA, I would like to thank you for your help and we have a car standing by to take you home. Need I say it but we would not want any of this information becoming public knowledge, so please do not talk to anyone else about it.'

John's jaw dropped. 'That's it? You don't want me to keep a listening watch out in case the girl calls again or provide any other help. At least tell me you actually believe me and are going to do something about it.'

The man smiled patronisingly. 'Mr Chester, the information is in the hands of the experts now. Please be assured, it will be acted on as necessary.'

'You are going to tell the Brits aren't you?'

'Mr Chester, that is none of your business now. Please do as we ask and just go home.'

John was ushered out of the building by another suit and put in the back of what looked to be the same car that had brought him here. For some reason he got the distinct impression that there was something he wasn't being told. His resolve slowly grew. He would take more direct action.

Chapter 40

Helen didn't know what to do. She had remembered the hawk nosed man's name now, it was Karim something or another. But that didn't exactly help her in her quandary. He was bleeding from a nasty gash to his head and seemed to be semi-conscious but the last thing she wanted to do was get close to him even if he seemed to be handcuffed pretty securely. She decided to wait. There was a small chair by the Captain's desk so she sat down and watched her prey. An age seemed to pass before he started to come round. Eventually, his eyes were focusing properly and he raised his head to look at her. For several seconds their eyes locked and then he tried to sit up snarling and fighting his handcuffed hands. He quickly realised that he couldn't even sit up properly with his hands secured behind his back to the low metal part of the bed's headboard. This only seemed to make him angrier and he started to rave and swear in some foreign language. Helen was scared that his efforts would allow him to break free but she soon saw that the metal bed frame was well capable of withstanding his efforts. She said nothing and waited for him to calm down.

Eventually, he lay back exhausted, muttering to himself and staring at the ceiling. He suddenly spoke. 'I suppose you take great pleasure in this, bitch.'

Helen decided the remark needed no reply.

He waited a few minutes and then spoke again. 'When I get free, I will take even greater revenge and you will be the first to suffer, believe me.'

'I don't doubt it but you have to get free first and it seems your friends have either deserted or even betrayed you.'

At the word betrayal, he started to swear again in Arabic. It was several minutes before he calmed down again. When he did, he looked at Helen again. 'Set me free and I will spare you.'

Helen just had to laugh. The remark was just so ridiculous on so many levels. 'What? From the man who just threatened my life. I don't normally swear but you Mister Karim can just fuck off,' and seeing the look of surprise on his face she continued. 'Yes, I know who you are. You knew of me and my naval connections, so you shouldn't be surprised that I know of you and your late brother's activities in Beirut. It's people like you who make life a misery for everyone else. And even if I wanted to set you free I couldn't but I could lift up this metal chair I'm sitting on and bash your bloody brains out, just remember that.'

His eyes narrowed as he looked at her. 'You may know my name but you know nothing about me woman.' He almost spat out the last word. 'You know nothing about me, my life and what I have suffered so don't go patronising me with your western arrogance.'

'I know you are a criminal, a kidnapper and a murderer. What else do I need to know? You are scum, you are beneath contempt.' Helen was finding it hard to hold on to her temper and with the man so completely immobilised, she found she could give vent to her feelings. She also realised she meant it when she talked about using the chair to beat the crap out of him if she had to.

Karim suddenly seemed to calm down. He lay back and looked at the ceiling. 'I wonder how you would have coped with the life I have been forced to live woman. You have no idea at all about what me and my people have had to suffer over the years. Protected in your western world, you just have no idea.'

Helen almost laughed again at the remark, it was so full of self-pity and self-justification but she also detected something else, some kernel of truth and even tragedy. 'Why don't you tell me then? Show me how hard everything has been, why it justifies all the crimes you've committed.'

Karim snorted in contempt. 'When I was twelve years old we lived in the Sinai. My father was a farmer, if you could call it farming, we mainly bred goats. At that time there was a war on between Egypt and Israel. It was nothing to do with us. No one asked whether we wanted to be part of it. But that didn't matter. I was lucky. I was out in the rocks looking for a lost goat. An Israeli jet, for no reason that I ever discovered, decided to bomb our house. It was a tiny stone house in the middle of nowhere and was no threat to anyone. That didn't stop the Israeli bastard from pressing his button. I discovered half of my mother and only bits of my father, rather like the meat you find in a market. I dug my brother out of the ruins and he survived. From that day on, we promised we would find out who did this to us and take revenge. That day defined my life.'

Silence settled over the room, Helen was amazed at the simplicity of the way he described such a terrible thing. Eventually, she forced herself to speak. 'That's dreadful but other people have suffered the same or worse and not become monsters.'

'Monsters?' he started to talk again as if he hadn't stopped. 'Khalid and I walked for miles after that. We almost died of thirst but eventually, we were found by a local military unit who passed us on until we found ourselves in a refugee camp. I wonder if you have any idea what a young boy has to do to survive in one of those with no adult to look out for them? We learned hard and we learned fast and we survived. Not only that, we eventually found out who had been flying the plane that day. Palestine and Israel were more open in those days and we managed to track him down. We could have killed him easily but instead we blew up his wife and children in their car. He committed suicide some time later.'

Helen felt sick. 'How could you do that? They were innocents. I could almost forgive you if you had gone for the pilot but to do that to children and the mother is disgusting, unforgivable.'

'Unforgiveable,' Karim said quietly. 'And what about my innocent parents? For that matter what about all the others killed in a stupid war that they had no interest in? A war with a country that your world created out of the homeland of thousands. I believe in an eye for an eye and in this case, we visited on that man what he had done to us. It was justice, nothing more. I would do the same again.'

'So how do you justify what you've done since? I know something of what you did in Beirut. I know exactly what you did to Jon Hunt and the French doctor.'

'That's a good question. What do you do after you've taken your revenge? Some turn to religion, indeed many do. Khalid and I could never believe in any God that would treat his creations in such a way so we decided to look out for each other. Beirut used to be a beautiful city but it soon turned into a cess pit. We did what many others did to survive. The difference was that we were very good at it. I am not a stupid man, I speak five languages, I have an education, mainly self-taught but none the less I am no ignorant peasant. I have a great deal of money. I wonder how many rich men in your world can say they have gained their wealth through totally legitimate means?'

'But you kidnapped people and for all I know did much worse.'

'We learned from an early age that we did what we had to, to survive. But when you've achieved that do you stop? No, you keep going to make your life better. And it wasn't just me. Khalid and I were a team. We worked together and then you bastards killed him. Now somehow I will have my revenge for that.'

Helen thought for a moment. 'And after that what will you do?' There is nowhere you will be able to hide this time. There will be no Beirut to go to ground in, no matter how much money you have.'

'So what? Do you have a brother or sister? For me, I might as well be dead anyway. Now let me get some sleep.'

But he didn't sleep and they soon started to talk again. Helen told him a little of her life. Growing up in an English household was so different from Karim's experience that he had difficulty even understanding some of it. However, her account of a set of loving parents and her relationship with three brothers struck a chord deep inside him, not that he would admit it, even to himself.

Helen realised that the gulf between them was so massive that it could never be bridged. She truly felt sorry for what had happened to him and his brother but despite all the hardships he had evidently endured, there was no way she could forgive his past actions. For his part, he realised he would never be able to comprehend her world but for him that hardly mattered. Their talking had passed the time but that was all. He needed to find a way to escape his confinement. The bomb in the engine room was still there and he knew how to detonate it.

Chapter 41

John Chester left his flat later that evening. He had called in sick that morning when the CIA took him to Langley. The last thing he wanted was the office to find out where and what he was doing. He had called in again and left a voice message for his boss just in case things got even more complicated. He used the underground and then a taxi. With no idea if he was under surveillance or how to counter it if he was, he just made the journey as complicated as he could. However, all too soon he found himself walking up to the doors of the British Embassy. With a quick look round and seeing that no one was taking an undue interest in him, he pushed open the large wooden doors and stepped inside. The entrance hall was lofty and ornate but the man sitting behind the reception desk looked very much the opposite, compact and sturdy.

John went up to him. 'Good evening Sir, I'm so sorry I'm so late but I have some information for you. My name is John Chester and I have some intelligence regarding the hijack of the British cruise ship Uganda which I hope you will find very useful.'

The receptionist looked at him and then nodded before picking up the phone. He waited for a few seconds and then repeated what John had said to the man at the end. 'Please take a seat, an attaché will be down shortly.' He indicated a row of plastic chairs along one wall.

John didn't have to wait long. A tall and rather thin man soon appeared out of the lift at the end of the hall. The receptionist nodded in John's direction and the man came over.

'Mr Chester, my name is Granger. How may I be of assistance?'

John had learned a lot from previous encounters and was very careful to explain how he had come by his information. To his relief the man seemed to accept his story almost straight away and although he had a great deal of questions, at no point did John feel he was being either patronised or disbelieved. When he went on to explain that he had already told the CIA the same story the man frowned.

'I think we had better stop there Mister Chester, maybe you would like to accompany me into the Embassy where you can repeat what you've said to my boss and also where we can keep you out of the way. I have a feeling you haven't made any friends with your own intelligence service.'

Jon was tired and fed up. He had been praying for the go ahead from London nearly all night. If they didn't go soon it would be daylight and another day would have been wasted. Conditions on the Uganda were probably fine as far as food and water went but the psychological pressure must be enormous. It would be the same for the hijackers and that would only make them more trigger happy and dangerous. Jon was feeling the pressure as well, along with all his people. He hadn't taken his own advice when he sent as many of them off to get some sleep and had only managed cat naps on a hard bench. Rupert was no better. They had tried several times to contact the hijackers but to no avail.

Brian's voice boomed across the small operations room. 'Jon, why don't you go to bed, you silly bugger, nothing's going to happen now. I can take over and call you if you're needed, which you won't be for hours yet.' Feeling the grit behind his eyes, Jon was about to finally give in, when Rupert bustled in looking a lot more alert than he had been some time earlier when he was called to the communications office. 'I've been talking to London Jon and things are changing fast. This came in at the same time,' and he handed a signal to Jon. All thought of sleep vanished. Jon initially thought it was the go ahead at last. He quickly realised it was something different entirely. He read it quickly then sat down and read it again more slowly.

'Yes, yes, well done Helen, what a girl.' Then turning to Rupert, 'Hang on, the message was received by this Yank HAM operator two days ago. What the fuck are the Americans up to? It says here he came to the British Embassy early this morning our time. This can't be right.'

'Sorry Jon, the signal doesn't tell the whole story. It seems the Americans are peeved that they aren't involved and wanted to use this as leverage to get invited to the party. They've got one of their assault carriers not too far away and it's full of marines and helicopters.'

'Over my dead body,' Jon responded angrily. 'The only thing the Americans do well is fuck up. Look at the mess they made in

Grenada or when they tried to rescue their own hostages. No way can they get involved.'

'Well they sort of feel that Israel is one of their overseas states, so I can understand why they feel left out,' said Rupert. 'It doesn't excuse what they did but hadn't we better consider the content of Helen's message? The diplomatic fall out will be well above both our pay grades.'

'Yeah you're right, we've got the information now,' Jon replied, handing it to Brian to read. 'Shit, I wonder why she only managed to get one message out. In fact how the hell did she get access to an HF radio in the first place? I just hope she's alright. There's nothing we can do now anyway. OK, so we now know that there are six of them but one is this bastard who kidnapped me. God, it puts a whole new slant on everything. This isn't just the PLF stunt that you thought it was Rupert. It means that they may well be out for revenge. That engine room bomb may well be for real for a start. Christ, I was right. The bombs in Cyprus must have been used to somehow get me to send some of my people out in the Uganda. I'll bet the bastards somehow managed to shoot down the Hercules as well. This whole situation just wound up more notches than I care to think about.'

Brian finished reading as well. 'Six of them, is that good or bad? I'm not sure.'

Jon considered the question. 'I'm not convinced that the numbers are that critical, it's their motives I'm worried about. Those bastards who kidnapped me were nasty pieces of work and one of them ended up dead. I'm guessing that the other one wants some sort of payback, hence the clever ruse to get us to put some of our people on the Uganda. Rupert, we need to consider what we say to them next time.'

'Damned right we do but we mustn't let them know. I am surprised though, because they are behaving as I would expect so far and there has been no hint that they want anything more than the hostage release.'

'Any news on that Rupert?' Jon asked. 'It will definitely draw their teeth if the Israelis agree.'

'Bad news I'm afraid. The Israelis have finally come to a decision and are flatly refusing to negotiate. Our government seems to be in accord. I know you wanted to go in tonight but London is now suggesting that we try and negotiate them off the ship with a promise of safe passage somewhere. Or rather they were. Unfortunately, this new information makes them far less likely to accept such a compromise.'

'So where the hell does that leave us now?'

'Up the bloody creek as far as I can see.'

'Let's sum up then,' Jon suggested with a grim look. 'We thought that they were playing to the crowd and we might have been able to talk them off the ship, which is why London wouldn't let us go in last night. Now we know there is another element to the whole thing and it means that at least one of the bastards is almost certainly after blood. So the chances of ending this without overt action are now far less.'

Rupert grimaced. 'I can't argue with any of that Jon but I can't see what we can do, can you?'

'Well, its been a long night and to pass the time I may have had a few ideas. Look, we've lost all our specialist equipment and people. We don't even have the right helicopters so using our standard tactics is just not going to work, is it?'

Rupert's brow furrowed. Brian, knowing his old friend started to look concerned. 'Why do I think you're going to suggest something that's barking mad and very risky?'

Jon grinned. 'Because that's exactly what I'm going to do.'

Chapter 42

The hours of darkness had been a nightmare for Helen. Despite their earlier talk, she had no intention of going anywhere near Karim. The passkey was under the mattress and she considered trying to retrieve it some time in the night but soon gave up on the idea. It was like having a tethered lion in the room with her, which meant there was nowhere for her to sleep except the floor. She had managed to get him to share some of the bedding but even so, she woke up exhausted and sore. Things had come to a head the previous evening when the requirements of bodily functions had forced Karim into asking for help. Persistent banging on the door had eventually alerted Mohammed who took some convincing to give Karim access to the small toilet and then to manacle him in a manner that at least allowed him to lie down. This meant handcuffing him with his hands in front of him. The problem was solved by locking another pair of cuffs to the link on those around his wrists and securing the other end back to the bed. All the time this was going on one of the other men was watching Karim like a hawk with his weapon trained undeviatingly on him. Helen realised just how dangerous they considered the man to be.

After they left, she asked him. 'They clearly don't like you, so why didn't they just shoot you and chuck you over the side?'

His laugh was tinged with anger. 'Oh, they need me. Guess who will get all the blame when this is over? They will say they never intended to hurt anyone. It was all in the cause of illustrating the plight of Palestine but this madman came with them and ran out of control.'

'So was it you who shot the officer on the bridge?'

He just grunted and didn't answer.

Helen took that as assent and her fear and distrust of the man went up yet another notch.

At last, the night was over and with light now flooding in through the small porthole she used the toilet and drank some water. No food had been provided and the rumbles from her stomach were quite audible. She would ask for food if she got the chance the next time someone looked in on them. When she went back into the cabin she saw that Karim was awake. He had been forced to lie on his side all night but that hadn't stopped him snoring like a hog.

'Good morning Helen,' he seemed almost cheerful. 'Could you get me a drink of water please?'

Slightly surprised by his affability, it nevertheless increased her wariness. She went into the toilet and filled up a tooth mug. When she returned, she handed it to him carefully and then backed off as soon as she could.

He grinned at her. 'Are you scared of me little lady?'

'I'll be honest, you scare the hell out of me. Everything you told me yesterday confirms that you are a psychopath with absolutely no concept of right or wrong. Anyone not scared of you is a fool.'

His eyes narrowed at the remark. 'Maybe that's because our concepts of right and wrong are different.'

Helen had had enough. She was tired, ached all over and fed up. 'No, you arrogant bastard, you use the excuse of your childhood to bolster your belief that the world owes you something and that excuses any behaviour on your part. Fucking grow up.'

He actually looked taken aback just for a moment. Whether it was her language or the fact that no woman had ever spoken to him in such a manner before, he roared with laughter. 'Very well, I can see we will never agree but at least you are not the one handcuffed to the bed.'

The rest of the morning passed in silence. No one came to see them until once more Karim asked Helen to bang on the door. This time only one man came. He gave the handcuff key to Helen and motioned her to release Karim from the bed. It was one of the men who didn't speak English and Helen felt a wave of disquiet while they waited for Karim to finish in the toilet. He seemed to be taking an inordinate amount of time but eventually they heard the toilet flush and the door opened. The guard stood back keeping his rifle raised. Karim said something in Arabic and the man motioned him back towards the bed. Once he was sitting down, Helen moved towards him and picked up the handcuff that was dangling from the bed frame. For just a second she was in line with the guard, blocking his view. Karim acted. He flicked his handcuffed wrists around Helen's neck and pulled her head forward into this chest. At the same time, he lashed out with his right foot catching the guard in the crotch.

Helen was surprised but at the same time, she had been expecting something. She was also having trouble breathing so hard was Karim holding her head into his chest. However, she still had her hands and she reached up raking her nails across his face. He cursed and released the pressure. It was only momentary as he forced her round and got the chain of the handcuffs around her neck and started to strangle her. At the same time, he lashed out with his foot again and kicked the guard's rifle across the room. The guard was doubled over clutching himself but started to straighten out. Karim continued the pressure on her neck and she realised she was losing consciousness. White specks were drifting across her vision and a great lethargy was building. With a savagery bred of desperation, she managed to reach behind her and grab Karim's crotch. She put every ounce of her fading strength into her hand and was rewarded by a slackening of the pressure and a grunt of pain in her left ear. Suddenly, he stood up, lifted the handcuffs from her neck and flung her hard against the steel wall. Her head hit with an agonising crack and her recovering vision started to fade again. The last thing she saw was Karim with the rifle in his hand repeatedly beating the head of the fallen guard and then she slipped into unconsciousness.

Some indeterminate time later, she opened her eyes and wished she hadn't. The pain from her left temple washed over her in a wave. Her throat felt as if it was on fire and in front of her was the bloodied face of the guard. It was quite clear he wasn't breathing but not because she couldn't see his chest moving but from the unnatural angle of his neck. She closed her eyes but it didn't help. She felt the vomit rise in her throat and tried to get up but only managed to get on all fours before throwing up all over the floor. Eventually, getting to her feet, she managed to reach the toilet before being sick again, this time in the toilet bowl. She ran the tap and rinsed her mouth out and then splashed water all over her head. It helped a little but she still felt like she had been run over by a bus. She filled a glass with more water and sat back on the toilet closing her eyes and trying to think. Swallowing was painful but she slowly found her thoughts clearing. Looking at her watch, she realised that, in fact, only ten minutes had elapsed since Karim had pulled his trick and it was now just past noon. As soon as she felt up to it she got to her feet and stepping over the inert body of the guard, she tried the door. As she expected it was locked. She went back to the bed and felt under the mattress. Sure enough, the passkey was still there. Although she still felt dreadful, she realised that staying in the cabin was not an option. She looked around desperately for some sort of weapon and her eye fell on the dead guard again. More in hope than expectation, she searched the body. His holster was empty and there was no sign of the rifle, she was hardly surprised but then she noticed something sticking out proud near this ankle. Lifting the trouser cuff up, she found a wicked looking knife about six inches long in a leather sheath attached to the ankle. Initially, she thought of just taking the blade but she would have nowhere to keep it. So, hiding her revulsion at touching the man's dead skin, she unfastened the sheath and put it on her ankle. Luckily, the loose trousers she was wearing concealed it well.

    With no more reason to stay, she carefully unlocked the door and eased it open. The short corridor to the bridge appeared empty. She slipped out and locked the door behind her, thinking it might convince Karim she was still locked in. She could hear voices coming out of the radio room but didn't wait to hear what they were saying. She had another destination in mind.

Chapter 43

The noon deadline for talking to the hijackers had arrived and Rupert was sitting by the radio with Jon and Brian in attendance. New instructions had been received from London. Helen's delayed message may have made a simple solution less likely but nevertheless Rupert had been told to try. There was a clear indication that if this didn't work and in the absence of a worked up British Special Forces team being available, then London were considering the American option. Dead on time, they heard the voice of Mohammed calling them.

Rupert replied. 'Good morning Mohammed, I hope all is well on board?'

'You can stop trying to be friendly Mr Rupert, I know some of the tricks you are taught. Now, what is the situation with the prisoners?'

Rupert looked at Jon and grimaced. 'Mohammed, they are not going to be released. I'm sure you are expecting me to say that. You know full well that the British Government never deals under duress. The Israeli Government have the same policy. Did you expect anything else?'

'Very well then Rupert, we have no choice but to carry out our promises.'

'Really Mohammed, is that true? You must have known that before you started. What will the world think of the PLF if you start murdering innocent children?'

'There are plenty of adults here to choose from, not just children.'

'Same thing Mohammed, does the PLF really want to be seen as cold blooded murderers?'

'You leave us no choice.'

'Oh no, there is always a choice Mohammed. The British Government is prepared to offer you and your team safe passage from the Uganda to a country of your choice.'

There was no immediate reply. Rupert drummed his fingers on the table and looked worried. Pushing things hadn't been his idea but his instructions were clear.

Mohammed came back on the radio. He sounded less sure of himself. 'How would you guarantee that?'

Rupert silently shook his fist in jubilation but kept his voice even. 'That's up to you Mohammed. You are currently only a few miles away from the coast of Egypt. We could allow a boat to come and take you off. You could then fly out of Egypt. Their government have already agreed to let that happen and you can choose your destination.'

There was another long silence.

'And what if we don't agree?'

'Mohammed, you must know that we have military contingencies for this sort of situation. We know the risks but if you leave us no choice we will have to act. Your chances of survival are not good. You must understand that if you leave us no option, you will be forcing our hand.'

Rupert waited a few moments. He turned to Jon. 'If Helen was right, I'm surprised that this is going so well. We've not heard from Karim at all.' Turning back to the radio, he continued. 'And we will want a guarantee that the bomb you say is in the engine room is disarmed.'

Silence greeted his last remark. Then Mohammed replied, 'we will give your suggestion some consideration Rupert.' Suddenly, there was a strange noise like a sharp explosion and the radio went dead.

'What the fuck was that?' Rupert asked.

'Sounded like a gunshot to me,' Jon replied.

Rupert tried calling again but there was no reply. 'Oh shit, something's happened and why don't I think it will be for the best?'

The radio crackled into life. 'Is that the British negotiator?'

The hackles on Jon's neck rose, he knew that voice. 'That's Karim, the guy who kidnapped me. I'd know that voice anywhere.'

'Yes, my name is Rupert, who am I talking to?'

'That is none of your business. The rules have changed, so just listen. The man you were speaking to may have been prepared to negotiate. He is no longer in a position to do so. There will be no further negotiation. If the prisoners are not being released in four hours, the first of my hostages will be executed. The first will be a young lady called Helen Barratt. I am sure you know who she is. After that, for every hour you delay, I will execute one of the five adults who boarded this ship in Cyprus. Again, you know exactly who I am talking about. If you still refuse to submit to my demands I will then start on the children. One of you knows me very well and also knows that I am quite prepared to carry out this threat. You have four hours no more. I will be on this frequency at sixteen hundred.' The radio went dead.

Rupert desperately tried to call back but there was no response.

'Fucking, fucking bastard,' Jon was beside himself. 'Four hours, not even the Yanks could respond in that time. Rupert, we have to act and act now.'

Rupert looked stricken, for a few minutes it looked like the whole situation was about to be defused. Now. it looked desperate. He couldn't see any other choice either. He looked at Jon. 'Can you do it in time?'

'Do we have any choice?'

Karim put down the microphone with a feeling of triumphant satisfaction. The pain from the scratches on his face and the ache in his groin were fading as he contemplated the future. He looked around the radio room. The radio officer, who was handcuffed to his chair, looked petrified and had been sick all over his desk. That wasn't really surprising as most of Mohammed's brains had sprayed across him when Karim had come in and shot him in the head. The three remaining PLF soldiers were on the bridge. They had come running when they heard the shot but not one was prepared to face down Karim. He had curtly ordered them out of the radio shack and was unsurprised when they obeyed. He now went back to the bridge. The Captain was still there handcuffed and sitting on the floor, Karim ignored him. He faced the three soldiers.

'Mohammed was about to sell us out, did any of you know that?'

Karim strongly suspected that they did. He also knew that they would do as they were told but he would need to keep them under tight control. 'Just in case you think I am weak, like Mohammed, your comrade is lying in the Captain's cabin with a broken neck. He is keeping the young girl company. If any of you want to follow him, then disobey me and you will find out just what I can do, do you understand?'

The three nodded warily.

'We have a new deadline, at four o'clock. If they haven't started to release our comrades then we start with the girl and after that the adults in the accommodation.'

One of the men looked as if he was about to speak. 'Go on, you want to say something.'

'Isn't that too tight? They will never be able to start releasing them in such a short time.'

'Of course not but it means we will be able to start some executions and then they will definitely realise we mean business. We were never going to be able to convince the bastards without spilling a little blood. So, now we show our true resolve.'

Helen was able to get back to the classroom with surprising ease. There were a few of the passengers about but they seemed to want to keep to themselves. It felt eerie and strange, the whole ship had been so lively. Now, it was like a morgue even though the majority of the passengers were not restricted. When she got to the classroom, she was relieved to find the radio was still where she had left it under a pile of other scientific bits and pieces. No one seemed to have been back there for which she was profoundly grateful. It only took moments to set it up again and as she had no idea what frequency she should use, she left it set as before and made a tentative call. To her astonishment, two people answered almost at once. At first, they spoke over the top of each other and all she could hear was a sort of mangled conversation with the odd word clear as one or the other stopped first.

Then a strong American voice managed to make itself heard. 'Other stations on this frequency, please get off the air.'

A British voice then broke in. 'This is British Intelligence operating in the clear. If the unidentified American on this frequency makes any further attempt to interrupt, it will be added to the catalogue of crimes that you have already committed and may I remind you that this a public HAM frequency that can be heard by others. Now you, get off the air you bastard.'

For a moment there was silence, then the British voice came on again. 'Is this Helen Barratt?'

Completely nonplussed by the earlier exchange, Helen was nevertheless relieved that this time she was clearly talking to someone who actually wanted to listen to her. 'Yes, this is Helen. I have escaped confinement on the Uganda and need to talk to someone.'

Arapaho

'Helen, that's fine. Now listen we have a ship not too far away and they have been told to come on to this frequency as well. You can talk to them in a moment. Can you confirm that all is still well on the Uganda?'

'No, not really, one of the terrorists is a known criminal and seems to have taken over. I assume you have heard my previous message from the other day, well he wasn't in charge then but I very much suspect that he is now.'

'OK Helen, well done, we have some information about that as well. However, I am going to hand you over to the Arapaho, who I am sure you know and they will take it from here. Good luck.'

The radio went quiet for a second and then an all too familiar voice started speaking. 'Helen, this is Jon on Arapaho, are you alright? You sound strange.'

With tears of relief starting in her eyes she answered, 'yes Jon I'm fine, although being nearly strangled might have affected my voice.'

'Oh my God but you're OK now?'

'Yes, I'm fine. I'll tell you the rest some other time. I don't know how long I can stay on the radio. You know Karim is free?'

'We know more than that. He seems to have taken over and says you are going to be the first hostage to be executed at four today. Does he know you've escaped?'

'I guess not. I was able to sneak clear. I'll tell you all about it later. Oh and Karim has killed one of his own people so there are only five of them now.'

'Actually, we think he must have shot the guy using the radio as well so there are probably only four.'

'You may well be right.'

'OK, now, do you know where the other squadron wives and kids are?'

'Yes, they're in an accommodation area near the stern, port side, five deck, Juliet section. Oh and Jon, I put a fire hose over the stern the other day in case you needed help getting on board. It's still there.'

'Clever girl, we saw it. Now listen, I can't go into detail we have very little time but we're going to do a boarding in daylight, in about an hour in fact, just a small team. If you can be at the stern to help that would be great but if you need to hide then do so.'

'In daylight Jon, how on earth are you going to do that?'

Arapaho

He told her.

Chapter 44

For Karim, the time before his deadline expired seemed to be dragging. At least he had managed to get some food and drink and was feeling a little better in himself. Soon he would be able to offer Khalid some of the revenge he had planned. The girl had caused him a great deal of grief. He decided that an hour before the deadline, he would pay her a visit and take some extra pleasure and then to keep his three men on-side, he would let them use her as well. Knowing the sort of tastes they generally had, she might even be grateful when her final time came.

Looking out of the bridge window, he was surprised that he could see so many other ships. He turned to the Captain who was still sitting bound on the floor.

'The area seems pretty busy with ships, Captain. Surely they would have been warned to keep clear?'

'We are very close to Alexandria now. It would be impossible to route them totally away from us. You'd better pray you don't see any grey ones.'

Karim laughed. 'Warships you mean. Oh, I'm sure they are out there somewhere but they are not stupid enough to come close, especially in daylight.'

'No and you won't see them in the dark.'

'What do you mean by that?'

'Come on, you can't be that stupid. You must know they won't let you get away with killing hostages. They will attempt a boarding at some time.'

Of course Karim was well aware of that but as far as he was concerned it would give him the excuse to blow the whole damned ship up. After that, he was prepared to take his chances, slim though they might be. However, he wasn't so sanguine about his other three men He was pretty sure none of them spoke English but kicked the Captain hard in ribs and told him to shut up, just in case. However, the Captain's words made him realise he probably needed to be more vigilant so he sent two of them out on to either bridge wing to keep a lookout and told the third man to keep his eyes out as well.

About half an hour later a large container ship was starting to get quite close. She had appeared well ahead and seemed to be crossing

Uganda's bow from starboard. However, at some point she must have slowed down because even to Karim's untrained eye it looked like they might collide. Karim turned to the Captain and hauled him to his feet.

'What is that ship doing Captain?'

'I've no idea but she is meant to keep clear of us by the international collision regulations because she crossing from starboard.'

Karim didn't really understand what the Captain was saying but was saved from asking. There was an enormous gout of flame from the container ship near the bow, which was followed seconds later by the sound of an explosion. Suddenly, the bridge radio burst into life. 'Mayday, Mayday, Mayday, this is container ship Southern Providence, we are twenty two miles north of Alexandria. We have had a container explosion and a severe fire. Request immediate assistance.'

Karim acted quickly. 'Captain, get us away from here as fast as you can, this is none of our business.'

The Captain ordered an immediate change of course away from the stricken container ship and increased speed to twenty knots. In a matter of minutes, they were drawing well clear. However, everyone on the bridge watched in fascination as the fire continued to burn, sending a large plume of black smoke into the afternoon sky. Other ships did seem to be responding but the Uganda was well clear.

Karim looked at his watch and was surprised to see it was almost three o'clock. He turned to his man on the bridge. 'I am going to pay our pretty little hostage a visit. When I've finished with her you and the others can treat her as you like. We will then check the radio but I'm sure she will be going for a swim. So make sure you leave her at least partially able to appreciate her fate.'

The man looked surprised and then a large grin spread across his face. Karim was content that there would no trouble from that quarter, for a while at least. He went down the corridor and after drawing his pistol, he unlocked the cabin door. The body of the dead soldier was the first thing he saw. He would have to move that into the toilet. The whole place stank of vomit but that wasn't anything new. Then he realised the girl wasn't there. She must be hiding in the toilet. Kicking the door in, he was amazed to find it was empty. Looking around he confirmed she wasn't hiding anywhere. The door

Arapaho

had been locked when he opened it. She must have had a key but where did she get it?

He rushed angrily back to the bridge calling for his men. 'The girl has managed to get out of the cabin. Go and look for her and when you find her do not be too gentle, understand?'

'What if we can't find her before four o'clock?'

'We will use one of the other women but I want this one found. You have over an hour, now go.'

The RIB felt extremely small, even with only four people in it, as the Arapaho steamed away from them. Jon and the three marines had been dropped off astern of Uganda and then the Arapaho had dashed off ahead, to get ready for her diversion. One of the Sea Kings was airborne, keeping eye on things, which gave Jon a bit more confidence. So much could still go wrong. Uganda needed to keep to her course and speed for a start. They only had four people in the RIB because a quick trial showed that any more and it just wouldn't go fast enough. What might have worked at night wasn't going to be effective in daylight, where speed would be the key. Rupert was extremely put out not to be included but as it was a military operation, Jon pulled rank and insisted he would be going. Jon was driving and Sergeant Smithers and his two marines; Thompson and Jones, were checking their weapons yet again. The sea was relatively calm which once Jon used full throttle would give them just about twenty five knots. In the distance, he could clearly see Uganda's stern but it looked a long way away. His hand-held radio broke into life.

'RIB this is Victor Bravo, Mother will be in position on time. Can you confirm you are ready, over?'

Jon looked at the target and if the calculations they had pored over were correct then everything was going as planned. Without an accurate method of measuring his closing speed, he would have to rely on those. 'Affirmative, Victor Bravo, looks good, we are continuing. Try to keep an eye on us both without getting near the target, over.'

'I'll do my best Jon. I'll call when you need to get going, good luck, out.'

Jon knew that to keep out of visual range of the Uganda the Sea King would be lucky to be able to see the two ships and the RIB with any clarity but any spare pair of eyes could be invaluable if anything changed.

Sergeant Smithers looked enquiringly at Jon, who responded. 'All set Sergeant, are you all ready?'

The Sergeant nodded. 'As we'll ever be, Sir.'

They sat in silence with the engine giving them about eight knots which should keep the distance from Uganda reasonably constant. Arapaho was turning now to start to cross the Uganda's bows and the radio came to life again 'Go, go, go.'

Jon gave a terse 'Roger' and pushed the throttle hard forward. The rib accelerated hard and came up on the plane. The marines were holding on and one of them turned and grinned at Jon. It was hard not to be exhilarated but Jon knew this was the most dangerous part of the approach. Anyone looking back now would see them and the game would be up.

Even though they were several miles away, they heard the explosion quite clearly and soon saw the tell-tale pall of smoke. Jon hoped they were enjoying themselves on the flight deck behind the containers. That was a lot of diesel they were burning as well as using up two of their precious stun grenades.

The gap was closing fast when the Uganda started to turn and Jon could see the wake behind her boil up. She was clearly increasing speed.

'Fuck, this could make thing rather interesting,' Jon muttered as he turned to follow. The marines had seen it as well. Jon shouted to them over the engine's roar, 'she's just getting out of the way as we expected. We know her top speed is twenty knots. We should still be able to get there.'

The range continued to close but now it was getting much harder to catch up with the cruise ship. As they started to encounter her wake, they were bouncing hard over the waves streaming from her stern and Jon was forced to move out to one side. Otherwise, he would have to slow down and they would never reach her. He prayed they wouldn't be seen and then with a lurch of fear he saw a face at the stern rail of the quarterdeck. A hand then appeared and waved at them and with a mixture of relief and anxiety he realised it was Helen. At the same time, he realised that climbing the fire hose was going to be just about impossible if the ship kept at the same speed. There was no way he could keep the RIB under control directly over the plume of the wake directly behind the stern. With agonising slowness they crept up on the massive ship, all the while being deluged with spray. Jon was even having trouble seeing now as the salt water was being blasted into his eyes with the force of a half gale. Waving desperately at Helen, he pointed to the starboard side of the ship as he drove the RIB clear of the wake and under the ship's counter. He pointed at the hose and then a point above where he was managing to keep station.

'Clever girl,' he muttered as she immediately worked out what to do and started to retrieve the hose. Within a minute, she had lowered it directly above them and then leant out and gave a clear thumbs up. Sergeant Smithers made several grabs at the wildly swinging hose and managed to get hold at the third try. Marine Thompson, the winner of the Arapaho hose climbing contest the day before, then got a hold and leapt up. Another line tied to the RIBs bow uncoiled from his backpack as he climbed. All the while, Jon was fighting the bucking RIB trying desperately to keep it as close to the massive wall of the ship and underneath her overhang. Thompson made easy work of climbing the hose, even though he seemed to bang into the side several times. Within a minute, he had disappeared over the guard rails. They saw him then hand the rope he had taken with him along the deck and eventually pull it tight and tie it on. Experimentally, Jon closed the throttle slightly. The RIB drifted back a few feet as the line became taught and then stopped. It banged against the steel side of the ship occasionally but the large rubber tubes of its hull seemed to give adequate protection. The next thing that happened was that Thompson lowered the rope ladder he had been carrying. Jon looked at the Sergeant who nodded back. Jon shut the engine down completely and made his way carefully to the side of the bucking RIB. The Sergeant handed him a Bergen which he put on his back and then he made a grab for the ladder. It was much easier to climb than the hose and Jon had practiced it when it was dangling from Arapaho's crane but this was altogether different. Firstly, it seemed a bloody long way and as he got higher the swinging and banging got worse. Forcing himself not to look down and taking each step with care, he soon saw the guard rail approaching. Once he reached it and before he could wonder how on earth he would actually manage to climb over, a strong hand grabbed the straps of his Bergen and he was lifted bodily over the rail and unceremoniously dumped on the deck. Breathing hard and infinitely grateful to Marine Thompson, he got to his feet to be confronted by Helen. She looked drawn and tired. The side of her head was matted with blood and there was a horrible livid red mark around her neck. Jon didn't care, she looked beautiful. He grabbed her quickly and gave her an enormous hug. 'Let's get the others on board, OK?'

She nodded. He pulled off the Bergen and went to help Thomson who had already been joined by Marine Jones. Between them, they helped the Sergeant on board. Thompson then went forward and cut the RIB's bow line, which drifted rapidly away in the wake. Helen then called to them to follow her and she led them into the store room behind the science classroom.

'Is this place safe?' Jon asked as soon as the door was closed.

'As safe as anywhere. They may be looking for me now. It's getting close to four o'clock. What are you planning to do?'

Jon exchanged a glance with the Sergeant and snorted, 'take out the bad guys, save the hostages, you know, just like in the films.'

They stripped off the lifejackets they had been wearing and opened their Bergens. Each armed themselves with a wicked looking sub machine gun and pistol. Jon handed one to Helen. 'You know how to use it don't you?'

She nodded and tucked it into a pocket.

Each of them took one stun grenade, the last of their stock and made themselves ready.

'Right Helen, what's the situation as far as you know it?'

'Karim was on the bridge when I last saw him or rather the radio room which is just behind it. I don't know the status of the other guys. I do know they had turned on him and were going to use him as a scapegoat. He told me that himself but then he got free. We were locked away together for a night. Jon, he's seriously paranoid and seems to only want to avenge his brother. You aren't dealing with a rational person but he's bloody smart. From what you said Jon, he took out the guy on the radio which was probably Mohammed the other leader. He's the one who has been doing all the talking. I don't think the others speak English. I've no idea where their loyalty lies. Otherwise, everyone on the ship has been given their normal freedom except for the squadron wives and kids. They've been locked up as I told you on the radio.'

'Thanks Helen, let me just check in with home.' Jon used their portable VHF radio to tell those on Arapaho that phase one was complete and they were safe and sound for the moment. He then looked at his watch. 'It's twenty to four, if they can't find you, then I suspect the families will be next so we need to get there first. Do you know the way Helen?'

Before she could answer, they heard the sound of footsteps and as they pointed their weapons at the door it opened and an angry face peered in.

Chapter 45

'Robert what are you doing here?' Helen asked the small boy who was staring in awe at the four machine guns pointing at him.

He ignored her completely. 'Hey, are those SMGs? They're really cool. I've seen them in my comics. Hey, are you here to take out the bad guys? My name's Robert and I'm the Science Monitor but I guess it's alright for you to be here.'

Jon and the others were a little bemused. 'Er, yes Robert now look come in and shut the door please. Now, tell us, is there anything going on in the ship right now?'

He screwed up his face. 'Well some of the bad guys have been running around looking for you Helen but we haven't seen them for a while now.'

'Right, that does it. We need to get to our people as soon as we can. Robert can you go back and tell everyone to keep clear of the back of the ship on five deck?'

Helen continued. 'Robert, it's just below us, a couple of decks down. Go and tell your teacher, Mr Spencer, wasn't it?'

'That's right. I'll go now shall I?'

'Yes off you go, there's a good boy, we're really grateful.' Jon answered, as he left with a look of determination on his face. 'OK Helen, lead on, time is getting really tight.'

She led them out through the classroom and into the passageway beyond. 'See that door there,' she said indicating a metal door a few yards ahead. 'It opens on a stairwell that goes from five deck up to here. Go down two decks and turn right to get to Juliet section. Oh and you will need this, it opens all the door locks in the ship.' She handed Jon the passkey.

'Good Grief girl, you are so full of surprises,' Jon said in admiration. 'Sergeant this is your call now, we follow your orders.'

It took only a few minutes to traverse the stairs and get to the locked door of the families accommodation. The whole place was eerily empty. Just as they reached the first locked door they felt the throb of the engines drop away and the ship slowed down. Jon gave the passkey to Sergeant Smithers who carefully unlocked the door. As he pushed it slowly open he called out to those inside. 'Hello there, we've come to get you.....,' he didn't finish the sentence as something heavy flew through the door and caught him full in the face. He fell back and a large suitcase dropped on top of him.

'Stop it,' yelled Jon. 'We're not the hijackers. Kathy, its Jon we've just got on board.'

Taking silence for understanding, Jon pushed the door open to be confronted by five angry looking ladies and one of the ship's officers all armed with an assortment of makeshift weapons. Jon was immediately recognised and frightened faces turned to smiles and then urgent questions. Jon held his hand up. 'Now listen, it's not all over. We think some of the hijackers will be down this way very soon. We need to get you all away from the doors and under cover. Where are the kids?'

Kathy stepped forward. 'They're all next door Jon. Should we join them?'

'Yes, anyone coming down will have to get past us first and believe me that won't happen.'

Sergeant Smithers re-joined them with a rueful smile. 'I don't know what's in that suitcase ladies but that was a good trick. Yes, please do as Lieutenant Commander Hunt says and go in with the children and keep down. Miss Barratt would you go too. Things could get nasty around here soon.'

For a moment it looked like Helen might argue but she saw the sense in the suggestion and went off with Kathy.

'Right Sir, this is what we're going to do.'

On the bridge, Karim's level of anger was slowly building. Instead of being able to enjoy the girl and then confound the British negotiator, he was stuck here with his men somewhere in the ship. He was just about to use the main broadcast to order them back when one returned.

'There is no sign of her Karim,' the man offered. 'This is a big ship and it would take hours to find her. I wouldn't be surprised if the other passengers are hiding her.'

Karim made his decision. 'Go and get one of the females from the cabin down at the back. That will have to do.'

'Which one?'

'I don't care. No, get that red headed one, the bossy one. She will have to do. And don't be too fussy how you treat her. Just drag her up here.'

The man nodded and left.

Karim turned to the Captain. 'Make us slow down old man we don't need to be going anywhere now.'

Sergeant Smithers had his men move down the corridor and take up positions. There were two avenues of approach to the accommodation area. Someone going there would either have to come down the stairwell or along the corridor from forward. There were more cabins along the corridor but a quick check confirmed they were all empty. He stationed Marine Thompson well forward behind a cabin door with instructions to let anyone past before breaking cover. Jones stayed aft just up from the cabin with the families in it. There was a toilet and bathroom that he could hide in. The Sergeant and Jon went into the stairwell and concealed themselves below the stairs themselves. Anyone coming down would have to turn and look behind them as they exited into the corridor which would be unlikely and almost certainly fatal. However, the Sergeant stressed the need to only use the guns as an absolute last resort. Discharging a weapon between the steel walls was a recipe for ricochets taking out as many good guys as bad.

The silence stretched out. Jon looked at his watch. It was now only ten minutes to four. Had they done the right thing? Had the hijackers just grabbed one of the passengers at random? His thoughts shut off as they heard the sound of voices coming down the stairs. Jon and Sergeant Smithers tensed as the footsteps echoed over their heads. There were several of them, Jon reckoned two maybe three individuals. As if reading his mind, the Sergeant held up three fingers and Jon nodded in confirmation. The chattering in what must have been Arabic continued. The men seemed casual almost happy. They reached the bottom of the stairs, opened the door and stepped into the corridor. The Sergeant and Jon followed once they were clear and stepped out into the corridor.

'Drop your weapons,' the Sergeant called in his parade ground voice while raising his SMG. The men spun around with various looks of astonishment as they stared down the barrels of two machine guns held by two soldiers who had no right to be there. A noise from behind made them realise that there was another soldier covering them from the rear. Two of the men didn't even have their weapons ready. They were slung across their backs. With no other option, they raised their hands in surrender. Unfortunately, the third man had his AK47 in his hands. Whether he acted deliberately or on instinct would never be known but instead of raising his hands, he pulled the trigger. The weapon was set to fully automatic. Over seventy five million AK47s have been made. One of the major reasons for the weapon's success is its reliability and it performed perfectly now. As it fired, the barrel flew up and a line of bullets hosed upwards catching Sergeant Smithers in his left side. With no other option to him, Jon pulled the trigger of his SMG at precisely the same time that Marine Jones opened up. The three terrorist were caught in the crossfire and didn't stand a chance. Unfortunately, before Jon could stop and as they had feared, several of his rounds hit Marine Jones in the legs and he also fell. Suddenly, the firing stopped. Jon was the only person still standing. The acrid smell of cordite filled the air and his ears were ringing from the noise of the weapons which had been made much worse by the confined space. Thompson ran up behind Jon and they both dropped to see what could be done for the Sergeant who was still conscious but there was blood seeping from his left arm and side. Jon realised he was completely deaf and indicated in sign language for Thompson to go and see to Jones, who also seemed to be conscious. Jon ripped open the shell dressing they all carried and pushed it firmly against the worst wound in the Sergeant's side just as the door to the cabin opened and Helen's face appeared. She took in the scene quickly, turned to say something behind her and then the women came out. She came up to Jon and said something but all could see was her lips moving. He shook his head and pointed to his ears. She immediately understood and took his hand off the shell dressing and replaced it with hers.

It took some time before Jon's hearing started to return. By which time the wounded had been taken into the cabin by the girls and were being expertly tended to. One of the wives was a nurse and several had been first aid trained, including Helen. It seemed that both the marines would survive. The Sergeant's chest wound was more of a graze although his left arm was badly broken. Marine Jones wasn't going to be walking anywhere soon but again he wasn't in any imminent danger. Of the hijackers, two were dead but one had survived and would probably pull through as well. One of the wives spoke a little Arabic and managed to discover that there were only the three of them plus the man on the bridge. And that was what was worrying Jon. It was now several minutes past four, the men hadn't returned to the bridge and the deadline was past. He had no idea what Karim would do now so he needed to act and act quickly.

He called over to Marine Thompson. 'Can you hear me?' he asked.

'Yes Sir, there's no need to shout.'

'Sorry but I was a lot closer to the guns. Look, there's one hijacker left and he's the most dangerous. We know he was on the bridge. We're the only two left, so we've got to go up there to try to find him and take him out.'

Helen had come up behind them. 'No Jon, I want to come along as well, I've got a score to settle with that man and I know him better than anyone else.'

Jon turned, she looked like she had been through a wringer. She still had dried blood on the side of her head and her neck looked dreadful. She also looked very determined. Jon didn't have time for arguments and anyway she knew her way around the ship better than anyone else. 'Alright but on one condition, you do exactly what you're told, is that clear?'

'Of course.'

'Right, have you used an SMG before?'

'No, I only trained on the SLR and pistol.'

'It's effectively the same. You cock it by pulling this slide back and this lever is for single shot or fully automatic as well as being the safety, got it?'

She took the weapon and nodded.

'OK this is what we'll do. Helen, you take us to the bridge. When we get close, you stay behind Thompson and me. If he's there, we try to take him out, no negotiating. What's worrying me is that talk of a bomb, so even if he's not there, we get the ship to go to emergency stations or whatever the civvies call it. That has to our first priority.' He turned to the Sergeant who was now sitting up. 'Sorry you can't join us Sergeant but if you hear an alarm you are going to have to try to get up to the boat deck. I'll try and get some help down to you if it comes to that.'

'Don't worry Sir we'll work it out. You just go and get that bugger on the bridge.'

It took longer than expected. There were some passengers about and Jon couldn't take time out to talk to them but every encounter delayed them a little. Finally, they reached the stairs leading up to the bridge. Jon motioned Helen to get behind and with Marine Thompson alongside. He readied his SMG and carefully climbed up.

The short corridor ahead of them was empty so they made their way carefully along it. There was a strange, unpleasant smell to the place, a mixture of cordite and vomit mixed with the more usual odours of diesel and paint. The door to the radio shack was open and Jon glimpsed a body lying on the floor but also a figure sitting in a chair. He quickly saw that the man in the chair, clearly a ship's officer, was also dead. He was slumped forward with his head on the desk in front of him in a pool of blood. Jon felt his gorge rise but waved Thompson past and gently closed the door. There was nothing to be achieved in letting Helen see what was in there. They reached the back of the bridge. Jon peered carefully in but couldn't see anyone at all. Motioning Thompson to follow, he crept carefully further in and immediately saw that their quarry wasn't there. What he did see was the slumped body of another man in uniform off to one side.

Fearing the worst, he approached the man and immediately saw his chest was rising and falling There was no sign of a struggle. As Jon approached, the man who he surmised must be the Captain, opened his eyes in astonishment.

'Captain Edwards? My name is Lieutenant Commander Hunt. We managed to get on board. We've dealt with three of the hijackers. Do you know where the other one has gone?'

'Help me up first, please.'

Jon and Thompson helped him to his feet as Helen also came in and joined them. 'Yes, I know where he is, it's the only reason I'm still alive.'

As he spoke, Thompson got out his knife and cut the cable ties on the Captain's wrists.

'Thank you. Yes, he heard the gunshots from down aft just before the radio call. I know because I heard him shouting into the radio soon after and then another shot. Did he kill Derek?'

'If you mean the radio operator, yes I'm afraid he did.'

The Captain closed his eyes briefly. 'The bastard, he killed another of my officers on the day they got on board. I hope you do the same to him.'

'So where is he?'

'With his bloody bomb.'

'It's in the engine room right?'

'I'm afraid so. They took me with them when they first took over the ship and showed me exactly where it was so I knew they meant business.'

'We did wonder about that because this ship is steam powered. Surely there would be ship's staff in there?'

'No, only in the boiler room in the next forward compartment. The engine room has two steam turbines and they're remotely controlled. They must have done their homework before they got here because they knew that already. It's the largest compartment in the ship and if it gets holed it will almost certainly sink us.'

'Shit, so what did the guy say?'

'He wants you, the leader of the boarding team and the girl Helen, to go to him in the engine room. He said he will wait for you but not for long. Otherwise, he will detonate the bomb and kill as many of us as he can. And I believe him. He's crazy enough to do it.'

'Alright, we'll do it his way. I was thinking of making the ship go to emergency stations but if I set off the alarm he will be alerted. Where are the other ship's officers?'

'They locked the deck officers in their cabins one deck down. There are five of them.'

Jon turned to Helen. 'Have you still got the passkey?'

When she produced it, he passed it to the Captain.

'I'll let them out.' The Captain said.

'Yes, get them all up here as soon as you can,' and Jon went on to tell him what he wanted him to do.

Chapter 46

Helen and Jon were arguing. 'You've got to let me come along Jon. If I'm not there he's going to set that bomb off.'

'Helen, he's going to set it off anyway. Surely you realise that? My job is to buy as much time as possible. Down in the engine room he won't be able to hear everyone moving about or even the helicopters at the bow. It's going to take time to get everyone off and I need to get us that breathing space. You being there won't help.'

'But it will. If he doesn't hear my voice he will get suspicious straight away.'

'Yes but I'm going to tell him who I am. He knows me remember? That should take his mind off you.'

'Are you really sure of that? Because I'm not and it's a risk we shouldn't be taking.'

Jon's real problem was that he knew that Helen was right but he really didn't want to expose her to anything more. She had done quite enough already. He tried to explain, 'look I just don't want you in any more danger. I want you off the Uganda and safe.'

'Well, that's not going to happen.' She looked him straight in the eye.

Jon gave up. He knew how determined Helen could be. 'Alright but we do this my way understand?'

She nodded but didn't say anything.

'The Captain says the bomb was in a suitcase sized container and they put it under one of the steam turbines. They opened it and showed him. There's some sort of timer on it. It will certainly be big enough to blow a hole in the hull. So what we've got to do is keep him talking as long as possible. There's only one hatch down into the engine room and he will be able to see us as soon as we start going down. I'll try to get a conversation going before we enter if that's possible. Marine Thompson, I want you to follow but well back. If at any time you feel you have a clear shot at him, you take it. Don't wait for instructions just do it, is that clear?'

Thompson nodded.

'It's not much of a plan but it's the best I can think of, any questions?'

There were none, so the three of them set off quickly back into the bowels of the ship. At the same time, the first passengers, alerted by the ship's officers, were rapidly going the other way to the lifeboat stations.

The engine room was near the stern and the raised access hatch was set in the floor. The hatch itself was held up by a large metal spring clip. John motioned Thompson to hang back as he and Helen cautiously approached. Looking down, Jon could see a large tangle of white lagged pipes and what he assumed were the two massive turbines and these were also clad in some sort of white lagging.

'Karim,' he called out loudly. 'This is Lieutenant Commander Hunt. You might just remember me, we've met before.'

Silence greeted his call but he wasn't surprised, the level of noise in the engine room was extremely high. Not just the turbines but various fans and pumps, all adding to the cacophony.

He tried calling louder a second time again with no result. He turned to Helen, 'I'll go down. You stay here for the moment.' He saw she was about to argue. 'No, there's absolutely no reason for us both to do this.'

'Oh but there is. I really want you both down there.' The voice was accompanied by the sound of a rifle being cocked.

Startled, Jon looked up, straight into Karim's eyes and the barrel of an AK47.

'You didn't think I would be stupid enough to just sit down there and wait for you? Oh, I see you did. Well, it's too late. Now, tell your tame soldier down the corridor to join us please. Don't think about moving. I will shoot the girl, so even if you might risk your life Mister Hunt, it will be her that goes first.'

With a feeling of despair, Jon called to Thompson to join them and Karim very quickly disarmed them all. He handed Helen a package of cable ties and watched carefully as she secured the two men's hands behind their backs. He then did the same to her before pulling the men's ties much tighter than she had done and carefully searching them for further weapons. When he was satisfied, he ordered them down into the engine room. Climbing over the hatch and down the steep stairs was no easy task and Jon did his best in taking his time but all too soon, all three of them were standing on the metal grating between the two turbines.

'I take it my men fell foul of your people a while ago? Did any survive?' He had to shout over the noise of all the machinery.

No one answered. Karim thought for a moment and swiftly backhanded Helen across the face. She shouted in pain and fell to the floor. Rage consumed Jon and he attempted to kick out at Karim who dodged him easily and then put the rifle to Helen's temple. Jon pulled back, his face a white mask of anger.

Karim smiled. 'So, now we have established that I really want my questions answered. I will ask again. What happened to my men?'

'Two are dead and one is wounded.'

'Thank you Mister Hunt, that wasn't so hard now was it?'

Jon stared stonily back. 'Typical isn't it, you bastard, always hurt the women. But there again you are a born coward, living off the proceeds of kidnapping.'

'Good try Mister Hunt but you won't goad me and for that matter, you won't delay me any more. You see my little bomb will be going off soon and I really don't want to be around when it does. You, on the other hand, will be able to watch the whole thing.' He checked his watch. 'After all, I am one of the ship's stewards and there is just time for me to go and get my uniform and evacuate with the rest of the ship, which I am sure is going on as we speak?'

Jon looked stonily back.

'Nothing to say? That's fine by me. Now, please sit down next to that railing.'

He pulled Helen to her feet and once again got her to cable tie the men's bound hands to the railing behind them before doing the same to her. He then checked the bindings and satisfied that they would never have time to get free, he simply started to walk away.

'At least your fucking brother wasn't a coward,' Jon shouted at Karim's retreating back. 'Mind you he got himself shot to pieces for being so fucking stupid didn't he?'

Karim halted in mid-stride. For a second, Jon thought he might have got through but then Karim shrugged, looked pointedly at his watch and continued up the ladder. Seconds later, a loud clang was heard as the metal hatch was dropped.

'Fuck, fuck, fuck,' Jon shouted at the room as he struggled against his bonds. Thompson was doing the same but Helen was sitting more calmly.

'Jesus, this is just like a cheap film with the baddie leaving the good guys to die. Shit except it's for real. Any luck Thompson?'

'No Sir, they're really strong these ties. We need a knife.'

'I've got one.'

Yeah, well in the films someone would have a hidden knife but this isn't a bloody film.'

'I've got one.'

'Fuck what do we do now?'

'Jon, will you bloody well listen to me.' Helen was almost screaming now. 'I've got a knife in a sheath around my left ankle.'

Jon looked at her in astonishment. 'You can tell me how later. Can you get your ankle behind me to where my hands are?'

'I'll try.' And with a lot of wriggling, she managed to almost turn round and push her left foot up behind Jon's back. He reached with his hands and felt the cuff of her trousers with the sheath below it. Carefully, he managed to pull the trouser leg clear and get a grip on the handle.

'Right Helen, I've got a grip on the knife but can't pull it free. You're going to have to pull while I hold the knife OK?'

Helen pulled her leg free and Jon felt the knife slide out of its sheath and immediately out of his fingers. It hit the grating below him with a clang. Terrified that it might slip through the mesh of the grating, he started to strain down with his fingertips.

'It's alright Sir, it's caught with the handle sticking up,' Thompson called. He had twisted around to watch what was going on. 'Move to your right a bit, now you're above it.'

With a massive effort that forced the plastic of the cable ties deep into the skin of his wrists, Jon managed to grab the knife. For a second he lay back and then very carefully reversed it so that the blade was upwards. He was then able to insert it up between his wrists and start sawing at the plastic strips. As the ones pinioning his wrists together parted, the point of the blade stabbed into his flesh. Ignoring the pain, he was able to pull himself free at last. Quickly he went behind Helen and then Thompson and cut them loose.

'Jon you're bleeding,' Helen exclaimed.

He was amazed to see how much blood was now pouring down his right wrist. Helen grabbed the knife off him and cut his sleeve back. The stab wound was quite deep but clearly hadn't cut an artery. It was also starting to hurt quite a lot. Thompson had ripped open a shell dressing and slapped it over the wound and then tightly tied off the straps. The pad started to turn red but the pressure was clearly working.

'Thank you Thompson, now we'd better find that bloody bomb. It's under one of these big turbine thingies.'

In fact, it wasn't hard to find at all. A large metal suitcase with its lid open was sitting under the bulk of the port engine. They could clearly see bundles of explosive with wires sticking into them and all leading back to some sort of timer. It was counting down with less than two minutes to go.

'Know anything about bombs Thompson?' Jon asked more in desperate hope than any anticipation that he would.

'They make a big fucking bang Sir.'

'Right everyone out, there's no time to grab it and chuck it overboard and I wouldn't know which bloody wire to cut anyway. And I've got an idea. Come on let's get out.'

They ran back up the stairs. Jon had a terrible thought that Karim might have somehow jammed the hatch but the locking clips opened quite easily and they heaved it open with the strength of desperation.

'Helen, Thompson, get the hell out of here. Helen, for once do as you're bloody well told. I know what I'm doing. Now for God's sake bugger off and quickly.'

Before she could protest, Helen was grabbed by the arm and Thompson dragged her down the corridor.

Jon turned to the hatch and prayed his idea would work. He unclipped the hatch and let it slam shut. On the bulkhead to one side of the hatch was a red emergency wheel with the word 'drench' written next to it. He had seen it on the way down and was pretty sure he knew what it did. He grabbed the rim and attempted to turn it but it refused to budge. The screaming pain in his wrist didn't help. Looking down, he saw a metal bar with a curled end clipped to the bulkhead. Grabbing it, he slid it onto the rim of the valve and levered with all his strength. It was clear the damned thing hadn't been maintained properly for some time or it would have been easier to move. With a lurch, it suddenly started to turn. Jon just prayed he was in time and it would work.

Superheated steam at five hundred and fifty degrees Centigrade is very different to the stuff that comes out of a kettle and Jon knew it. It's very dry and very hot and pushes any oxygen swiftly out of the way, which is why it useful as an emergency fire fighting system. In this case, Jon was hoping it was also an effective bomb destroying system. The heat alone should cook both the timer's electrics and the explosive itself. He would find out very soon whether his theory was correct.

Suddenly, realising that he no longer needed to be standing over a bomb, he scooped up the weapons that they had been forced to drop and then ran down the corridor while praying that there wouldn't be a large bang at any moment.

There wasn't.

Chapter 47

Jon caught up with Helen and Marine Thompson just as he realised that his idea had worked. It was now two minutes after he had turned on the steam drenching and so the bomb, if it was going to work, would have exploded by now.

As he reached the other two, half way up to the boat deck, he stopped to catch his breath. Suddenly, he heard the roar of a Sea King as it transitioned away from up forward.

He told them briefly what he had done to stop the bomb and then continued, 'we need to keep the evacuation going. If Karim tries to get off with the passengers we should be able to find him and if he stays on board then we can quarantine the ship and search for him at our leisure. He must have realised something is wrong by now but won't know why. So grab your guns and we'll split up. Thompson, you go with Helen and I'll go on my own. My guess is that he won't go up to the bow, climbing into one of our aircraft would be pretty daft. So he'll be on the boat deck. I'll take port, you take starboard. He said he would be dressed as a steward so there won't be too many to check. Right, off you go.'

Jon ran up two more decks, which were deserted, to the port boat deck. There were five lifeboats each side but the rear two were not being used as the Captain had been concerned that if the bomb had gone off in the engine room then they could be damaged in the explosion. The engine room was right in their path to the water. It was for this reason that the Sea Kings were being used to take off the people assigned to these lifeboats. Two boats had already been lowered into the water. Jon looked down and saw two people in stewards uniforms, one in each boat but neither looked anything like Karim. The third boat was just being swung out and again he couldn't see anyone of Karim's description.

He ran across the ship and met the other two coming the other way. 'No sign of him.'

'Nor our side either Sir,' said Thompson.

'Sod it, he must be trying for one of the aircraft.' Suddenly, he caught sight of the Captain coming down from the bridge.

'Captain Sir, over here,' he called.

Arapaho

'Ah, there you are. I take that as we're still afloat and you are here that you somehow defused the bomb?'

'Yes, no time for details now. The hijacker has escaped and we thought he was trying to get in a lifeboat dressed as a steward. But there's no sign of him in any of the boats.'

'Where have you looked?'

'Down both boat decks.'

'What about the forward boats? Ah, I can see from your face you didn't know about them. We've got two more boats, one on either side, ahead of the bridge. As your helicopters have been operating from near there, it's taking a lot longer to launch them. Come on, follow me.'

They followed the Captain through to the front of the superstructure and there on either side were the two lifeboats, both swung out but still waiting to be launched. Each had a small crowd of passengers waiting to embark. Jon immediately spotted their quarry standing in line for the port lifeboat and trying to look inconspicuous. Unfortunately, just at that moment a Sea King arrived and approached the bow of the ship. To Jon's surprise, it wasn't deploying the winch but rather it hovered close to the bow and put one main wheel onto the deck. A crewman, who must have been dropped off earlier, then marshalled passengers into the aircraft by the main door. Jon would have to give a serious chuck up to whoever was flying the aircraft. Luckily, the sea was calm but even so it was some serious flying and it would be speeding up the embarkation enormously. Unfortunately, the noise was deafening and Jon could understand why they were having trouble with the lifeboats. Pulling the others back into the relative quiet of the superstructure, Jon told them what he wanted to do.

Helen, Thompson and at his insistence, the Captain as well, went across to the other side of the ship and pushed through the people waiting for the starboard boat and the Captain had a quick word with the ship's officer manning it.

Jon gave them a couple of minutes and as soon as the Sea King had departed, strode onto the deck and shouted. 'Karim you bastard. Looks like you've run out of options now you murdering sod.' And he pulled out his nine millimetre pistol and pointed it.

Karim looked startled for a second and then he ducked down into the crowd which was starting to realise something was up. Jon walked steadily forward and the crowd parted for him. Wearing military uniform and carrying a pistol worked like a charm. All of a sudden, he was facing his adversary who had pulled his own pistol out of his clothing and was pointing it straight at Jon.

'I don't know how you stopped the bomb and got away but you won't leave here alive.'

'That's fine,' said Jon. 'And neither will you.'

'I wonder. Just how long will you be able to hold that pistol? Your hand must be really hurting, judging by the amount you're bleeding.'

Someone from the crowd shouted out. 'We've had enough of you. If you shoot, we will tear you to pieces.'

For a moment, a flicker of fear shot across Karim's face. 'Then many of you will also die with me.'

Jon was impressed by the anonymous man but really didn't want any help just now. He took several steps towards Karim who automatically moved back the same amount and then a few more until he was where he wanted him. Then, the roar of another approaching helicopter was what he was waiting for as well as the flicker of movement behind Karim. He now needed the man's full attention. 'Either way, you will soon be with that stupid fuck up of a brother of yours.' He had to shout over the increasing noise.

Karim's eyes narrowed. 'That's the second time you have insulted the memory of my brother. I promise you, you will regret it.'

It was the last thing Karim said before the jib boom of the foredeck derrick, swung with the strength and anger of three very pissed off people, flew around in an arc and hit him in the back. The gun flew from his hand as he was flung forward and straight over the side of the ship, missing the swung out lifeboat by inches. Jon rushed to the side as Karim hit the water. He stayed face down and didn't move as the ship slowly swept past.

Epilogue

The Fleet Air Arm memorial church at Yeovilton rang with the peal of bells. All the officers of 844 stood in their best uniforms, arms raised and swords drawn, to make a ceremonial arch for the couple about to come out of the doors. As they opened and the organ could be heard, Lieutenant Commander Jonathon Hunt DSO and now with a Bar, walked out. On his arm was his wife, Second Officer Helen Hunt WRNS, OBE. A cheer went up from all the other squadron staff and families waiting outside. There had been far too many to cram into the small church. Inside, were Jon and Helen's families, two doctors from France as well as Rupert. The couple stopped at the end of the arch and Jon kissed Helen, to the great delight of the crowd, who started to throw all the things the vicar had asked them not to.

The aftermath of the Uganda incident, as it was universally being called, had taken weeks to sort out. A Bomb Disposal team had entered the engine room and confirmed that Jon's unique disarming solution had indeed done the job. In fact, it was now spawning a whole new area of enquiry in various Defence Research Establishments. Once cleared, the passengers and crew were allowed back into Uganda and sailed home to a welcome not unlike the one she had received when she returned from the Falklands. One little boy, in particular, received a great deal of attention.

COMAW finally arrived on the scene and once again, Jon expected a major bollocking and didn't get it. Arapaho was ordered home. There was some serious thought needed about how to stop the hangar flooding and the Met shack from attempting to go absent without leave. On top of that, quite a lot of repainting and some repairs to a rather scorched part of her flight deck were in order. She also got a rapturous welcome back and Jon had to put up with far more media attention than he wanted.

A week after they got back to Yeovilton, Jon finally managed to make room for some leave and asked Helen to go with him. They rented a small cottage on the cliffs, near St Ives in Cornwall and had a blissful week walking the coast and drinking in small local pubs. On the last night, Jon had taken Helen out for a quick drink but when they got back she found he had arranged some outside caterers to come in. The little cottage had been transformed. The dining room was lit with candles and a special meal was waiting on a heated trolley. Jon opened a bottle of Champagne while Helen looked at him warily.

'Come on Jon, this isn't like you. What's with all the romantic crap?'

'It may not be like me normally but you've got to have the right atmosphere, haven't you?'

With an inkling of what was about to come she answered him, 'for what?'

He didn't say anything for a moment and rummaged around in his pocket muttering for a second until he pulled out a small box.

'For proposing marriage of course.'

The reception was in the Wardroom but Jon had special dispensation to allow the whole squadron to attend. It was going to cost a fortune but he had been so busy in recent years, the opportunities to spend money had been few and far between. Anyway, he owed it to his guys. Brian was best man and true to form had made a speech that was close enough to the truth that Jon couldn't really argue but so hilarious and often quite rude that Jon wondered if it really was him he was talking about. To his embarrassment, Brian even mentioned the first time he had met Helen in this very bar but somehow Brian twisted it and had everyone roaring with laughter. Then, all too soon, it was time for them to leave.

Just before they left the mess, Jon took Brian aside. 'I know you lot, you'll be in the bar till God knows when. So tell GG not to drive his bloody car into the foyer or at least tell him to open the sodding doors first this time.'

'Yes Boss.'

'And no explosives, I really mean it.'

'Yes Boss.'

'And that statue by the doors is not to be painted drab olive green with roundels on her tits.'

'Yes Boss.'

'Oh and no pianos are to spontaneously burst into flames.'

'Jon?'

'Yes.'

'Just fuck off. Go on honeymoon and leave the boys to me.'

'Right.'

Even now they weren't allowed to do it their own way. One of Jon's Sea Kings was parked outside the front of the mess. They were both given helmets which looked a bit daft over Jon's number five uniform and Helen's white wedding dress. At least Jon was relieved to see that the pilot was not from 844. He doubted there was one capable of standing properly, let alone flying a helicopter. The last thing they saw as the aircraft took off and flew all the way across the road to a car waiting to take them to Jon's house, so they could change for the trip to Heathrow, was a sea of smiling faces waving at them. They didn't see the large white ensign hanging underneath the helicopter with 'Just Married' embroidered all over it but they saw it later in the photographs.

Brian and Kathy watched the aircraft as it left and Brian gave his wife a hug. 'Well, I really hope they'll be happy together.'

There was something in Brian's tone that alerted his wife. 'Do you know something I don't?'

'Well it's probably nothing and I deliberately didn't tell either of them but a signal came in this morning from the Second Sea Lord's Office. As of the first of January next year, for the next few years, the Women's Royal Naval Service is going to be wound up and women will be asked to go to sea as full members of Her Majesty's Royal Navy.'

'Oh.'

'Yes, Oh.'

Author's Notes

As with all my books which have an element of my own service experience in them, I will now try to extract truth from fiction.

Project Arapaho was real, as were all the problems I mentioned. The ship was originally MV Astronomer, a container ship. She was taken up from trade for the duration of the Falklands War but stayed on in RN service as RFA Reliant. The Arapaho concept originated in the US and was reactivated by the RN after the Falklands. You can never have enough helicopters and so you also need the decks to operate them. I decided to keep the name Arapaho as it sounds more exciting than Reliant!

The main issues that dogged her short operational life were the leaking hangar, the wayward met shack and the very rough flight deck. When they tried to use her down south she proved to be totally unsatisfactory and the whole project was shelved. However, before that she did go to Beirut and operate in the evacuation as I have described. I was the Air Engineer Officer of 846 Squadron at the time and as usual we were given two minutes notice to put several aircraft on an experimental ship for a potentially dangerous operation, so nothing new there then.

844 Squadron doesn't exist but I needed to give Jon his next step up. However, I mention the Achille Lauro hijack in the book and use elements of that incident in the fictional Uganda hijack. In the original case, it was four hijackers and they actually killed a disabled passenger before negotiating a 'safe passage' off the ship. It didn't work as the Egyptian aircraft they were in was intercepted by US fighters and forced to land in Sicily.

The lecture by the American Vietnam veteran is as accurate as I can remember it. He was a Naval Lieutenant Commander and a very, very brave man. We all left his talk a little shocked. And it's actually true that the only nationality that survived in the North Korean POW camps with ease were the Turks.

The 'cheap shot' about all air combat kills since WW2 being carried out by carrier based Fleet Air Arm aircraft is true. Makes you wonder about the decision to get rid of our Harriers and the carrier force.

Being thrown out your seat in a helicopter crash has happened several times. It happened to a colleague of mine in a Wasp helicopter, as he came into land and I know of at least two other incidents. One, where an RN Lynx flew into the sea at one hundred and twenty knots and a similar incident in an American Sea King, in both cases the pilot survived with only minor injuries.

The C130 Hercules is an aircraft that escaped the rigours of a full scale fatigue test. Many years ago, when I was in the MOD, I sat on a panel called the Military Aircraft Structural Advisory Group (pronounced Massage by all and sundry). Because this lack of testing came to light, the aircraft was subjected to quite a lot of additional checks and of course the crash I described never happened. Sorry but I needed it for the plot.

Beirut – what can I say? I tried researching what actually went on over the period in question. Actually, I'm not sure that even the people there at the time really knew what was going on. There were indeed at least twenty two individual factions squabbling and continually changing allegiance and sides over the period. However, the 'war of the camps' did happen. The PLO had taken them over and Syria wanted them out. It seems no one bothered to ask the Lebanese Government what they thought about it.

Kidnap was rife. Much was heard in the west about some of them but it was a cottage industry in its own right for much of the time. Hostages often passed through several hands and a British military officer would have been very valuable.

Uganda was of course, a real ship and was used for educational cruises. Many of my school friends spent summers on her in the Mediterranean. She was the British hospital ship during the Falklands War. Anyone who has read my Falklands Blog will know that she gave me a few grey hairs during the war. Her navigation radar had very similar characteristics to the search radar of an

Etendard aircraft which the Argies would switch on just prior to Exocet launch. She had been told to keep it off but one day, as I was flying my Lynx towards the Islands, we picked up a couple of sweeps and had no choice but to call an alert. It must have cost the fleet quite a lot in Chaff rockets and brown trouser laundry bills.

After a refit, the ship returned to educational cruising again but only for a few months as in January 1983 she returned to duty as a troop ship serving between Ascension Island and the Falkland Islands. Two years later, she was laid up in the River Fal and sold to Taiwan for scrap. She was driven ashore by Typhoon Wayne on 22 August 1986 near Kaohsiung Taiwan and there she lay until broken up in 1992.

The Women's Royal Naval Service was finally wound up in 1993 but I was serving at CinC Fleet in Northwood from 1988 to 1990. It was a time of good economic growth and we were having real trouble keeping male bums on seats, so the decision was taken to allow girls to go to sea. It was nothing to do with political correctness although that was how it was dressed up. It caused enormous controversy at the time. Ships had to be converted with separate showers and messes. Many of the men resented it, not the least because many girls were not strong enough to meet the physical standards set at the time, particularly during training. Then there was the dreaded spectre of 'sex at sea'. I never served in a ship with women as part of the crew but from all I've heard it was a bit of a storm in a tea cup and nowadays everyone accepts it as the norm.

The little graveyard in Gibraltar, with the graves of some of the sailors from Trafalgar, was still there when I last looked. It's just outside the old Dockyard Main Gate, on the way up to the Casino. One grave is of one of the powder monkeys and it always brings a lump to my throat…….

Bog Hammer

Jon and Brian sail together again:

The Gulf at the end of the eighties is a powder keg. The war between Iran and Iraq may be over but tension in the whole region remains high. Having been forced reluctantly to the negotiating table, Iran is still looking for revenge. The Frigate HMS Prometheus is tasked to maintain the safety of British interests in the area as part of the Armilla patrol. Now commanded by the newly promoted Commander Jonathon Hunt with his friend Brian Pearce as his Operations officer, they are thrust into a situation that requires all their courage and ingenuity. The threat of 'Bog Hammers', small armed speedboats that can cause chaos far in excess of their size, as well as that posed by shore based missiles puts Jon and Brian in a precarious position as they try to counter an audacious attempt by an Iranian faction to bring chaos to the whole region.

Printed in Great Britain
by Amazon